D1356781

NIGHT ACTION

NIGHT ACTION

ALAN EVANS

Hodder & Stoughton

LONDON SYDNEY AUCKLAND TORONTO

This is a work of fiction and resemblance of any character to a real person,
living or dead, is coincidental. The locale of St. Jean is also fictional but not
untypical.

British Library Cataloguing in Publication Data
Evans, Alan, *1930–*
    Night action.
    I. Title
    823′.914[F]

ISBN 0-340-42929-1

First published in Great Britain 1989.

Published by Hodder and Stoughton,
a division of Hodder and Stoughton Ltd,
Mill Road, Dunton Green, Sevenoaks, Kent TN13 2YA.
Editorial Office: 47 Bedford Square, London WC1B 3DP.

Typeset by Hewer Text Composition Services, Edinburgh.
Printed in Great Britain by Biddles Ltd, Guildford and King's Lynn

Acknowledgments

When I first had the idea for this book its title suggested itself and only later did I find that the late Captain Peter Dickens had used it for his fine work on the subject: *NIGHT ACTION – M.T.B. Flotilla at War* (published by Peter Davies). However, Mrs Mary Dickens has kindly said that she has no objection to my using it.

I am also grateful to the Coastal Forces Veterans' Association, in particular Peter Bickmore, Jim Saunders, Len Bridge and Bernard Coote, to the M.T.B. 102 Trust, the Imperial War Museum and the staff of Walton Library.

But, as always, any mistakes are mine!

Contents

1

November 1940

The girl was blonde and pretty, thin-faced and wide-mouthed.
She sat at a table outside a café and smiled into the camera
and the sun. Her long legs were crossed and the skirt of the
cotton summer dress hitched back over her knees. Teasing;
this was a nice girl being naughty for her lover. Then the
picture was lost in the blink of an eye as the boat rolled in
the swell, a pencil skittered across the chart and he trapped
it with one big hand.

Lieutenant David Brent was tall so he stooped under the
deckhead of the wheel-house. It was used as a chartroom
now because the captains of the motor torpedo boats preferred to con them from the bridge; they could see better
from there. The bridge was right over David's head and he
could hear the scuff of boots on the gratings.

He stared down only at the stained chart of the Channel
and the coast of France; there was no photograph. He had
torn that up but he could not erase the picture of the girl
from his mind. Now he told himself: You'd better forget it.
But that was not easy though the parting had been months
before when she stood by the train in Paris and told him,
"It's over, David . . . finished."

His wet oilskins, glistening under the light, hung open
over old blue trousers and sweater, dripped sea water
onto the deck. He took off his battered cap and ran long
fingers through the thick black hair that needed cutting. He
scowled, the brows meeting over the dark eyes, not liking
what the chart showed.

His was one of three boats engaged in a raid on the
French coast. The other two boats had landed a party of
twenty commandos at a village that lay a mile up a river,
although for navigational purposes it was little more than a
stream. The estuary spread wide but shallow between low

9

banks and mud flats. There was only one buoyed passage with water deep enough for the boats to manoeuvre up to the jetty which ran out from the village. After putting the commandos ashore the boats would have hauled away from the jetty, and would now be lying out in the deep-water channel until the soldiers had to be re-embarked.

Intelligence reports said there were no German troops in the estuary and it seemed that information was correct because the commandos had gone ashore without any sound of firing. Their objective was a power station set by the side of a dam a half-mile upriver from the village and again it was reported as unguarded. They were to blow up the machinery in the power station and then return.

David wondered at the lack of defences, decided it was because the Germans didn't think they were needed as the village was so far upriver and only consisted of a dozen houses. Besides, the French population had not resisted so far and these commando raids were a new idea. Just the same, he was uneasy about this job and he wasn't the only one. The senior lieutenant in overall command of the three boats had told Brent, "I want you to stay outside and watch the back door. Besides, there's no sense putting all our eggs in one basket so I'm only taking two boats in. It looks quiet enough but if it goes bad on us then you pull out."

The leader had gone in – David glanced at his watch – just an hour ago. He climbed quickly from the wheel-house to the bridge, went to the starboard side and stood in the corner next to the coxswain at the wheel. Here he could see the boat for all of its seventy-foot length. She was nineteen feet in the beam but up here the bridge was barely five feet wide. The torpedo tubes were mounted on the deck either side of the bridge, while aft of it was an open-topped turret in which were mounted twin Vickers .5-inch machine-guns.

The night sky was overcast, with neither moon nor stars. That was a blessing because a fine summer night with a moon would have exposed the boats on the sea as on a lit stage. His boat lay two miles outside the estuary so he could not see the lift of the land broad on either side of the bow.

He asked the coxswain, "Anything seen on shore?"

"No, sir." Leading Seaman Grundy was a head shorter than Brent but stood solidly at the wheel on thick legs. At just twenty-two years old he was still the senior non-commissioned rank aboard and the link between David and the lower deck. Grundy had just been promoted coxswain and into Brent's boat. Easy trust was still to come; each was still on trial in the eyes of the other.

David thought uneasily: All right, so far. It was his duty to watch the back door so he stepped away from the bridge screen and lifted his voice to remind everyone: "Keep a good look-out all round." But he himself saw it less than a minute later, just a creeping, darker mass against the background of the night sky. He asked the signalman next to him, "Port bow, one mile. What d'you see?"

The signalman's big binoculars swung to follow the line of his own: "Something there, sir . . . ship . . . maybe a trawler? Steaming very slow."

Not a warship, not a destroyer, but certainly an enemy, armed and inshore, between him and the estuary. Brent wondered: A trap set? And as if in answer the signalman said, "I think she's stopped, sir."

Brent was sure of it. She lay a bit less than a mile ahead now, on his port bow and on the left side of the estuary. He had been ordered to watch the back door and now it had been shut in his face. He shifted the binoculars to peer past the ship into the black valley of the estuary. He did not see any flash but heard the far-off rumbling of the explosions at the power station almost three miles away.

The signalman muttered, "Hear that, sir? Sounds like they've done it."

Brent grunted agreement. The soldiers had done their work – but had some cunning local *Wehrmacht* commander received a report that they were ashore and guessed that someone would be waiting to bring them out? If this ship was one jaw of a trap then the other would be on the shore.

His gaze returned to the ship and he lifted his cap, ran fingers through his hair then settled the cap again. Grundy

11

was coming to know the gesture that marked stress – or decision. Brent said, "Attacking." He spoke on the voice-pipe to the engine-room, "Auxiliaries." The little V-8 motor would only give around six knots but was quiet, while the three big main engines would be heard for miles.

He was again at Grundy's side, wedged in that starboard corner of the bridge and watching the ship as his boat stole in on her. You wanted the range to be about five hundred yards so there was some way to go – and in near silence. If you made a noise the enemy would hear you and use your boat for target practice. And that boat was fragile, with a thin skin that would not keep out a rifle bullet, and two thousand gallons of high octane petrol in its tanks. Murmur of the engine, soft lap of the water under the bow . . .

The ship was under way, moving again from left to right, easing out slowly to lie off the centre of the deep-water channel. He thought she was making no more than six knots and he set that, and her course, on the torpedo sight on the front of the bridge. He looked ahead, reckoned the range at six or seven hundred. The ship was still on the port bow but he had to "lead" her and he ordered, "Starboard a point."

"Starboard a point, sir." Grundy's eyes were glued to the compass, the glass in the binnacle no bigger than the top of a teacup, glowing faintly. His hands turned the spokes of the small wheel, the "coffee-grinder". His mouth was clamped shut but in his mind he cursed steadily. She was a right cow to steer at this creeping pace; every gust of wind or thrust of wave sent her drifting off course.

Brent was crouching knees-bent beside Grundy to peer along the sight. He growled again, "Starboard . . . steady. *Steady!*" as the bow wandered too far to the right.

"Flare, sir! In the river!" That was the signalman behind him but Brent had already seen the light from the corner of his eye. He straightened, grabbing the binoculars and lifting them to his eyes.

The flare had burst high above the estuary, a brilliant pale green that was almost white, lighting up the two boats and the jetty as they closed to take off the commandos. The village at its back was just a huddle of dark buildings. Then the guns opened up, tongues of flame licking out from the darkness that was the left bank of the river. Brent listened to their rapid banging and thought: 40mm. cannons, like the Bofors gun.

The leading boat was hit at once; David saw the bursts high on her bridge. She slewed off course then stopped dead and he knew she had run out of the channel and gone aground. The second boat was turning to render assistance to the leader, but now she too came under fire, was lit by the bursts, exploded, burned. And there was fighting around the village, the pin-pricks of flames speckling the darkness there. Then the guns ceased firing and Brent heard the distant growl of engines. Three E-boats, the German counterparts of his own craft, showed in black silhouette against the glare from the burning boat. Their guns flamed, taking up the task of finishing off the two trapped in the river.

Brent lowered the binoculars and crouched to the torpedo sight once more. He rubbed shoulders with Grundy who had held to his course. They were so close as to hear each other's breathing. Brent judged the range was now down, almost, to five hundred, but held on just a little longer – "Starboard a point" – because he still needed to lead the ship by a fraction more.

"Starboard a point, sir." Grundy eased the wheel around.

"Steady . . ." Brent pulled at the triggers, first starboard then port, heard the pound of cordite in the impulse charge in each tube explode with a dull thud. The torpedoes slid out of the tubes and over the bow, plunged into the sea, dived then rose and ran. He straightened and watched their twin but diverging tracks of phosphorescence. His eye and his instinct told him the starboard one had missed; he had fired too soon, led by too much.

He glanced quickly towards the firing in the river, saw the one boat burning, the other being shot to pieces where it lay stranded. His friends were dying in the estuary. His eyes came down to the silver tracks and he stooped to the engine-room voice-pipe, "Stand by for crash start."

13

"If it goes bad on us then you pull out." That order had been given to Brent in the presence of his sub-lieutenant so no blame would be attached to him if –

Pull out. Save this boat at least. He had already come to know every man aboard and his worth. Leave any survivors from the other boats, and the soldiers, to take their chance. But what chance did they have without him?

The starboard torpedo ran past the bow of the ship but the port struck in a sheet of flame and an explosion that felt like a blow on the ears. The ship stopped dead and sagged, listed at once. Brent worked the handle of the engine-room telegraph, calling for main engines. The engineer below was waiting for that and the engines fired with a deep roar. The boat surged ahead as Brent thrust the throttle levers forward. As she swung past the bow of the stricken ship he saw she mounted a gun forward and another aft, both trained into the estuary. The other jaw of the trap.

The ship dwindled in size as they left her astern and the boat worked up to full speed, bow lifting and stern dug in. Brent ordered, "Starboard twenty . . . midships!" The bow swung, steadied as the boat swerved away from the course that led to the buoyed channel. So for a bare half-mile, then he worked the engine-room telegraph and the roar of the engines died, the bow of the boat dropped and she slid to a halt.

He watched, and saw what he had expected to see, had gambled on. The three E-boats had seen that flash, heard the torpedo strike and they were racing out to the aid of the stricken ship. He saw them first against the light of the flames far up the estuary, coming up the deep-water channel in line ahead. Then they emerged from it to pass him a quarter-mile away. They were not outlined on the backdrop of light now but he saw the grey plumes of their bow-waves. He could see them but they would not see him, lying still. Past him now – "Start up! Port ten!"

The boat was accelerating and swinging back towards the channel. Brent could picture how it had happened. The E-boats, lying still at the side of the estuary, had seen the

M.T.B.s enter and set up the trap with a wireless signal to their base. That had brought the mobile guns tearing down to the bank of the river and the ship to the mouth of the estuary. The guns could not have been far away, the ship already close by, probably on patrol. But they had been quick, efficient – and lucky. Brent and his friends had been out-manoeuvred.

He turned to bawl to the sub-lieutenant standing aft of the bridge, "Tell the gunner to concentrate his fire on those two guns on the shore!" The sub lifted a hand in acknowledgment and Brent turned forward.

They were entering the estuary and Brent had to be able to follow the bobbing buoys that marked the channel. He eased the boat's speed to cruising and heard above the roar of the engines the hammering of the twin Vickers machine-guns aft of the bridge. The lines of red tracer soared away towards the flashes of the two guns on the left bank of the river.

Those flashes disappeared. They had been firing again at the boat stuck helplessly aground and the other that was aflame along its length. But the sweeping tracer had stopped them. Shooting at someone was very different to being shot *at* and the startled German gunners had ducked as the bullets whined round them.

Brent ordered the coxswain, "Port ten." The craft turned to conform to the channel as it bent around to close the jetty, about a half-mile away now. They were running close to the burning boat, lit by its glare and he shouted, "Look out for survivors!" But he saw none, heard no sighting report. No one could have lived through that sudden explosion as the boat's petrol tanks ignited.

The guns on the shore flared again but the shells screamed high overhead. They ceased as Brent raced out of the lake of red light and ran down to pass the leader. She also had a fire aboard her now, aft of the bridge, but no sign of life. She was listed and down by the stern, so probably not only aground but flooded for half her length, holed where the shells from the guns had ripped into her as she lay a sitting target. And then the E-boats had raked her.

Brent saw the jetty ahead, silhouetted against a fire now burning in the village. The twin Vickers were no longer firing and he demanded the reason, watching the narrow jetty standing out of the water on its piles. It had been empty a moment ago but now four men were running out along it. They appeared from the houses of the village and they moved stiffly and jerkily as if very tired. They bent over as they ran as if afraid of moving in the light from the burning house.

The sub came to the bridge and said breathlessly, "The gunner ceased firing because he can't see the guns on the river bank. They're masked by the leader's boat out there."

So Brent's boat was hidden too and would be while he lay at the jetty. He thought: Thank God for that, anyway. He told the sub, "Get down and be ready to take those men aboard."

" – sir!" He dropped down from the back of the bridge and Brent heard him yelling orders at the hands. He appeared forward of the bridge as Brent reached out to work throttle levers and engine-room telegraph. The boat slowed, the engines went briefly astern as he took the way off her, then he and Grundy brought her in alongside the jetty.

Men forward and aft leapt ashore with lines and made them fast. Brent stood on the bridge in the wavering yellow light as the soldiers began to climb aboard. At first they slumped on the deck but Brent bellowed at the sub, "Get 'em below!" Then they were herded down through the hatches.

There was still firing all around the village and Brent thought: Somebody is still organising a defensive perimeter, sending his men away a few at a time. Now another group of five came trotting out from the village, trailed by one who swayed as he ran but his mouth was open as he shouted at the others, urging them on. He wore a pistol holster on his belt but he carried a rifle.

Brent judged, Officer, and called to him, "When are the rest coming?" They had to get out of this. The E-boats would return –

The young officer peered up at Brent on the bridge and answered, "I'm the last."

Brent swallowed. Ten? Out of twenty! He shouted, "Cast off!" The two seamen stationed on the jetty by the bow and stern lines threw them aboard and jumped after them. Brent took the boat out astern then set one engine ahead, turned her almost on her axis and shoved the throttle levers forward.

He sought and found the buoys marking the channel, as the bow lifted and the boat cruised out from the protection afforded by the stranded wreck. The guns on the river bank flickered at them and the twin Vickers chattered tracer in reply. That silenced the guns for a time but then the boat ran into the huge circle of light from the burning craft. The guns found her and then she was hit. Brent and Grundy hunched down as the cannon shells screamed over or burst on the hull. The Vickers fired briefly then stopped.

The sub came to the bridge to report, "The gunner's been killed."

Brent snapped at him impatiently, "Put another man on it!"

"The guns are wrecked, sir."

"Then get off the bridge and into cover if you can." No sense in all of them standing up here to be shot at.

The sub went away and Brent did not see him alive again. But at last the boat ran out of the light, the darkness hid her and she sped away. The guns lost her. Brent peered ahead into the darkness. He could not see the ship outside the estuary but closer, much closer, was the grey moustache that was the bow-wave of another boat headed towards him. The E-boats had seen him as he passed through the circle of light, were coming in after him. He held to his course, took a tight grip on the bridge coaming and saw Grundy stretch out one hand from the wheel to do the same.

The gap between the boats closed in seconds and Brent saw the other looming in front of his bow, then she swung aside. The gratings leapt under his feet as his boat rode over the bow-wave and wake of the other, bucking, pitching and rolling wildly. That was a heart-stopping progress for several mad seconds as they flashed past each of the three E-boats, then it eased as they ran into less turbulent water.

The E-boats were lost in the night astern. Brent circled past the torpedoed trawler outside, now listing and down by the head, her stern high out of the water and soon to slide under and sink. Then his boat was free on the open sea.

So they came home. Grundy was relieved at the wheel for a time and he gulped hot soup from a thermos. The bouncing of the boat at high speed spilled a lot of it but the rest went down, warming him. He wanted something in his stomach now because he knew he would not be able to eat later. He was back on the bridge at the helm to take the boat into port in the dawn light.

When she lay alongside the quay the young army officer came to stand below the bridge. He looked up at Brent and introduced himself, "Chris Tallon." He was a stocky young man with a direct look. He had swayed as he ran out on the jetty but he stood straight now.

"David Brent."

Tallon said thickly, "It went like a clock right up to blowing the power station. But as we got back to the village we came under fire. I think there was a company of infantry. Don't know. A lot, though. Managed to hold on just long enough. It was good of you to bring us out. Thanks."

"You're welcome."

There was no more to be said. They had been kicked out of France and were just glad to be alive. Chris looked up at Brent leaning casually on the bridge coaming, old cap pushed back from his brow, but eyes bleak, searching, seeing everything aboard the boat.

Brent returned Chris Tallon's salute and watched him march off along the quay at the head of his men. Then he turned to look the boat over from stem to stern. She was filthy, stained by smoke and sea-water, torn by gun-fire. The turret behind the bridge was holed and dented as if by a huge hammer. He told Grundy, "She's a dockyard job, of course, but you'll clean her up for now."

"Aye, aye, sir." Grundy thought that as soon as he could he would send a man off to the requisitioned houses where the ratings were quartered. He could light a fire so there would be some comfort for the rest of them after the work was done.

David Brent knew this, and the hardship of the men's lives. He had to make his report now, but then he would go to the hotel where the officers were billeted, for a hot bath and breakfast. Grundy and the men would clear away the bloody débris. He said, "Well done, cox'n."

"Thank you, sir." Grundy watched him walk away. Brent had a duty and Grundy had his. He led the hands in hauling the torn body of the gunner out of the mangled turret and laying him gently on the quay with the others, then hosing down the deck. At the end of it he felt more dead than alive. He had lost friends, almost his life. But his boat was tolerably clean now and he had found a captain.

2

December 1941

In the early afternoon of Friday the twelfth of December, a slender, long-legged girl walked on tapping high heels through the rain-wet streets of the new town of St. Jean on the coast of Normandy. The new town was so-called because it had grown up in the last hundred years and to distinguish it from the old port of St. Jean which had existed before the days of William the Conqueror.

Suzanne Leclerc wore a trenchcoat belted at the waist and a kerchief knotted over her blonde hair against the misty drizzle that drifted in from the sea. Her heart had been broken over a year before, in the spring of 1940, but she had gone on with the business of living. Her strength of character had served her well and she needed it now. She was British but had spent half her childhood with her French grandmother and most of her adult life in France. She was an agent of the Secret Intelligence Service, playing the part of a Frenchwoman in this German-held country.

The main streets of the new town were wide, tree-shaded and the rain dripped from the trees to fall cold on her face. She passed the barracks looming sombre on the other side of the street. A German soldier stood sentry at the gate in his grey-green tunic, iron grey trousers stuffed into the tops of jackboots, a rifle slung over his shoulder. Suzanne cast a quick glance over the parade ground and the barrack blocks beyond but saw only a few soldiers at work and no unusual activity nor sign of a strengthening of the garrison.

She walked on along the street that ran arrow-straight to a distant square and the bridge leading to the old port. Her thoughts were of the man she was to meet that night, whom she knew as "Michel". She had not known him before the war but he had known of her. When the Germans overran France and marched into Paris, Michel searched her out and recruited her. She lived and worked in Paris but he sent her to Normandy because she knew the region and had contacts there. Paul, the wireless operator, joined her later, landing from a motor torpedo boat on a winter night.

She had rarely seen Michel, but had received messages from him. Then two days ago, on Wednesday, he had come to her in the room she rented. It was above a shop and chosen because she could take calls on the telephone downstairs. He was in his early thirties, of average height and slight build, shabby and nondescript so he would be lost in any crowd. His face was haggard with strain as he sat on the bed in her room and told her, "I brought a man out of Germany. He has papers in the name of Max Neumann. On Sunday I left him in a safe house in Le Havre, went to my wireless operator's apartment and coded the message for London, that I had Max Neumann. Then I went back to him but I found the safe house being raided by the S.S. and saw my man being taken away with the others. I ran all the way to my wireless operator to cancel that message to London but the S.S. were at his apartment as well. There were two vans with aerials on their roofs: detector vans. They'd picked up his transmission and tracked him down."

Suzanne felt sick, swallowed. Michel rubbed at his face with his hands then blinked at her, "S.S. is short for *Schutz Staffel* and means guard detachment because the first ones were a bodyguard for Hitler. Did you know that?" And when she shook her head he said grimly, "But the branch working around here are called *Gestapo*. I've no doubt you know that." He went on, "You'd better warn your operator about the vans. Remind him to keep on the move." She nodded, and he carried on: "I spent that night in a rented room. Next day I got a new set of papers out of hiding and destroyed my old ones. Then I looked up my connection in the S.S." He saw the flicker of surprise on Suzanne's face and his lips twisted wrily, "I helped him get a Jewish relative out of Germany before the war. That Jewish relationship would have got him thrown out of the S.S. He still wasn't pleased when I saw him in Le Havre a

21

few months back and got in touch with him. But he produces the goods."

Suzanne asked, "Can you trust him?"

"As much as anybody. He knows if I'm caught and talk, he'll be for the high jump." Michel dug a crumpled pack of cheap cigarettes out of a pocket and lit one with a match. "He told me my operator had taken poison and was dead." He sucked on the *caporal* quickly, nervously and talked through the blue smoke, "He said the safe house was raided because they'd had a tip-off that Jews were using it as a hide-out. That turned out to be true. I hadn't known, but the family there had hidden a Jew because he was an old friend."

"Is this Max Neumann a Jew?"

Michel shook his head impatiently. "No. But he was there and they'd know he was German as soon as he opened his mouth. They'd want to know what he was doing there and why he wasn't registered." He pointed the cigarette at Suzanne. "Now the point is this: Max Neumann is being deported to Germany with a batch of prisoners. My contact didn't know when, but it will be soon. There'll be some extra wagons coupled onto a regular night freight and because it's regular I've got the timings along the route. I'll give them to you. I want your help to find a place where that train can be stopped by a party landing from the sea. I've looked at the map and picked out one possible place, but you know the country around here."

Suzanne asked, "Can London do a thing like that?"

Michel said flatly, "If they want Neumann, they'll have to. It's our last chance to save him."

"Why do they want him?"

"I don't know. I was ordered not to try to find out. Can *we* do it?"

And after thinking and poring over the map with him, Suzanne took him to the bridge fourteen kilometres south of St. Jean. There the railway ran through near-empty countryside and a bare kilometre from the sea. From there they went to the landing place on the coast. Finally they selected a rendezvous, between the two and at the corner of a wood, for when they met again.

Paul set up his wireless that night and sent the message Michel had drafted, though he was already on his way back to Le Havre. The message told of Max Neumann's capture, the timings of the train that was to carry him, then the suggested places for a landing and for stopping the train.

On the Thursday London replied: a landing would be made and they only waited to be told which night, but requested a guide. Paul sent an affirmative. Then on this Friday morning Michel telephoned Suzanne in the shop under her room and she told him, "Everything's fine."

He answered, "It needs to be. They're sending him tonight."

Suzanne said, "I'll tell Uncle and see you this evening." "Uncle" meant London; they used a code because they believed the S.S. might be tapping the telephones at the exchange.

This night the soldiers would land and she would lead them to the bridge.

Now she walked down the last steep slope of the street and came out on a cobbled square. She turned right and passed the fronts of several houses and shops until she saw a young man standing in a doorway. Suzanne grabbed at the kerchief over her hair, as if it was about to blow away, and stepped aside into the shelter of the doorway. She took off the kerchief and shook out its folds, saying softly, "Tell them it's tonight. Send straight away. I'm going to meet Michel. You know where."

Paul, her wireless operator, was slight and pallid. He wore a felt hat and his sodden raincoat, too big, hung baggy on his frame. He asked, "Will you wait for confirmation?"

"No. I have to see Albert, then go to meet Michel. I can't wait; there isn't time."

"Suppose I don't get through?" Reception was always bad and sometimes Paul failed to make contact at all.

"Then we will have wasted our time." Suzanne was silent a moment, thinking of this man, Max Neumann, being taken back to Germany – to what? She went on, "When you've finished transmitting, get out. You've sent too often from there. Remember Michel's operator was traced by detector vans."

Paul grimaced, "And we know what happened to him. Don't worry, I've found another room and I'll move. But it's a hell of a job moving so often with two damn great suitcases."

Suzanne said, "Just the same, do it." Ahead of her and across the cobbled square was the harbour of the old port, crowded with the drifters of the fishing fleet. On the far side the three E-boats were tied up in a line, one against the quay and the others outside of it. The Germans called them S-boats, *Schnellboote*, and they were the equivalent of the British motor torpedo boat. The quay stretched back for thirty or forty yards to a long terrace of buildings, houses, offices, stores and chandlers that ran in a line parallel to the harbour and out to the sea-wall. Though the terrace was continuous, each building joined to its neighbour, they had been built and rebuilt over the course of eight hundred years.

The furthest house, that standing on the sea-wall, was the residence of *Oberst* Erwin König, the colonel commanding the *Wehrmacht* battalion in St. Jean. It stood at a right-angle to the others, like the foot of a long L. The second house from the other end was the headquarters of the S.S. Once, a century or more ago, it had belonged to a butcher and the name stuck. It was still "the butcher's house". Its windows looked like glazed, blank eyes staring out at Suzanne across the harbour. She knew the layout of the house very well, from the redecorated sleeping quarters of the S.S. men on the upper floor to the cellars newly converted to cells in the basement; she had listened to the talk of some of the local painters and masons employed to do the work. She had also walked, and learned the layout of, the maze of narrow alleys and streets behind and around the house.

Suzanne shivered and turned her gaze away. A hundred yards to her right was the bridge carrying the road over the

river that ran into the harbour. There were two German
sentries, as always, standing in their open-fronted wooden
shelter at this end of the bridge. Further right still was a
bend in the river. It ran down from the north then turned
at that point to pass under the bridge and into the harbour.
She heard a train's piping whistle and saw its puffing smoke
above the houses, marking where the railway ran through
the new town. She glimpsed the engine and its coaches for
a few seconds as they ran parallel to the river flowing down
from the north, then they were hidden by the houses of the
old port on the opposite bank. The railway track ran close to
the river for almost a kilometre to the north before turning
inland.

She adjusted the kerchief to her satisfaction, saying, "I'll
see you tomorrow or the next day, same time, opposite the
baker's in the rue de Rochelle."

"Right." And Paul, in love with her and afraid for her,
added, "Good luck tonight."

But the girl was already tapping away through the rain.
She walked back up the street but after fifty metres turned
left to climb steep stone steps to another street on a higher
level. It was narrow and she turned right for another fifty
metres then entered a café. It was a long room running back
from the street, with a bar on one side and a succession of
booths down the other. The lamps were lit on that dark
winter day, shedding pools of light and making shadowed
caves of the booths.

As she walked the length of the room some of the dozen
or so men scattered along the bar lifted a hand and called
a greeting. One of them was a gendarme while another
worked on the quay in the old port and smelt strongly of fish.
Suzanne knew them all and they knew she would exchange
banter but a man would be put in his place if he went too far.
They also knew she had come to St. Jean in July of 1940 after
the German occupation of Paris and that she was a teacher
of shorthand, typing and other secretarial skills. She taught
them privately, as a self-employed tutor, which meant she
kept irregular hours and travelled about the countryside.

Suzanne slipped into the booth farthest from the door. Albert was already slouched on the curved wooden bench-seat; they met in this place twice a week. He grunted, "*B'jour*". He was aged around sixty, a skinny, leathery peasant, erstwhile smuggler and poacher who ran a café-cum-general store ten kilometres to the north of St. Jean. He was a simple, gentle man, honest by his own elastic standards, and shaved on Sundays. Suzanne had known him since before the war and he had hated and distrusted the Nazis then. She had sought him out in the July of 1940.

Now she said, "I've had a message from London. There is to be a landing tonight."

Albert glanced at her sharply, "At our place?"

Suzanne shook her head. "Our place" was a secluded inlet close to Albert's café and they had marked it as a good site for a landing. "No. South of St. Jean. I have to meet a man at a rendezvous tonight, then we go to the boat."

Albert shifted worriedly in his seat. "This landing place, is it safe? Are there no sentries?"

"There should not be, but a friend will let me know." A doctor who lived close to that stretch of coast, which was patrolled infrequently. That was one reason why it had been selected for the landing; the other was because it was little more than a kilometre from the bridge. Suzanne said, "Don't worry."

Albert muttered under his breath so she could not hear the obscenity. Aloud, but his voice still low, he said, "We are in a dangerous business. This of tonight could be very dangerous. And the man is important. Yes?"

Suzanne hesitated a moment, her grey eyes meeting his scowl, then with a half-smile she agreed. "It could be."

"Then you, and this man you are meeting, need some protection. Take me." And when she declined with a shake of the head, he persisted, "Then – better – take Louis. If there is danger, a sentry, he can handle it. He is a good man with a gun."

Suzanne thought: Or with a knife or a boot. Louis was Albert's nephew and a thug. Suzanne knew his type, did not like it but used it if she had to. Certainly he could deal with an unsuspecting sentry. She had seen Louis as she entered the café and he had winked at her then turned back to the girl serving behind the bar, leaning across it to whisper to her. He was a tall, muscular young man who carried himself with a swagger. When he first arrived from Paris he affected a thin moustache, and his hair was artificially waved and grew down to his collar. Now he was clean-shaven and his hair was cropped short.

Suzanne said, "I see you have him with you."

Albert shrugged and spread his gnarled, brown hands. "He is a city boy and he finds the country too quiet. He says it drives him mad and he likes to come into town. His mother, my sister, was the same. She ran away to Paris and the bright lights when she was less than your age, and she died there."

Suzanne knew Albert had a soft spot for Louis as he had been fond of his sister. Suzanne thought her a slut who had sponged off Albert. But she could understand a "city boy" being bored. Albert's café was a tiny bar, dark and spartan, in a hamlet of a few houses. Louis had turned up there a month or so ago, down at heel and broke. He had told Albert, "I am in trouble. The Germans in Paris are looking for me. I killed one of them and had to run for it."

Albert had believed him and had gone to Suzanne. She had cross-questioned Louis and he seemed genuine. Not satisfied with that she checked his story and found it true: the S.S. and the *Gendarmerie* in Paris had put out calls for Louis' arrest. Albert had given him shelter and Suzanne provided fresh identity papers, including the pass, initiated by the Germans, granting permission to live or move in the coastal zone.

Louis had accepted the papers gratefully and with a wink: "You are Resistance, yes?"

Suzanne truthfully denied that; she was not Resistance. She told Louis, "I know someone who can obtain these things. We do not speak of it." She trusted Albert and Paul but no one else.

Louis said, "If ever I can do anything to pay you back, just call on me."

And Suzanne had thought: Well, you never know when you may need him. So, later, she gave Albert a map of the area and suggested Louis found his way around and learned the lie of the land. The old man reported that Louis had seized on the chance to go roaming. Suzanne had seen him in St. Jean on several occasions.

Maybe she could trust him . . . But "maybe" was not good enough. She hesitated, Albert's insistence making her uncertain. Suppose she was injured, or picked up by the Germans for some reason? Then the landing would fail. Suzanne said, "All right. I'll take you with me." She told Albert where they were going and said, "You'll need a bicycle, of course."

Albert nodded, "I know where I can borrow one."

"Then meet me on the road by the churchyard in an hour. No later; we have a long way to go before dark."

"That is understood." His face was serious.

Suzanne wondered if that was because of the possible danger, or at the thought of the hours of pedalling ahead. She slid out of the booth and left the café. Louis did not look at her as she passed but she saw he had a drink in front of him, and was watching the girl behind the bar with greedy eyes.

But Louis had seen her go. A few minutes later Albert pushed himself up from his seat and walked stiffly to the door. He paused outside and Louis caught up with him there.

Albert said, "I have a job to do tonight."

Louis asked, "With the girl?"

Albert did not answer that. "You know where to meet the cart."

Louis scowled, "Sure. But three hours sitting behind that horse's arse in the pouring rain! I wish I could go back on the barge." They had come downriver to the town in a barge that had spent the night tied up near Albert's café. The barges ran down into St. Jean and discharged their cargoes every day.

"The one we came down on started upriver again two

28

hours ago. It'll be past my place now. You know that."
Albert turned impatiently and started away. Louis spat in the
road and followed him. Albert went on, "You go home. I
should be back sometime tomorrow."

Louis asked, "Where are we going now?"

"I must borrow a bicycle."

"Going far?"

"Yes." Albert came to the head of the steps leading
down to the main street and started down them. Almost
immediately he tripped and fell, threw out his hands to try
to save himself but tumbled and rolled to the street below.
Louis ran down the steps and helped him to his feet. The
old man was shaking and cradling his right arm with his left.

Louis half-carried him to the shelter of a doorway then
stepped back to eye him and say flatly, "You're in no
condition to go cycling for miles. I'll tell Suzanne you can't
do it. Where will I find her?"

Albert shook his head, pain and worry pinching his face,
"No. She has to have someone with her, and the time . . ."

Louis patted his shoulder, "All right. She has to have
someone with her and you can't go, so I will. What kind
of job is this, anyway? She said you weren't Resistance."

Albert shook his head, "We are not."

Louis shrugged, "What the hell. It doesn't matter what
you are. We're all against the Boche and I wouldn't like
anything to happen to that young girl."

Pain throbbed in Albert's arm. He saw the sense in Louis'
words and said, "She has to meet a man."

"A friend?"

"Yes."

"But you think it might be dangerous?"

Albert muttered, "It could be very dangerous for her to
go alone."

Louis nodded, "And you want me to go along as muscle.
O.K. That's my kind of work and I'll be able to earn my
keep. Where are we going?"

"She'll tell you later."

Louis stared at him in disbelief. "Are you kidding? Before

I start a job like this I want to know where I'm going, every step of the way, so I don't make a wrong turning or a wrong move. In a strange place, once you're lost or in doubt, you're dead." He dug into the pocket of his jacket, pulled out and unfolded a worn map. "You told me I had to get to know the country around here, remember? Well, I've tried. With a bicycle and this." He tapped the map. "Now you show me. I'm ready to put my life on the line but not wearing a blindfold."

Albert wondered how he himself would react if asked to go to a rendezvous at night, breaking the curfew and risking being shot, ignorant of his destination and whether the enemy were there. He admitted that Louis' demand was no more than reasonable and put his finger on the map: "You go there."

Louis said again, "Are you kidding? The bridge? And she's meeting him there? That's guarded day and night by a pair of German troops. I've seen them."

"You're going to the bridge first because she wants to see it again." Albert's broken-nailed finger moved across the map then stopped. "And she'll meet him here, after dark."

Louis peered at the map a moment, and muttered, "I think I know that place as well. There's an old house opposite the corner of that wood. It's a ruin, been falling down for years by the look of it. You could break a leg or your neck in there at night."

Albert nodded and winced, "You've got the right place. Don't worry about the house; he'll be waiting in the corner of the wood nearby."

Louis folded the map and put it away then slid his arm around Albert's shoulders. "Come on, old man, show me where I find this bike."

Suzanne went back to the room she rented, changed into low-heeled shoes, picked up a torch and took the Mauser pistol from its hiding place under the floor. She checked the load and that the safety catch was on, then tucked it away in the special pocket inside her trenchcoat. She cast one final glance around the room, ticking through a mental check-list to ensure nothing was left which, if found, might give her away. Satisfied, she closed the door behind her.

She cycled to the churchyard on the road south of the town and waited there. A few minutes before the appointed time she saw a solitary cyclist riding out towards her. Louis stopped and dismounted. He was serious and businesslike as he apologised for Albert: "He fell down those steps coming from the café to the main road, and he's not a young man. He was worried about you so I said I'd come along. It's the least I can do. I owe you a lot."

Suzanne asked worriedly, "Where is Albert now?"

"I got his wrist dressed – I think it's only sprained – wrapped a blanket around him and gave him some cognac then put him up on the cart. He'll be home before it's dark. Don't worry. I'm sure he was all right."

Suzanne was relieved at that. Louis waited and she asked, "He told you about this?"

Louis nodded, "He said it might be dangerous. So I could be useful." He opened his jacket and lifted the sweater beneath so Suzanne could see the Luger pistol thrust in his belt. "That did the business in Paris."

He was talking of the murder of a German soldier. Suzanne knew all the details. She said, "No shooting unless we are fired on or in danger of being taken. Understood?"

"Of course." Louis pulled down his sweater and buttoned the jacket. He swung his leg over the saddle of the bicycle and followed Suzanne. They rode south on side-roads, not talking, saving their breath for the cycling. And they were busy with their thoughts.

Paul had locked himself in his small rented room at the top of the house in the new town. The other rooms were empty during the day, their occupants out at work. He packed all his belongings into one of the two big suitcases then opened the other that held the wireless. He leaned out of the window and strung the aerial along the overhanging guttering, then coded the message, short and to the point:

"Tonight. Guide present." He bent over the key and tapped out his call-sign.

He was afraid now, remembering the warning of radio detector vans. He wondered how long they took to get a cross-bearing on an illicit radio, to send the troopers running up the stairs and smashing down the door. He wondered how long he would have to send before his call-sign was heard and acknowledged – *if* it was heard? And he had to keep trying. Suzanne had emphasised that this operation was vitally important. But he did not know what was involved, only where she was going to meet Michel tonight, and that there was to be a landing.

He heard the faint crackle of morse in his headphones: they had heard him in London. He sent the signal and only had to repeat it once for it to be passed in full. He took a deep breath of relief and packed up the wireless.

He carried the two suitcases down the stairs and along the street. There were few taxis still running at this time of petrol shortage but one stood waiting for business. The cases dragged at his arms but he would have declined help because he did not want anyone to wonder at the weight of the case that held the wireless. Help was not offered. The concierge was a woman in her seventies and the driver of the taxi did not move from his seat. He watched out of slitted eyes as Paul manhandled the cases into the taxi, climbed in after them and panted the address of his destination. The driver grunted around the smouldering stub of a cigarette dangling from his lips, then swung the taxi away from the kerb.

Paul sank back into the sagging, cracked leather cushions of the rear seat. For a moment he relaxed, then stirred uneasily. Here in the car he could smell the rum and he knew it was borne on the breath of the driver. The taxi was travelling at no great speed but these side-streets were narrow and it swayed wildly as it rounded each bend. Paul clung on, hesitating, then leaned forward to protest, "Slow down! You'll kill somebody!"

The driver's head turned and he peeled the cigarette from his lip. "Shut your row. I've been driving for twenty years."

He faced forward again, hauled on the wheel to turn into the main street and Paul lurched sideways into the door as the taxi heeled over. He glimpsed through the opposite window another car, a black Citroën, charging down on him. There was a squeal of brakes then the shock of impact as the Citroën rammed into the side of the taxi.

Paul still leaned against the off-side door and now this burst open, swung wide. He was somersaulted out of it into the road and a split-second later his cases followed. He stopped rolling and lay face down, gasping as he caught his breath and partially stunned, his vision uncertain so that the street tilted, rose and fell as his gaze wavered.

The black Citroën had in fact been the leader of three travelling in a speeding convoy. Its front had telescoped against the side of the taxi and it was packed with S.S. troopers who now climbed dazedly out of the wreckage. The driver lay still, collapsed over the wheel.

The second Citroën had swerved to avoid the first and halted alongside it. *Sturmbannführer* Schleger, chief of the S.S. in St. Jean, and Ostmann, his second-in-command, swung quickly out of the car. Like the others, they wore the grey-green service dress and jackboots of the S.S., Schleger with the four silver stars of his rank on his left collar-patch. His narrow face tight with rage, he shouted at the men from the wrecked Citroën, "Find a telephone and call H.Q. for another car!"

But Ostmann, big and burly, with a wide, red, humorous face, walked around to the other side of the taxi. He went to toss the suitcases aside, frowned at the weight of one and yanked it open.

"See what we have here!" he called and stood there, fists on his hips.

Schleger strode around the taxi to join him and stared down at the suitcase. He looked from the wireless packed in the case to Ostmann and shrugged.

"The detector vans reported a fix just before we left. We'd have traced him anyway." They both turned on Paul where he lay in the rain.

A crowd had gathered and some of them were stooped around him, trying to see the extent of his injuries. A woman was on her knees beside him, trying gently to turn him onto his side. Ostmann thrust his way through the crowd, scattering it. He lifted the woman one-handed and shoved her after the others then jammed his boot under Paul and kicked him over onto his back. That wrenched a cry of pain out of the bruised and dazed wireless operator. He stared up wide-eyed and swallowing with fear. Ostmann told Schleger, "He's alive. He'll talk."

Schleger beckoned the *Scharführer*, the sergeant in command of the first car, and pointed at Paul: "Put *that* – " his finger shifted to indicate the wrecked car, " – in there. Then telephone for two cars. One is to take him back. He goes in the cellar and we want to know who he is, his address, contacts. Understood?"

"*Ja, Herr Sturmbannführer!*"

"Then you and your men follow us in the other car. Your driver knew where we're going. Do you?" But before the man could answer, Schleger snapped impatiently at Ostmann, "Check his map and make sure he knows the way. And if he's late, then Christ help him!"

He strode back to his Citröen, standing with its engine ticking over softly. Ostmann grabbed the map from the *Scharführer* and ordered, "Show me!" The man peered, then jabbed a finger at the map. Ostmann threw it back at him: "Right!"

Schleger shouted from the Citroën, "Come on!" Ostmann ran to it, ducked inside and the black car roared away as he reached out to pull the door shut behind him.

3

"At all costs!"

The four motor torpedo boats sailed in the evening of that Friday and David Brent commanded in the leader. The last long year, of monotonous patrolling interspersed with flashes of sudden action, had changed him. He was leaner, the face and eyes harder.

Memories still returned to haunt him. Of the girl, smiling in the sunlight or a breathless voice in the dark. Or pale-faced and eyes shadowed with grief, sending him away. And of the motor torpedo boats closing the shore in the night, the flare bursting and hanging high and the cold, hard light. Then the enemy guns opening up and hell taking over.

That was in the past and these were different boats. The girl was lost forever and that action of a year and more ago was just a fragment of history now. The nightmare pictures ran through his mind but he looked out on, and was aware of, reality as he stood on the narrow bridge of this M.T.B. with the other three cruising astern of him in the arrowhead formation. There were six in the flotilla but two were in dockyard hands. That was not unusual.

The boats were clear of Folkestone, on the open sea in the last light of the day and working up to thirty knots, bound for the French coast again. The girl's face came into his mind at odd times, at sea or in a crowded street, but he usually only remembered the action when there was talk of such. This time the picture was called up by sight of the soldier, Captain Chris Tallon, standing at the back of the bridge. Brent could tell by Tallon's bleak stare that he also remembered the horror of their last meeting. And now the spectre of this new mission hung between them. They were only warned of it yesterday, had met this afternoon and been ordered to sea scarcely an hour ago after a wireless message had been received from France.

The four M.T.B.s carried, shared out among them, a platoon of commandos, thirty-two men, led by Chris Tallon. Seven of them were sappers of the Royal Engineers, trained in demolition. His orders were to land in Normandy, destroy a railway bridge a kilometre inland, stop a train there and rescue a man held prisoner aboard it. David Brent's orders were to put the commandos ashore where they would be met by a waiting guide. When they completed their operation he would take them off, together with the prisoner. The priorities of Brent and Tallon had been spelled out to them by an admiral with brutal clarity: "The man to be taken from that train is more valuable than the agents working over there, the commandos – or your flotilla. So swim back with him if you have to – but bring him!"

David Brent would carry out his orders, but he thought now that it was one thing to determine priorities in the distant seclusion of a headquarters, another to be faced with the choice in action. He prayed he would not have to make that choice. He glanced at Chris Tallon. They had talked little, had no pleasant, shared memories but Tallon had said, "This operation came up at short notice. I suppose they couldn't be choosy and we were handy."

Brent replied, "Looks like it."

"So we're the second team." Tallon had shrugged and smiled, "Still, should be interesting."

But both knew they were thinking of that night in the estuary under the guns. Each was a reminder to the other.

Brent looked out at the boats slicing through a sea the colour of lead. Of their seventy-foot length nearly half the space below decks was taken up by the three huge Packard 12-cylinder engines that could push them up to forty knots. At that speed they were exhilarating, like flying over the sea. David thought they were sleek and lovely. The crews they carried were men he knew, though not as well as he would have wished; he was a comparative stranger, new to this command and this was the first time he had led these boats in action. What if he was called on to sacrifice one or all of them?

He thrust the thought aside; that was a bridge he would cross when he came to it, and please God, he never would. He ordered, "Test guns!"

The signalman on the bridge lifted the Aldis lamp and the beam flickered pale in the last grey winter light. The sun was setting somewhere astern, hidden by low cloud. The guns, twin Vickers .5-inch machine-guns mounted in a small open-topped turret aft of the bridge of each boat, hammered in short bursts, red tracer curving out to sea, then were silent. Brent turned to face forward and nodded acceptance, not satisfaction. The machine-guns were the sole armament of the flotilla. The torpedo tubes mounted either side of the bridge had been left empty for this operation to lighten the boats.

He stood, bulky in oilskins, in the right-hand corner of the narrow bridge. He rubbed shoulders with Grundy, the coxswain, standing at the wheel in the centre of the bridge, eyes intent on the compass. It was a silent intimacy. They were a team now, still divided by rank but joined by that year of shared hardship. Their conversation was sparse and formal, limited to the working of the boat, but talk had nothing to do with respect and liking.

Lieutenant Jimmy Nash, next in seniority to David Brent and his second-in-command, stood at the back of the bridge. He was "spare skipper" for this trip because his own boat was one of those in the dockyard. He would take command if any of the four captains became a casualty. Jimmy was a raffishly handsome young man, curly-haired, confident and humorous. Before the war he had sold cars and raced them – and power-boats.

He watched Brent, curious and assessing, because the commander of the flotilla was an unknown quantity, a stranger. He had come only two weeks before, bringing Grundy with him. He was tall and lean, taciturn. Jimmy thought: He doesn't look tough but you never can tell. Nash believed he was in line for his own flotilla and looked forward to it with eagerness tinged with apprehension. He had been disappointed when Brent was given command although he came with the reputation of being a fighter, a victor in savage encounters with the enemy. Fair enough, but he had to prove himself here and Jimmy would watch him.

Brent turned and caught Nash's speculative gaze. He guessed at Jimmy's thoughts, knew he had that reputation but believed it had come by chance; he had simply faced crises and dealt with them as best he could. He wanted only to come out of this operation alive. Correction: he wanted all of them out of it alive. He grinned at Jimmy and then faced forward.

Nash found himself returning that grin, then his eyes shifted to Tallon. He did not look a soldier at that moment, anonymous in oilskins like the rest. He was short and broad, square-faced and sharp-eyed.

This was a "silent" patrol, which meant they were to avoid action at sea and go for their primary objective: land the commandos and bring off the prisoner from the train. Jimmy thought: It's silent, all right. Brent and Tallon knew each other, that had been obvious to Jimmy when the soldier came aboard, but he and Brent had only exchanged nods, had not spoken a word to each other except on matters of duty. There was distance and silence between them.

Now Chris Tallon turned on Nash and snapped at him, "What are you staring at?"

Jimmy replied mildly, "Just day-dreaming, old lad."

Tallon glared, "I hope we don't have any of that when we're on the other side."

"Don't worry about it."

"I don't. I just make damn sure it doesn't happen."

Nash shrugged and moved away. The soldier was on edge and Jimmy didn't blame him; he would be landing on the enemy coast before long. Jimmy stopped at David Brent's shoulder and raised his voice above the roar of the engines, "You said you knew this stretch of coast around St. Jean."

David Brent did not turn his head, answered only "Yes."

Jimmy waited, but Brent said no more, offered no explanation of the source of his knowledge.

In one of the rooms in the warren beneath the Admiralty a tall man in a tweed suit sat erect in a straight-backed wooden chair and watched the officer at the telephone on the other side of the desk. The two men were of an age, in their early fifties. The sleeve of the navy blue uniform of the man behind the desk bore the thick and the thin gold rings of a rear-admiral. He said into the telephone, "Thank you." Then he put the receiver back on its cradle and told the man in the tweed suit, "They've sailed, General."

There was still formality between them though they had worked together for some weeks and their countries were now allies; Pearl Harbor had been attacked only the previous Sunday.

The general nodded and was silent for a moment, then asked, "They're your best men?" His voice was deep and the accent was that of New England.

"They are the best available."

The general noted that careful choice of words, and questioned: "Available?"

The admiral spread his open hands, palms up. "The cream of the commandos are already committed to a raid on the Lofotens. It would be impossible to bring any of them back in time. The flotilla of boats I would have used, experienced and with a brilliant leader, were the targets of a dawn air-raid yesterday. The boats were badly damaged, crews decimated, their captains killed."

"So these really aren't the best."

The hands lay still on the desk now and the admiral conceded, "No."

"I see." The general kept his tone neutral, but thought, *Jesus*! "Do they know?"

The admiral hesitated, then admitted, "I think they do."

"All right." The American was silent for a minute, thinking he would have to report this. But the point was . . . He demanded, "Can they do it? Can they bring that man back?"

The admiral looked down and used one finger to open the slim file on the desk. He read again the orders given to him and phrases jumped out from the page: 'At all costs' . . . 'No price is too high to pay.' He thought that he had got that across to Brent and Tallon, remembered their faces, expressionless, not looking at each other. He said, "I think so." The initials scrawled at the foot of the curt directive read W.S.C. He said, "Your President spoke directly to Churchill about this operation. Why does Roosevelt want this man brought out of France? Why is he so important?" The American stared back at him, not answering, and he smiled wrily and nodded, "I see. I have no need to know and you aren't permitted to tell me. That's right, of course."

The general asked, "When will we hear from your men?"

"If all goes well, around one in the morning. They'll be home then. They'll maintain wireless silence throughout."

" 'If all goes well,' " the American repeated. Then: "I went down to Southampton a couple of days ago. The train was late both ways. This train they're going for, suppose it's late?"

"It would make the job more difficult, even more dangerous." The admiral explained, "They must be clear of the French coast and well on their way home by dawn. If they are still on the other side at first light they will be bombed and strafed out of existence."

"That's what I thought." The American also thought: I'm not a bloody fool, to have the obvious pointed out in simple words. Maybe his dignity is hurt because I couldn't answer him a minute ago. Tough. Aloud, he said, "A lot of things can go wrong."

"Any operation is subject to chance, or the enemy not acting as you expected, and amphibious ones are the devil. You can lose a lot of good men." The admiral stopped abruptly, shook his head then smiled. "You must excuse me. You know all that. I think possibly your suit deceived me. I sometimes have to explain military or naval decisions to ill-informed civilians."

"O.K." The general had suffered that experience and he

returned the grin sympathetically but did not relax in the chair. "But you know these men and you still think they can do it?"

The man opposite met his stare, thought a moment, then said slowly as if marshalling his thoughts, reasoning his way to a conclusion: "The commandos are well trained and their officer is brave. The man in overall command believes himself to be a conventional naval officer, but he can behave in unconventional fashion. He is resourceful, can retrieve a situation that is apparently lost." He paused, then answered definitely, "Yes." But it was not only down to the men.

In the old port of St. Jean, *Kapitänleutnant* Rudi Halder tucked his cap under his arm and entered the fishermen's café on the quay. He was a tall man in his mid-twenties with crinkly hair the colour of copper. He was not handsome but a humorous grin was never far away. His men knew him to be a strict disciplinarian, but fair. The girl Ilse knew him to be strong but gentle.

He ordered a glass of beer and drank it standing at the bar and looking out to the harbour. The fishing fleet, a score of drifters, were putting to sea. They were broad-beamed little boats with a wheel-house aft, a mast forward and a hold between for the fish. They slipped past the guardship moored just inside the entrance to the harbour, another drifter like them but armed with a 40mm. cannon in the bow. They threaded one by one through the narrow gap between the grey sea-walls and their masts stood like a forest of bare poles against the dull yellow glow of the sun setting behind the low cloudbase. This was a brief interlude of peace and Rudi savoured it.

He glanced around the bar and saw the few Frenchmen in there were deliberately not looking at him. Rudi was used to that, and the thin beer, and was prepared to put up with both. 'Count your blessings,' he told himself, 'that bastard Ostmann isn't in tonight.'

He drained his glass, left the bar and walked down past

the S.S. Headquarters on the quay to the three *Schnellboote*
where they were moored side by side in a trot against the
harbour wall. Rudi halted on the edge and stood frowning
down at the boats, his eyes sliding, searching, over each
one in turn, from the 20mm. cannon in the bow and the
torpedo tubes flanking it to the second cannon aft of the
bridge. The crews were lined up in the waist of each boat
and Rudi examined them, too. He was not merely looking
for smartness of dress, but at faces and how the men bore
themselves. And after a minute he nodded, satisfied. He
could find no fault with the boats and the men looked fit
and confident.

He stepped down to the deck of the inshore boat, saluted
and ordered, "Carry on!" The rigid ranks broke up and the
decks swirled with activity as Rudi crossed the two boats
nearest the quay and so came to his own. Bruno Jacobi, his
first lieutenant, short, broad and swarthy, waited for him and
saluted as he came aboard.

Rudi said, "I take it we're ready for sea; no problems."

"Ready for sea, sir." And Bruno added, "It could be a
good night."

Rudi nodded agreement, "Dark and dirty with some fog."
He grinned at Bruno. "A good night for hunting *Tommis*
and I've got a lucky feeling. Let's get after them. Start up!"

The sun was sinking behind low clouds as Suzanne and
Louis dismounted from their bicycles at the top of a rise.
The road before them ran down gently to the railway and
ended at a siding. There was no station or platform, just a
spur-line leading off from the permanent way. A train could
be shunted off into the siding, to get it out of the way so
another train could pass, or to load it. Beyond the siding
was the bridge carrying the railway over a defile. This was
the one place, near the sea and in open country, where the
railway was vulnerable and the rescue could be made. Or
might have been.

The bridge was a quarter-mile from where Suzanne and
Louis stood but there was no need to go down to it. There

was no train in the siding but one was to be loaded there. A battalion of infantry was bivouacked around the siding and down to the bridge. Some of their vehicles were close to Suzanne and she saw that these troops were not middle-aged nor stoop-shouldered clerks. They were young and smartly turned out; they looked tough and efficient, a thousand men of a crack fighting unit.

Suzanne turned away and Louis asked, "Why did we come here?"

"It doesn't matter now." The soldiers would not land tonight; the raid would not take place. Suzanne felt a load of responsibility lifted from her shoulders, and then was ashamed. She had not thought of the man on the train who would now die. She said, "Come on, let's get out of here."

Louis shrugged and they cycled back along the road. Suzanne led the way to a café she knew and they found it crowded with men from the battalion. The proprietor was too busy and harassed to talk but Suzanne managed a few words with Madame in the kitchen, who told her, "They are on their way north. They entrain tomorrow, going back to Germany." She lowered her voice to add, "I wish they were all going back."

The fresh-faced, fit, noisy young men turned their heads to watch Suzanne and she kept her eyes cast down as she went to the telephone. The doctor answered from his house near the coast and Suzanne asked, "How are you this evening?"

"I am well. I took a short walk and got back only a few minutes ago. It is fine and clear." That meant there were no sentries at the landing place this night. When that area was to be patrolled a section of six men and an N.C.O. took up occupation of a guard-hut in the last light of the day.

Suzanne pushed through the crowd of soldiers, evading their hands, shaking her head at the invitations. She rejoined Louis who waited outside the café and they cycled away through the gathering dusk.

It was full dark when Suzanne gestured to Louis and the soft hiss of tyres on the wet road ceased as they dismounted. They hid the bicycles behind the hedge then Suzanne led the way off the road and up a narrow, rutted track. After two hundred yards the wood loomed ahead as a rough-edged hump against the night sky. To the right was the square black shape of a house but they turned away from it and towards the corner of the wood close by. They halted when they were just short of the overhanging branches of the trees and Suzanne called in a low voice, "We're here!"

They heard the rustle of movement in the blackness of the wood and then a voice demanded, "Who's that with you?"

Suzanne answered, "Louis. He's here to give extra protection."

Louis lifted his right hand above his head to show the pistol he held, pointed at the sky.

The voice asked, "Why do you have that out now?"

Louis answered, "In case somebody else was in there instead of you."

"You don't know who I am."

Louis jerked his head at Suzanne, "She does."

She did, and had recognised Michel's voice at once. Now he stepped out of the blackness of the wood and she told Louis, "Stay where you are and keep watch on the track."

She moved close to Michel but before she could speak he glanced over her shoulder, saw Louis was out of earshot and whispered, "I saw my Gestapo contact just before I left Le Havre. Six S.S. men will travel as escort in the last coach of the train, the prisoners in the next two. But the time of the train leaving there has been put back by three and a half hours because they want to send more deportees."

Suzanne said flatly, "It doesn't matter." And when he looked at her questioningly she told him of the crack battalion bivouacked at the siding: "The raid is impossible now."

Michel's shoulders slumped and he sighed, "Well, I told you this was our last chance to save that man and now it's gone." He was silent a moment then added, "I liked him."

Suzanne said softly, "I'm sorry, but now we have to meet the boat." She turned back to the track.

Louis eased in front of her. "I'll lead," and he explained, "in case we run into trouble."

"You don't know where we're going."

Louis paused, and turned his head to ask, "Not back the way we came?"

"No."

Louis shrugged, "All right. You two stay back about ten metres. Just tell me when to turn left or right. Which way now?"

Suzanne pointed towards the distant, unseen coast and Louis nodded. He led back along the track until it forked and there took the left turning. The other two followed. Suzanne glanced down to make sure of her footing. She had passed this way before and knew the ditch at the side of the track was deep. She saw she was walking a metre clear of the black void that was the ditch and looked forward again.

They were passing the derelict house that was roofless, the beams making a black lacing against the sky. The shutters hung askew by the windows that were no more than holes in the walls, like embrasures –

The track was suddenly flooded with light and there was a shouted order, "Stand still!" Louis half-turned, pistol lifting to point at the lights but the firing came from behind the glare, three shots, the reports running into each other: *crack! crack! crack!* Louis spun away and fell on his face in the mud, arms splayed wide. Suzanne threw herself down. A bellow came from the outer darkness, "Stay where you are or we'll shoot you down as well!" But she remembered the ditch, rolled towards it and over the edge to fall into a foot of water as another shot crashed out and ricochetted, whining, off a rock.

All the time she was praying, "Oh, God! Oh, God! Oh, God!"

45

4

"We've done this before"

David Brent's four boats were running at near full speed now, tearing through the dark night at close to forty knots. Their square sterns were tucked down and their bows lifted high out of the sea, splitting it in two flaring white waves that flashed past either side of the bridge. At times the spray drove in like a torrential rain to run salty down Brent's face. That of Grundy, poised above the glow of the compass binnacle, glistened with salty rivulets.

David glanced to right then left and saw the other M.T.B.s were neatly holding the arrowhead formation. Crozier's boat tore along to starboard and astern of Brent, while little Dent and Tommy Vance were in echelon to port. The arrowhead formation was to avoid the turbulence encountered by boats steering in the wash of that next ahead. This way the M.T.B.s on either side of David Brent were running just in front of his boat's wash and in clear water.

Jimmy Nash pointed out over the port bow. The roar of the boat's three big engines was to some extent left behind but he still had to raise his voice to be heard: "The fishing fleet!"

David nodded. The pin-pricks in the darkness were the masthead lights of a score or more of drifters out of St. Jean. They carried the lamps partly to illumine their work, partly to mark the position of each for the benefit of the German boat patrolling around them like a policeman. If her commander saw a light was missing then he would investigate, because drifters had been known to try to sneak away to England. One had succeeded and supplied the information that the German boat was a drifter like the others, no bigger nor faster but armed with a 20mm. cannon and equipped with wireless.

The lights were slowly sliding back from the bow down the

port side. The boats would pass wide of the fishing fleet and about four miles to the south. David saw Chris Tallon climb onto the bridge and guessed that the soldier had been below to see how his commandos were faring. Jimmy Nash turned and called, "Are they all fit?"

Tallon nodded, then asked, "What are the lights over there?"

Jimmy explained and then told him, "We're about twenty miles out. Won't be long now."

Tallon said nothing in reply to that, only stared out over the bow at the darkness hiding the distant, enemy shore where he was to risk his life again.

He would be thinking about Brent, standing near him now, and of the previous disastrous action from which they had barely escaped with their lives. David Brent was sure of that. And Jimmy Nash had asked, "You know this coast?" It would be more accurate to say Brent knew a part of it, had spent just one week of his life there and could not forget it, though God knew he had tried . . .

He brought his mind back to the present: "Pass the word for Cullen." He heard the signalman relaying that message to the deck below.

Grundy thought: Cullen. Young for a leading seaman, smart up top but casual in his turnout. He liked to argue but Grundy would not have that. He knew the kind of ship Brent wanted and his own ideas were in accordance. Cullen would have to learn.

He had come aboard late, just before they sailed, and Grundy had demanded, "Where the hell have you been?"

"Had to phone one o' me girls, 'Swain." Defiant. Insolent.

Grundy had not believed him but they were on the point of sailing so: "First Lieutenant's report when we get back. Think of some better excuse before then."

When Cullen came onto the bridge he saw Grundy at the wheel. The coxswain did not look around from the compass but Cullen thought: He knows I'm here. The bastard has eyes in the back of his head. If the skipper hadn't brought him along I might ha' been rated cox'n. Should have. I know

47

my stuff, good on the wheel, get on well with the lads. He's always picking at the rest of us: "Get your hair cut. Smarten up."

And tonight Cullen had waited ten minutes in the telephone kiosk on the quay before he got his call through to his worried parents in the corner shop they kept in London's East End. He tried to reassure them: "That's all right, Dad. I'm fine. Don't worry about me. Wangled myself a cushy number, haven't I?" Cullen thought that maybe he should have told Grundy the truth, but the coxswain put his back up. He'd ask for a transfer to another boat after this trip.

Brent turned to him and said, "Cullen, the coxswain thinks you're the best man to send in with the dinghy. Take one man with you, carbines for the pair of you. Look over the dinghy now and make sure it's ready to put over the stern. You'll be bringing back one agent from the beach, maybe two. Understood?"

"Aye, aye, sir."

Rudi Halder turned as Bruno Jacobi came onto the E-boat's bridge. Bruno's hoarse bellow cut through the deep boom of the big diesel engines: "Nothing seen yet."

Bruno was talking of the enemy. Rudi answered, "The night is very young." And you could go for nights on end without making contact. Then it was sudden.

Bruno said, "The fishing fleet."

Rudi nodded. The lights were tiny, fine on the starboard bow and he reckoned the drifters were close on ten kilometres away. The three E-boats were cruising at thirty knots and were abreast of St. Jean, fifteen kilometres to port but invisible in the night. The spray flying in over the bow spattered the men at the 20mm. cannon just below and forward of the bridge. It drove into Rudi's face.

He said, "We'll run south for another twenty kilometres then lie still and listen for a while." In this kind of night warfare, when visibility was severely restricted, it was a useful tactic to stop the big diesels, then in the quiet use another sense and listen for the sound of the enemy's engines.

He recalled the night a year ago when he had stopped the boats at the mouth of the estuary and they had heard, then seen the two *Tommi Schnellboote* run in along the deep-water channel. Rudi had guessed they were going to make a landing and he sent a wireless signal to his base, reporting, saying he was going to follow them in.

That had been a mistake. He had been told to wait. The tactical geniuses at base had thrown together a trap to make certain, sent the army to the bank of the river with guns and an armed trawler to close the mouth of the estuary. They had been quick, efficient, he gave them that – but it was all unnecessary. Both *Tommi* boats were destroyed but Rudi would have seen to that anyway. The trawler was torpedoed by a third *Tommi* who got out those soldiers still left alive. Rudi's neat operation had been elaborated into a cock-up. He scowled. But the basic tactic was correct: when you can't see, lie quietly and listen.

It had been quiet in Ilse's bed, just their breathing and their whispers. Her father, the *Oberst* commanding the *Wehrmacht* battalion stationed in St. Jean, had toured his area all that day. Rudi had gone to the house on the sea-wall in the afternoon and was passed by the sentry outside the front door; the young naval officer was a regular visitor. The other soldiers of the guard were in a room at the rear but never entered the house proper. Ilse was alone. She took Rudi to her room and he left her half-asleep and sated in her bed when it was time for him to go down to the boats.

Rudi grinned at Bruno, "I still feel lucky tonight."

Suzanne ran crouched along the bottom of the ditch with the track on her right until she saw the ragged outline of bushes lifting on her left. She scrambled out of the ditch and into that cover. Looking back she saw the track bathed in the light of a dozen torches that blazed from the holes that were the windows of the ruined house. So the S.S. had waited there in ambush.

Louis lay as he had fallen, arms outflung and face-down in the mud. Michel stood on the track with his hands raised above his head. He had not known of the ditch, had been given no chance. Could she have saved him? No. A second's delay would have cost her life and not saved Michel. The trap was complete. Figures were closing in on him now and others running up the track towards her hiding place.

She ran.

Michel stood frozen for vital seconds, squinting into the glaring lights, hands lifted to shield his eyes. Then the S.S. troopers swarmed around him, the stubby, short-barrelled Bergmann carbines held two-handed across their chests. They strapped his hands behind him and searched his body for weapons. Rough fingers probed his mouth for a poison capsule and he gagged from revulsion and fear. Then they hustled him away down the track between two of them, another close behind. Michel stumbled as they passed the mud-splashed body of Louis and he felt the muzzle of a carbine stab into the back of his neck.

He was English but had been brought up in France, where his father served in the diplomatic service, and he spoke French as a native. The shock of the ambush, the lights and the shooting – the capture – were wearing off now. He had always been prepared for the possibility of capture but that had only been a theoretical exercise. He had no practical experience because he had not been caught before. You were only caught once and that first time was also the last.

Finish.

The first realisation that he was caught, would die, and quickly only if he was lucky had temporarily paralysed him. He was starting to think again now, though his breathing was still rapid and shallow and his heart thumped. He had a story ready, of course, but it would not be believed because they had been betrayed. This was not like being arrested on suspicion, when you might convince your questioner that you were the innocent man you pretended to be. This time someone had pointed a finger. Who had the girl told?

Two cars, black Citroëns with hooded headlights casting pools of light, bumped down the track. One of them halted by Michel and his escort while the other ground on. His guards threw him into the back of the car and crowded in after him. He lay on the floor and they rested their boots on his back and ground his face into the dirt of the carpet. His head bounced in erratic rhythm as the car turned and lurched away along the track.

Louis lay still in the glutinous clay of the wet, rutted lane outside the ruined house. The lights and the shots, when they came, had startled him although he had been ready and thrown himself down. He lay without moving as Michel was hustled past him by a group of S.S. troopers, listened to the retreating scuffle of their boots in the mud, then the distant grinding of the cars coming up from the road. He saw the glow of their lights but still did not move. Until Schleger said, "All right. He's gone."

Louis shoved himself up to his feet, brushed mud from his clothes with his hands then picked up the pistol. He checked that its safety catch was on, wiped it with a dirty handkerchief then put it into his jacket pocket. He still had that self-confident swagger but he was deferential when he spoke to Schleger: "It went well?" That was only half a question, sure of his answer and seeking congratulation.

He got it: "Excellent. Fine work." They stood in the glare of the lights from the house and satisfaction showed in Schleger's face. He now wore a grey-green service raincoat. He took off his high-peaked cap, with its badge of a spread-winged eagle above the death's head, and mopped at the rain on his narrow face with a handkerchief. His thinning hair was oiled and brushed flat with a carefully straight parting. He was smiling now, delighted with the night's work.

Ostmann, Schleger's lieutenant, trudged up to them. He wore no overcoat and was jamming his pistol back into its holster on his belt. His service tunic was stained black with rain from his waiting in hiding under the holed roof of the ruined house. He rubbed his meaty hands together.

"The girl got away but they're after her. They'll soon pick her up. I'm looking forward to getting hold of her."

Schleger's eyes shifted to Louis, "Where were they going?"

"Towards the sea." Louis shrugged. "That's all I know. She's close, that one. She wanted Albert to come with her, so I made sure he couldn't." He chuckled, recalling how he had tapped Albert's heel so that the old man's legs tangled and he fell. That was an old trick Louis had often used in Paris when stealing wallets: trip the mug then help him up but slide your hand into his pocket as you did it.

Louis went on, "But then I had to persuade Albert that I had to know where the rendezvous was and why we were going there. He told me we had to meet somebody here. That was all. But I knew it had to be somebody special if she wanted my extra gun. I had hell's own job getting to a phone to pass the word to you."

That was a lie; it had been easy, standing in the corner of a crowded bar, noisy with talk.

Schleger ordered Ostmann, "Tell them to sweep towards the coast."

Ostmann tramped away into the darkness and then his voice lifted, bawling at some N.C.O. Schleger walked to the car with its engine throbbing softly, and ducked into the rear. Louis waited until Schleger called impatiently, "Well, get in!"

Louis joined him in the back of the Citroën, but sat stiffly in a corner so that Schleger had most of the rear seat. Ostmann came hurrying back, swung into the seat beside the driver and the car rolled forward.

When Louis had talked with Schleger in Paris he had asked the *Sturmbannführer*, "What do you want me to do in Normandy?"

Schleger had replied, "I hope you might flush out the enemy agents operating there."

"There are agents? How do you know?"

"I can smell them." Schleger's eyes were cold and un-winking, watching Louis. "I can sense when they are there: enemies of the State."

Louis did not question that claim, only nodded acceptance at the cold stare.

Schleger went on, "Besides, they are using a wireless set. We have intercepted coded messages but the radio detection vans have not been quick enough to pin-point the area where the set was operating. And it moves around. But they must have friends, people – traitors – who hide them. I want you to pose as one of that sort, become one of them. Will you do it?"

He knew Louis had no option but to try, as did Louis. He needed the job to have the *gendarmerie* taken off his trail. They were seeking him for another offence. He was eager and boasted, "I think I may have a contact already."

He had travelled down to St. Jean then north to the hamlet where Albert ran his tiny bar, and told the old man his story: "I am in trouble. The Germans in Paris are looking for me . . ." It had been easy for Schleger to arrange for the S.S. in Paris to put out calls for Louis' arrest.

He had only hoped that Albert might have suspicions of those in the district who might be engaged in Resistance work. He could hardly believe his luck when Albert introduced him to Suzanne and she found forged papers for him. They denied being members of the Resistance but that only meant they were lying or up to something else. But what?

The luck seemed to run out then. Louis believed there must be others in the network but he was not told about them and dared not ask in case he raised suspicions of himself. He knew he was not trusted, at any rate by Suzanne. When she and Albert met they always talked alone and Louis was left out. They never let slip any mention of a wireless operator.

Louis reported regularly to Schleger in St. Jean by tele-phone, counselling patience, promising results soon, but saying only that he had made a contact. He refused to give any details, told nothing of Albert or Suzanne. It was wise to keep some cards up your sleeve.

Then he saw the chance to take Albert's place as escort to Suzanne. He telephoned Schleger and told him of Albert, Suzanne and the rendezvous: "We can sweep them all up." He wanted the job finished. The longer it lasted, the longer he was at risk. Besides, he was bored with life in the country, though he contrived to escape to St. Jean on occasion. And he wanted the money.

Now Schleger said, "We have had another success tonight. We pulled in the wireless operator. He was riding in a taxi with his wireless, presumably moving his hiding place, and his drunken driver ran into one of our cars."

Ostmann turned to laugh at Louis in the back of the car. "You'd have been on your way to the rendezvous about the time we hit him. Poor thick-head was terrified. I put the boot into him and he knew that was only a sample! He's being questioned in the cellar in St. Jean now."

Louis knew what that meant. "It's fortunate there is a cellar; quieter."

Ostmann said, "All those houses on the quay have cellars. I hear the *Herr Oberst* keeps a good one."

Schleger said coldly, "Is that so?"

Ostmann grumbled, "Stiff-necked swine. Regular army, officer corps."

Because neither were invited to König's house.

Louis sensed the change in atmosphere. If they sulked about something they would take it out on someone and he was nearest. He tried to restore the mood of elation, "The wireless operator asked for it."

That brought the grin back to Ostmann's meaty face. He nodded, "*You* know which side your bread is buttered."

Louis grinned back, because it was expected, sat up straight in the corner, because it was expected. He thought: Bastards. Arrogant pigs. They held the whip hand. If you

wanted money or power – *anything* – you had to toe the line
they drew. You've done all right, Louis, you were well paid
while you worked for the S.S. in Paris and Schleger is being
generous, maybe because it isn't his money. But I still hate
these bloody Germans . . .

Well, not all of them. Talk of the *Oberst* reminded him of
the woman in the house on the end of the quay in St. Jean.
The colonel commanding the *Wehrmacht* in St. Jean lived
in the house and the woman, girl rather, was his daughter.
Louis lusted after her, wanted to take her and not only to
humble that German arrogance.

Schleger broke in on Louis' erotic mental images: "I think
we have uncovered a network of British agents. The man
appears to be the most important, but we also have the
wireless operator." He ticked them off on his fingers: "We
will have the girl soon and a squad will be picking up Albert
any time now."

Albert had been gruffly kind when Louis' mother had
taken him to Normandy on occasional, infrequent visits.
She did not like the country, either, but Albert had always
given her money when she left for Paris again and he never
forgot a tip for Louis. The boy had not taken long to realise
that Albert never knew how much cash was in the drawer he
used as a till in the bar – and to profit from that knowledge.
Now he shrugged, "He's another one who asked for it." To
hell with him.

David Brent gripped the throttle levers and eased them
back. As the power was cut the bow of the boat slumped
from its racing lift to butt into the sea. David worked the
handle of the engine-room telegraph. It was no use speaking
on the voice-pipe because the engineer and his two stokers
would not hear a word, shut up in that cavern below with
the now muted but still rumbling engines. But they could
see the repeater dial of the telegraph and its warning light.
Now, obedient to that signal, the main engines died and the
V-8 auxiliary motor cut in. The boat slid on quietly, no faster
than a man trotting.

The other boats were still in the arrowhead formation and now matching the slow progress of his own. David took the torch from his pocket and flashed it astern, twice, an orange, ember glow. The three boats stopped and were slowly lost in the night as David Brent went on towards the coast of France, less than a mile away now.

Rudi Halder told Bruno, "Stop engines." The boom of the diesels died and there was only the wash of the sea alongside as the last of the way came off the three E-boats, until they stopped. The other two boats had manoeuvred to close on Rudi so they lay together in line abreast. The two captains, Hans Petersen and Ernst Fischer, waved to Rudi from their respective bridges.

There was a general mutter of conversation, a stirring of movement running through the three low craft as gunners eased and stretched. Bruno said, "So now we listen – "

He broke off as Rudi snapped, "*Silence!*" The command cracked like a whip and the men froze, voices stilled. Rudi and Bruno stood with heads lifted, turning, and they heard the distant rumble of engines.

Rudi said softly, "Astern of us; north of us."

Bruno nodded, "Between here and St. Jean. *Tommis*. Has to be. There's only us and Gunther's lot out tonight and the area his boats are patrolling is twenty kilometres or more north of St. Jean." Then: "They've stopped!"

The rumble had faded and died. Rudi could hear Bruno's breathing in the silence and saw the dark face turned towards him with an unspoken question.

Rudi answered it, "We know about them. They don't know about us. We wait."

Suzanne ran around the edge of a field, found a gate and rolled over it into another lane beyond. Now she knew where she was and set off up the lane. She had slipped the pursuit, left the troopers shouting and searching the ground around the old house. She ran on, panting, until she came to the cottage and fell against its door.

The doctor came to answer her hammering, an old man, gaunt, in a shapeless old cardigan and felt slippers. He peered at her over pince-nez set crookedly on his nose and recognised her despite the darkness; because of the black-out he had switched off the light in the passage behind him before opening the door. He held it wide for her and she slipped in quickly and gasped, "The telephone. Please?"

"Of course." The old man gestured. "You know where it is."

Suzanne went on to the room at the end of the passage where the telephone stood on the desk. She spoke to Albert: "There's been an accident. I'm going to tell Papa, if I can find him, and I'll meet you at our place later tonight."

Albert's voice croaked fearfully over the wire: "A serious accident?"

"Very." Suzanne took a shuddering breath. "I'll explain when I see you." She put down the instrument and saw the old man staring at her from the door, realised her raincoat hung soaking wet, her shoes were smeared with mud and she had carried it into this room, leaving a trail from the door. She said, "I have to go. I'm sorry about the mud. Please make sure you clean it up in case anyone comes here looking for me. If they do, then you haven't seen me, don't know me."

The doctor nodded, "That is understood."

"Thank you." Suzanne kissed him on the cheek then hurried to the door.

He called after her, "God bless you!"

Albert had taken the call standing at the end of the wooden bar in his darkened café. He had returned from St. Jean on the seat of the farm cart, a bandage of vinegar and cold water wrapped around the injured wrist. Then he spent a long hour drinking with the two men from the barge tied up in the river for the night. He was friendly with all the men who worked the barges, had often crewed for them when they needed an extra hand. He knew the shoals and currents as well as they did, could talk of the river and their work on equal terms.

But tonight his conversation was forced, his thoughts with Suzanne and Louis. When the bargemen left he locked the door, put out the light and sat by the old black stove. The pain in his wrist had eased until it was only a dull ache, and he could use the hand.

When the call came he listened to Suzanne's voice, breathless, hurried and stumbling over phrases in the rough code they used. "I'm going to tell Papa" meant she was going to try to meet the boat as planned. "Our place": she intended to be put ashore on the beach she and Albert had marked for landings – if she could. And the "accident" was serious. Albert knew he had sent his nephew to his death and was heartsore, could have wept.

Now he stood with heart thumping in the gloom of this place that had been his home for over twenty years. He had marched into the carnage of the battle for Verdun in 1917 when he was not quite forty, a man in the prime of his life. He had staggered out of it prematurely grey and when he was demobilised he came back here. Now he was to leave again and he was an old man. This time he would not return. He took one last, long look around and sniffed the familiar smell of tobacco, spirits, cheese and ham, then moved.

The old Lebel pistol he had from the last war lay by his hand on the bar and he groped for and found the torch that rested on a shelf under it. He tested the torch to see that it worked then put that and the pistol into his jacket pockets. He broke a fist-sized chunk of bread from a long loaf, picked up a wedge of cheese and a flat bottle holding a half-litre of cognac. He stuffed these into the bag that held the tools he would need and grabbed his old raincoat from its hook by the back door. He shrugged into it, swung the bag over his shoulder and let himself out.

He made straight for the trees and undergrowth standing thirty yards from the back of the café. When he was in their shelter he worked around the little hamlet of a dozen houses until he reached the track that led down to the river. He paused there as he heard the growl of a car's engine on the road. Seconds later it swung around the bend and the engine was cut. The headlights, dimmed because of the black-out, still glowed but the car rolled silently down the slope into the hamlet and halted with a soft squeal of brakes. Four men spilled out of the doors and two waited at the front of the café while the other two ran round to the back. There was the shrill of a whistle and the men at the front kicked the door open and charged in.

Albert turned away and walked down the track for five minutes until he came to the river. When he reached its bank he could see the black rectangle of the wharf. It stood two hundred metres upriver on the opposite bank, with the low, flat shape of the barge moored alongside it. His own small boat was tied up where he stood. He stepped down into it and sculled across the river that flowed swiftly and gleamed like basalt. On the other side he set out on the kilometre-long walk to the coast.

The night was dark but Suzanne would not use the torch. She could just make out the path snaking through the scrub that grew low and thick on the cliff-top. The fear nagged at her: had the S.S. known about this landing place, too, and laid another ambush here, hidden from the eyes of the old doctor? Were they waiting for her now?

The scrub tore at her legs that shook with fatigue and she had a searing pain in her side. She had run a long way but she dared not stop to rest. Then the scrub ended and she stood on the edge of the cliff, the chalk face showing pale in the night and falling sheer to the beach below. Away to her right the headland with its solitary tree lifted against the night sky. The track ran on, angling steeply and narrowly down the face of the cliff. Suzanne paused just long enough to take off the low-heeled shoes then started the descent. She thought she heard, above the low rumble and suck of the sea on the shingle, the sound of voices calling a long way behind her. She did not wait to listen.

The path tilted not only downward but outward and it was greasy from the rain that still drizzled fitfully. Her bare feet gripped a little better than the shoes would have done but she still slid at every other stride. She went with one hand always grabbing at the side of the cliff to steady her – and ready to fall on the path rather than from it.

The last few feet were easier and she ran down them to the shingle then out to where the sea broke in a line of foam and phosphorescence. Her feet crunched on the shingle and she winced as the sharper stones cut her skin but she did not slacken speed until she stood in the surf. Now she finally reached for the torch in the pocket of her trenchcoat, flashed a signal out to sea and waited. She could see no craft out there.

David Brent leaned on the coaming of the bridge as the motor torpedo boat crept along the line of the shore, marked by a silver line of breaking surf. No light showed aboard her except the faint glow from the compass binnacle. It was barely enough to illumine the intent face of Grundy, the coxswain, hanging above it.

The coast was visible now, the grey loom of the cliff standing out of the darkness of the night. Bill Emmett, the navigator, was on the bridge, binoculars at his eyes and his lips moving but making no sound. Brent thought: Praying? He lifted his own glasses again, searching for the landing place as he and Emmett had done for the past five minutes, casting northward along the shore. But now, slowly sweeping the line of the cliff, he checked, swung fractionally back, stopped. He said softly, "There it is, off the starboard bow: headland with a lone tree."

Emmett said quickly, "Right! Got it."

David lowered his binoculars, "Congratulations, Pilot, you've made a near-perfect landfall. I'll stand you a drink when we get home."

Emmett blew out his cheeks in a puffing breath of relief, "Could do with it now, sir. But thank you." He ducked below, going back to his chart.

David thought: *When* we get home? He remembered closing this coast once before, but a long way farther north. He remembered how the guns had torn open the night with long tongues of yellow flame. One of the two boats had caught fire and burned like a torch. The other had been blown apart, nothing left of it but a shattered, stranded hulk. And on the shore the soldiers waited to be taken off.

He shuddered and Tallon muttered sardonically behind him, "Somebody walking over your grave?"

"Something like that." Brent glanced over his shoulder at Tallon. The soldier's face was no more than a grey smudge in the night but Brent knew he was restless – or nervous?

Tallon stared past David at the shore. "We've done this before."

"Once." With other boats and other men. "Going the other way."

"This way might not be so bad, but once is more than enough." Tallon knew a guide was supposed to lead him and his men to the railway but it would be a night march of a kilometre or so through enemy-held country. He did not know how many wagons or coaches would make up the train, nor how many escorts would be aboard it. There could be a dozen heavily-armed men, or a platoon, a company – a thousand of the bastards! He wondered if David Brent knew how frightened he was.

Jimmy Nash said urgently, "There's our signal!"

A light flashed briefly from the shore. David used his torch to send the reply then ordered, "Starboard. Take her in, Cox'n."

"Starboard 'n' take her in, sir." Grundy's hands on the wheel turned the bow to point at the shore and they crept in towards it.

When it was barely a hundred yards away Brent shoved past Tallon to reach the engine controls set on the panel to the left of the cox'n. He ordered Grundy, "Hard aport." The cox'n spun the wheel and as the boat came around Brent rang down the engine-room telegraph. The way came off the boat and she stopped with her stern pointed towards the shore. "Send away the dinghy." Brent turned and watched it lowered over the stern then it pulled away rapidly, Cullen and another seaman tugging at the oars.

The engine still muttered softly but the boat lay without forward motion, rocking gently as the sea rolled her seventy-foot length. Tallon said, "I'll bring my chaps up, ready to go." He turned to leave the bridge.

Brent told him, "No. Leave them below for now. Wait till we've confirmed the guide is there and the other boats have come in with the rest of your blokes." Tallon halted and shifted restlessly from one foot to the other. Brent watched the shore. He could make out a figure standing on the line of the surf and the dinghy was close, would ground in a second or two –

The firing came from the top of the cliff, a staccato, ripping burst of flickering flame. Brent shouted, "Engage that fire!" The figure still stood in the surf, but now was bowing, blending into the greater, lower black outline of the dinghy that had grounded. Another burst came from the cliff but then the gunner in his turret aft of the bridge, ready and waiting for action, brought his sights on and opened fire with the twin .5-inch machine-guns. The lines of red tracer curved up to the cliff-top and the muzzle flame up there was snuffed out. The gunner continued firing, in bursts of two or three seconds, sweeping left and right across the face of the cliff. There were some answering shots – Brent saw the flashes from the weapons in several places along the cliff – but none came near the boat and he could see the dinghy on its way back, the men at the oars pulling strongly. Brent thought: Who wouldn't?

He called, "Hoist that dinghy in!"

There was a lull in the firing and Tallon said savagely, bad-temperedly, "That's scuppered my little jaunt!" Brent thought he could understand the soldier's anger, primed and ready to go – and now anti-climax. Because the raid could not go in now, with the coast defences alerted. But was there also a hint of relief, satisfaction, in that statement? Was Brent himself relieved?

Jimmy Nash thought he detected that relief in both of them and his confidence was shaken, but then he said, "Here's the agent – Lord, it's a girl!"

David Brent was working the telegraph, calling for a crash start on the main engines, and as they roared into life, shoving the throttle levers forward to full ahead, but he swung around now. The girl had been brought up to the bridge and stood close to him. He stared at her, disbelieving. Suzanne's face, pale and wide-eyed, was the last he wanted to see yet he felt a flare of exhilaration. And she knew him, despite the gloom, the sharp jerk of her head told him that. But she only said, "You were sent for by – Michel." Brent marked that hesitation but Suzanne went on: "I wasn't supposed to come aboard; I was the guide."

Brent said, "Michel? That's the name of an agent?"

"It's the name I know him by, but he uses others. He has been captured by the S.S. and another man was killed. I got away."

Their voices were lifted now to make themselves heard above the bellow of the three big engines. Brent stared at Suzanne, thinking: Why her? And that this night's operation, for which he was responsible, was washed out. The raid could not be made, the bridge would not be blown, the railway not cut. But worse, far worse than that, was the failure to rescue the prisoner aboard the train: *"More important than the commandos or your flotilla! Bring him!"*

Tallon and Jimmy Nash – and the girl – were watching him, waiting for his decision, his orders.

He thought she had not changed, was as he remembered her. His memory had been true.

5

". . . A damn fine action!"

Brent's boat was roaring out to sea at better than thirty knots now, bow riding high out of the water and stern tucked down, spray flying past the bridge. He wondered what the hell he could do? Tallon could not even reach the prisoner on the train, let alone Brent carry him back across the Channel. The situation would have defeated a Nelson while Brent and Tallon were only the "second team".

Then there had been that reaction of relief when he knew the raid was aborted. Was it some instinct warning him that it was doomed? Or just fear? Probably that. He was no stranger to fear, lived with it. He snatched off his cap, ran his fingers through his hair and clapped it on again. The girl: they had to talk about themselves, but not now. At the same time he needed to know all that had happened ashore.

He turned to Jimmy Nash and told him, "You've got her for a minute. I'm going down to the wheel-house. Pick up the other boats and hold this course." He glanced at the girl and jerked his head, a summons, then edged past Tallon where he stood with shoulders hunched in bad temper. Brent dropped down the short ladder to the wheel-house below the bridge and the girl followed him.

The wheel-house was a cramped box and they stooped under the low deckhead. The chart-table took up a lot of the room and they perforce stood close. Once inside, the hatch shut and the light on, he said, "Tell me about it." Suzanne hesitated, again, and that irritated him. He snapped, "I know you Secret Service people are a close-mouthed lot and I can understand that. One careless word could give away a friend, kill him. But I was ordered to bring this prisoner out whatever the cost, so you can tell me what happened."

Suzanne's shoulders lifted then fell in a shrug. Her hands were dug deep in the pockets of the trenchcoat, one holding the torch, the other curled around the butt of the pistol. The already wet coat glistened afresh with the spray that had flown over the bridge. She said, "That raid would have had to be cancelled anyway. Michel had got the timings of the train all along the route and gave them to me, but this morning he found it had been put back by more than three hours because the S.S. are rounding up more deportees. Then when I went to the bridge this afternoon I found a first-line battalion of infantry bivouacked there for the night. They are entraining tomorrow on their way north."

David thought bitterly that everything had gone wrong with this operation, but he did not speak and the girl continued: "After checking on the bridge I went on to meet Michel at a rendezvous and I took another man with me as an escort." She told him of the ambush, the shooting, the capture of Michel and her escape. "I ran. Away from them and heading towards the sea, praying you – the boats – would be there."

Now she looked at David Brent. "I want you to put me ashore again, ten kilometres north of St. Jean."

"What!" Brent was shaking his head.

Suzanne insisted, "You must! I have to warn another agent, tell him to run for it." She was talking of Paul. She was supposed to meet him tomorrow. Michel knew where the wireless operator had been staying and the S.S. would soon trace his movements after leaving there. They had only to question taxi-drivers. She did not know that Paul was already in the cells below S.S. headquarters in St. Jean. She explained, "Michel's orders are to hold out for twenty-four hours before talking, to give others time to get away, but whether he can, when they start 'interrogating' him . . ." She left that unfinished and went on: "A friend will be expecting me, waiting on the beach. It is a place we'd chosen as good for landings. I managed to telephone him – "

Brent broke in: "Telephone! How?"

"From the house of a friend." So Albert would be waiting for her, she was certain of that, but she had an awful fear of what would follow later.

65

David did not like the idea. Put this girl ashore again? She was watching him, leaning back into one corner of the little wheel-house with her legs braced against the pitching of the boat as it raced out to sea. Brent's arms were outstretched to the bulkhead to hold himself steady. The girl was determined, he could tell that from her set face, her hair clinging damply around it. She was slender in the tightly-belted trenchcoat, seeming fragile, but she was strong. He knew the strength of that slim body.

Suzanne urged, "I only have to go from the shore to the river and that's little more than a kilometre inland. Then I'll go down the river to St. Jean." She stopped, had nearly said, "You know it", but checked herself in time.

David Brent remembered the river and how it ran down to the town. He remembered how she had looked the first time he saw her. He said harshly, "I'll have to think about that." He would say no more and led the way back to the bridge, the tearing slipstream and drenching spray.

He stood at the front of the bridge by Grundy. The other three boats were now in company and had fallen into the arrowhead formation. Crozier's boat tore along to starboard while Dent and Vance had taken station to port. All four boats raced out to sea, bows lifted and sterns squatted on cushions of foam, engines bellowing.

Brent narrowed his eyes against the lash of the spray. He was conscious of the girl behind him. She had followed him up to the bridge again but had the sense to stay at the back out of the way. He glanced around and saw a seaman clambering up to the bridge with one arm wrapped round a huge bundle, the other clutching dexterously at one handhold after another. That was Cullen, experienced and sure-footed on the pitching deck. Grundy said he had the makings of a good man and only needed "straightening out a bit".

Cullen handed the bundle to Jimmy Nash, who shook it out. The oilskin flapped on the wind, clapped like thunder but then he helped the girl to put it on and fastened it about her waist. David thought how true to form it was that Gentleman Jimmy had sent Cullen below to fetch it. He grinned.

The outsize oilskin hung about the girl like a tent. When he had first seen her, at the party in the embassy in Paris a year ago, she was demure but shapely in a little black dress and gloves. He was on leave, waiting for an appointment to another ship. She told him she was British by birth but held French nationality now. She was a bi-lingual secretary and had come to the party with her boss, head of a French firm that did a lot of business with Britain.

He remembered he had said, "I've had enough of this place. Let's go out on the town."

She had looked up at him seriously for what seemed a long time and he had wondered: What the hell? Then she had given him a small smile and said, "I'd love to." And when he left her at the door of her apartment in the early hours of the morning she had said, "I'm going to Normandy tomorrow for a few days. Will you come with me?" And that was the start of the affair.

He remembered how the river ran close to the coast at the place where she wanted him to put her ashore, and how it meandered down the ten kilometres or so to St. Jean. He stared out to sea, thinking. Suppose . . .

"Lights! Starboard bow!" That was Jimmy Nash making the report: "The fishing fleet again."

The drifters were three to four miles distant. Brent turned his eyes away from the lights and instead searched the outer darkness to starboard and port. Blackness. There could be another fleet out there, invisible without lights. All you would see of another boat would be the white blaze of her bow-wave and wake. And those of an E-boat showed less than those of a M.T.B. because the E-boat ran lower in the water.

His eyes changed focus and found Chris at the back of the bridge. Brent wondered about Tallon's relief and his own as they'd raced away from the shore. Fear? Or a healthy respect for danger and gratitude for a narrow escape? And he thought again of the river winding down to St. Jean. Suppose . . .

Rudi Halder lowered the binoculars and let them hang from their strap on his chest. He balanced easily on the bridge of the E-boat as it rocked gently in the swell. The three boats lay with engines stopped, still, within yards of each other. So he could hear, above the soft wash and slap of the sea, the occasional low murmur of voices aboard the boats on either side. Their captains, Fischer and Petersen, stood on their bridges as Rudi did on his, watching, listening. Their heads frequently turned to look to him, waiting for his orders. These were Rudi's boats and he had trained their crews, led them and driven them. He was proud of them.

He estimated the fishing fleet was about ten kilometres away and to seaward. His boats had stopped twenty minutes ago. At that time he had heard the distant rumble of engines, but the sound had receded and died, tantalisingly. Rudi thought they had been headed for the coast, and waited.

Now his head turned quickly and he knew he had been right. There was a crackle of firing from the direction of the coast, muted by the miles of sea between, and he saw tiny red sparks of tracer floating in the night sky. Then he heard the engines again, distant but approaching from the land.

Bruno Jacobi's voice came deeply: "Sounds like the same boats coming out."

Rudi grinned at him. "Right." For a few seconds longer he stood with head cocked on one side, listening to the engines, the sound rolling over the sea like far off thunder, the herald of a storm. He saw the other two captains turned to him and he lifted his voice to order, "Start up!"

David Brent saw the mist as a floating greyness ahead of the boat then a second later they ran into it. He blinked, and as quickly the mist had gone. He glanced out to starboard and saw the lights of the fishing fleet clearly. So the mist was drifting in on the wind from the port side, had been left astern but there might be more of it ahead. He stepped around Grundy at the wheel, gripped the throttle levers and eased the speed to twenty-five knots. That would give them

68

all a little more thinking time if the mist suddenly thickened about them.

The fishing fleet was abeam now and soon he would have to make the turn to take the boats around the drifters. He had to make a decision about the girl and his course of action, talk to her again, and to Tallon and the other captains. Time was precious. Whatever he decided to do, he had to bear in mind that the boats must be well on their way home before the dawn. Otherwise they could be caught on the open sea by enemy aircraft.

He glanced astern and saw the other boats had conformed to his reduction in speed, were neatly holding the arrowhead formation. In the night they were dark silhouettes riding the silver furrows they cut in the sea. Beyond them was the outer darkness with visibility of about five hundred yards at most.

He saw Suzanne Leclerc tucked away in a corner at the back of the bridge, beckoned her to him and asked, "You said the time of the train was put back? You know the timings?"

The girl nodded, "All along the route. It was delayed three and a half hours, but that only made the raid more dangerous. It was the battalion bivouacked around the bridge . . ." She stopped because David Brent no longer seemed to be listening to her, was peering into the night.

He muttered, "Bloody fog!"

She went back to her corner, wondering.

The E-boats ran into the fog and Rudi Halder cursed softly as the boats on either side of him disappeared. He was aware of Bruno Jacobi glancing quickly at him then turning away to peer ahead. He would be wondering if Rudi was going to reduce speed. Rudi was not. He had decided on this interception course and speed and he would hold both. But this fog was the devil! He could miss the *Tommis* – he was certain there were British boats ahead of him, somewhere – or he could run right into them. He could hardly see beyond the E-boat's bow, let alone penetrate the grey curtain. If another craft appeared before him now he would collide with it: *Smash!*

Bruno Jacobi bawled, "Damned fog!"

Rudi nodded but did not turn his head, leaned forward, arms on the bridge coaming, eyes narrowed against the mist streaming past . . .

They burst out of it. One second they were wrapped around by the fog and the next they were tearing through open water straight towards the *Tommis*. Rudi had time only to see there were four boats, two in front of him and two more beyond them. Then he snapped into the voice-pipe, "Hard aport!"

The coxswain in the wheel-house below the bridge spun the wheel. The boat heeled in the turn and as she straightened out of it he saw the boat astern and to starboard swinging to follow him. The *Tommis* were barely more than a hundred yards away on the same course and now the 20mm. cannon in the bow below Rudi opened up, followed a blink later by the other aft in the waist. He was almost blinded by the muzzle flashes and the flying tracer. He could not make out the other two E-boats but saw their guns firing. Now he was leading them in echelon, both of them astern of him and a boat's length between each. That way they weren't bumping in each other's wash.

There were strings of red tracer coming the other way now as the *Tommis* replied, and he saw from the angle of the tracer that he was drawing ahead of them, making better speed. Something beat like a hammer on the cupola around the bridge and he knew that was the enemy fire hitting. He held the course another few seconds as the 20mm. cannons banged away, then ordered again, "Hard aport!" He laid a steadying hand on the coaming of the bridge as the boat heeled, his head turning to look astern. He still could not see the *Tommi* boats, would not get his night vision back for some minutes, but the white blazes of their wakes and the lines of tracer showed their position. He could not see any fires but they had been mauled, he was sure of that.

The cannons of the three E-boats had hosed the *Tommis* at point-blank range.

Then he was into the fog again, the guns ceased firing and Bruno Jacobi was bellowing congratulations. Rudi nodded, grinning. It had been a good attack. The entire action had lasted less than a minute.

The attack had achieved total surprise. David Brent saw the E-boats duck back into the fog that came down behind them like a shutter. He could charge after them into the fog, pursue them blind on the chance that he could bring them to action again. At another time he would have done so, wanted to do it now, but his orders were to avoid action, to carry out his primary task. "Starboard twenty!"

Grundy spun the wheel again and Brent's boat swerved away from the fog. The others followed and fell into the arrowhead formation again. Brent glanced to starboard and then to port. The three other boats were maintaining course and speed, not making any signals for help. That did not mean they had escaped damage. They must certainly have suffered.

Jimmy Nash had expected them to hunt down the enemy and fight it out. Then he remembered Brent's orders to avoid action – but also his relief when the raid was aborted. Nash stepped close to David Brent and ground out, "The bastards jumped us!"

Brent thought that was the whole idea and Jimmy knew it, was only voicing his anger. So David just nodded acknowledgment and looked past Nash to where the girl stood at the back of the bridge. She was all right but had been lucky. He reproached himself for not sending her below – but that would have been no guarantee of safety. A shell from a 20mm. cannon would rip through the hull as if it were paper.

He wondered where the E-boats were now.

They were clear of the fog and Rudi Halder had altered course so that they were running out to sea. Bruno Jacobi, braced on thick legs against the bucking of the boat, shouted,

"That was a damn fine action! In – *bang!* – and out again before they knew what the hell was going on!"

Rudi grinned at him. The fog had helped; that had been lucky. But the boats had been well handled, the attack carried out perfectly. Rudi answered above the boom of the engines, "We're not done with them yet." And as Bruno looked questioningly at him: "When they've finished counting the damage they'll head for home. We're going to lie out along their probable course and hit them again, when they're already dreaming about their beds and their girls, and their eyes are growing tired."

Bruno laughed.

David Brent saw that the lights of the fishing fleet were far astern now and he ordered the change of course to take the M.T.B.s circling around the drifters and then northwards. The boats heeled in the turn and settled on the new heading and he knew that would not be lost on the girl. She would conclude that he was going to put her ashore as she had asked. She might be right.

Suzanne had been deafened and blinded, shaken by the fire-fight between the boats. But now her sight and hearing had returned, her hands did not shake because she gripped the side of the bridge to hold on against the pitching of the boat. The terror had receded. Now there was only the bellow of the engines, the black night all around and the cold, driving spray.

She saw David's face turned towards her, as he had looked down at her in the darkness outside her flat in Paris when she asked him to go with her to Normandy. She had driven them down in her open two-seater the next day, her hair flying on the wind as they slipped out of the blaze of sun into cool shade beneath the trees marching along the roadside. Her hands on the wheel were slim and brown, innocent of rings. She had told him, "I was brought up in this part of the country. I could find a job here any time I wanted." And: "I keep the cottage as a place to get away to." She did not tell him why she needed to escape.

The cottage had only one room. You could lie in bed with the window open and listen to the sea, watch the dying fire in the hearth and imagine pictures in the flames . . .

Suzanne became aware that David Brent was at the throttle levers, easing them back, and the boat was slowing, stopping. The engines were suddenly silent and the bow slumped from its racing attitude so the boat wallowed low and level in the sea. The other three boats stopped close alongside and edged in closer so that a man could make a long stride from one to the next.

David turned to the girl and, as if reading her thoughts of a moment ago, said, "You talked of travelling down the river to St. Jean. I want you to tell me about sentries, patrols, defences. There's a map below in the wheel-house."

Suzanne nodded: "I can do that."

He watched her drop down the hatch, then he turned to the other boats. Crozier, lying close on the starboard side, had little to report. He had seen even less of the action than had Brent and his boat had not been scratched. Dent and Vance had borne the brunt of the attack by the E-boats, both had taken hits but all on the upperworks so they were not making water and their engines were unaffected. Little Dent had one man slightly wounded, and Vance two. All were minor cuts from flying splinters. None of the eight commandos aboard each boat were hurt.

Tommy Vance had one man dead. The blanket-wrapped body was now being lashed to the deck in the stern. David Brent asked, "Who?"

Tommy answered, low-voiced, "Garbutt, sir."

David remembered Garbutt as a thin, cheerful youth of no more than eighteen. He sighed bitterly, but thought they had been lucky, might easily have suffered worse damage and casualties. He wondered about the action's effect on the morale of the crews. That kind of reverse might destroy confidence, instil an unhealthy excess of respect for the enemy. But he did not think that was the case with these men of his. They were not silent and brooding. They were working or keeping a look-out but there was a low murmur of conversation and someone was humming softly. David picked out the tune: "A Nightingale Sang in Berkeley Square". He called drily, "You won't hear any nightingale out here," and heard chuckles.

Brent told Jimmy Nash, "I want to see all captains in the wardroom in five minutes." He glanced at the soldier. "And you, Chris, please."

Tallon replied ironically, "My time is yours. I've a highly trained, wound-up platoon, seven of them with enough explosive and know-how to blow up the Forth Bridge. But you might say we're all dressed up with nowhere to go now."

Brent looked at him thoughtfully, then said, "We may need them all."

He swung down through the hatch to the wheel-house and Tallon looked at Jimmy Nash. "So what is this for? And why are we hanging around here?"

Jimmy said, "We'll find out in five minutes."

Tallon muttered, "It looks like a wash-out to me."

Jimmy Nash privately agreed, but said nothing, remembering Tallon's relief when they had to flee from the coast.

Chris Tallon scowled bad-temperedly. He wondered if his relief had shown, though he was sure he had seen the same reaction in Brent. Tallon knew the reason for his. He was ready to fight but hoped for a fighting chance, not to be thrown in hastily in an attempt to save a lost cause. But there was also bitterness. He was retreating again. He would have to tell his men and he knew what they would say: "Just like one more flaming exercise then, sir." They had trained enough, had keyed themselves up for this.

But David Brent had said, "We may need them all." So . . .?

Brent turned Bill Emmett out of the wheel-house and replaced the navigator's chart with a map of the area ashore. Chris Tallon, up on the bridge, had another. Both were marked with the site of the intended landing now abandoned, and the bridge that was to have been blown.

Suzanne looked at the map. It was small scale and covered a section of country around St. Jean some forty kilometres square. Suzanne sketched quickly on a spare sheet of paper as she talked: "St. Jean and the region around it have been quiet. There's been the occasional arrest of someone caught listening to the B.B.C., or making rude signs at the Germans, but no actual resistance. So there is just one battalion of infantry based in the barracks in the new town, here, across the bridge from the old port." The pencil tapped the sketch.

"The *Oberst*, that is the colonel, who commands in St. Jean lives in the old port. There's a row of houses facing the harbour and he has the one at the end, right on the sea-wall." The pencil blocked them in on the sketch. "The S.S. Headquarters is in the butcher's house, that's this one, second from the other end of the row. It belonged to a butcher at one time, a hundred years or more ago, then it became offices but the name stuck. Now the S.S. have requisitioned it for the headquarters. They will take Michel there." And she knew what awaited him. The pencil shook slightly then, but was stilled as the long fingers tightened their grip.

"The *Oberst* has deployed most of his battalion as sentries on the coast or as patrols and left only a hundred men in the barracks. There are scattered patrols of two or four men in the town after the start of curfew, and sentries on the bridge over the river joining the new town to the old port."

Brent pictured it in his mind as he remembered, watched the girl's slim fingers move over the sketch, listened to her even voice: "The river runs down from the north then swings westward to pass under the bridge and so into the harbour. The railway – the same railway we were meant to cut tonight – comes up from the south, passes through the station in the new town then goes on past the bridge and the old port. It runs close by the river, and inland of it for a kilometre, then turns away to the east."

Brent asked, "The river traffic, the barges, still goes on?" He looked up and saw the girl watching him, puzzled, curious.

She answered, "Yes. Every day except Sunday, and even

then if the Germans want a cargo urgently." She quickly turned her gaze to the map now and her pencil marched across it: "There are similar patrols out in the country. On the coast there are posts of seven or eight men housed in a shed or a hut. They send out sentries through the hours of darkness, two at a time: one patrolling north along the coast for a mile or so, one south. They can only cover about half of the battalion's section of coast on any night, so they keep changing, operating from different posts. Sometimes a stretch of the shore is patrolled for a week, or not at all for nights on end." The pencil paused: "There is a gun, an 88mm., on the headland overlooking the approaches to the port. A guardship is anchored at the harbour mouth, an old drifter with a 40mm. cannon mounted in the bow. Three E-boats are based in the port but they are at sea almost every night, except when the weather is bad."

David Brent said wrily, "We know about them."

Suzanne nodded. "They have maintenance crews who live in the barracks and go down to the port every morning to work on the boats. The Naval Headquarters is thirty kilometres north up the coast and there is another flotilla of E-boats based there."

Brent asked, "Is the guardship moored there all the time, out in the harbour and near its mouth?"

"Nearly always. She goes to sea occasionally, out to the fishing fleet, or moves about the harbour, but most of the time she lies near the mouth."

Brent nodded and Suzanne moved the pencil again, set its point down on the map. "I've told you of all the defences. I want to go ashore here, just north of this cape. It stretches out to sea for eight or nine hundred metres and stands high. It's sheer rock and very prominent." David silently agreed with that, at least; the cape stuck out from the coast like a pointing finger. Suzanne said, "There may be a sentry, maybe not." She shrugged. "If a sentry is patrolling then there is a prepared plan for dealing with him. So will you do as I ask, please?"

Brent replied with questions of his own: "You said you

had the timings of the train? And can I ask you about the old port? I remember St. Jean but I think you know the place inside out as it is now."

Of course he would remember. Suzanne said, "I'll tell you all I can." She thought: We're both so bloody formal as if it never happened. But what else can we do?

She answered his questions.

The wardroom was on the port side and flattered by its name. It was a cabin like half of a railway compartment, with a long seat down one side on which a man could sleep. A table was mounted on the opposite bulkhead and there was just room to edge between the two. The map and sketch were on the table, David Brent and Suzanne Leclerc standing either side of it, when Jimmy Nash, the three captains and Chris Tallon crowded into the wardroom. Tallon and little Dent were the last to enter and stood by the door. The others sat on the bench, hunched forward to see the map.

Brent said, "I expect you're wondering why I've got you here. There are E-boats out there and the sooner you're back aboard your own boats, the better. So I'll make this short." Then he told them all he knew, all Suzanne had told him – and laid out his plan.

He watched them, waited for their reactions. He was the only regular officer. Crozier was big, burly, weather-beaten and an artist in civil life, while Dent was an erstwhile bank clerk, short, thin and pink-cheeked. Tommy Vance, a solicitor, was little taller than Dent but looked twice as wide and was black-bearded. Under the oilskins, now hanging open, they wore a miscellany of old reefer jackets, sweaters, even a bridgecoat: that was little Dent's and hung past his knees. They were only alike in their youth. Not one of them was over twenty-six.

The three captains looked at each other, then at Jimmy Nash. He saw he had been elected spokesman, cleared his throat and said diplomatically, "It's an – unconventional plan, sir. A bit risky?"

Chris Tallon said baldly, "I think it's bloody mad." He

stood in silence for a moment, returning Brent's expression-less gaze, then he went on slowly, "I'll say one thing for it: if the impression made on us is anything to go by it should have the advantage of surprise."

The girl did not speak. Tallon and the captains were all aware of her, of course. She was out of place in that wardroom, anyway, and besides that she was an agent, a strange breed. It called for someone unusual to live day after day under the hand of the enemy, playing a part, your life always at risk. She was bedraggled now, the oilskin like a bulging sack tied about the middle, but she was pretty.

David Brent did not look at her. He had been in the front line since the summer of 1940, with the boats fighting to hold the narrow seas between Britain and the continent. He had been ready to land and take off the commandos, to face familiar dangers. And now? He saw the risks in his plan, the odds against success and they were daunting. But resolution was forming out of necessity. "Can you think of any other way?" He waited, but when no answer came, said flatly, "This is not a council of war. I'm not canvassing opinions. I've told you what we are going to do."

They stared at him, their minds running parallel now, thinking that he was the senior officer and could give these orders to his captains, and to Tallon. But, by God! He would have to answer for them later.

He was ready now to answer the questions Chris Tallon put to him – and Tallon's one suggestion: "We should go on foot before then." Brent turned that down and Chris glared silently, then finally asked, "Assuming we get in, how do we get out again?" He stared unwinkingly at Brent and was remembering. He would never forget: he had commanded the rearguard of only five men spread thinly among the houses of the village. He had sent the rest of his command down to the shore to embark, but when the first two M.T.B.s were destroyed he believed he was going to die . . .

Brent held Tallon's stare, guessed at the soldier's thoughts, had his own pictures burnt into his mind. The petrol from the tanks of the burning boat had spread out over the sea to make a lake of flame that lit up the approach to the jetty as bright as day. Brent's boat had to pass through that glare to reach the shore. They had gone in and come out with the soldiers. It had seemed like a miracle, though the Sub and the gunner were killed.

Now David Brent grinned stiffly at Tallon. The soldier had said "assuming we get in". So he saw the risks, accepted them, would attempt this "bloody madness". But his eyes had never left Brent's and his question still hung in the air: "How do we get out again?"

Brent answered him, then carefully folded the map and sketch, pocketed them. He said, "Now it's time for a little piracy. I told you we needed a drifter . . ."

Rudi Halder leaned in the corner of the bridge, cradling a steaming mug of coffee between his hands. Bruno Jacobi screwed the top on the thermos and stowed it away in a locker. The three E-boats lay side by side and rocked slowly to the Atlantic swell. The drifters of the fishing fleet, fifteen kilometres or so inshore, were hull-down over the horizon but their lights shed a glow like a faint, false dawn.

Rudi was well pleased with his night's work – so far. And he was confident the *Tommi* boats would pass not far from his present position on their way home. He was proud of his Service, his profession, and that he was making a success of it.

He shifted restlessly now as an uncomfortable thought intruded: *Oberst* Erwin König, the tall, spare commander of the *Wehrmacht* battalion in St. Jean, had said of the *Führer*, "You can usually judge a man by his friends."

Rudi had asked, "What do you mean by that?"

The *Oberst*'s bony face was contemptuous as he answered, "Himmler, Schleger, Ostmann. Those friends."

And Rudi had his own doubts about the S.S. Only a day or two before, in the bar down by the harbour of St. Jean and close by where the E-boats lay, a semi-drunken Ostmann had boasted to the young E-boat captain of how he and his chief, Schleger, made their prisoners "sing".

He had gone into obscene detail. Rudi had turned away, sickened.

Later, when he was alone with Ilse König, the *Oberst*'s daughter, she had asked what they could do.

Rudi had had to answer bitterly, "Nothing. The S.S. is a law to itself."

Now he shoved away from the bridge coaming and dug his hands into his pockets. Still no sound of engines, but there was time; the *Tommis* had to sort themselves out. His mind turned yearningly to Ilse. She was twenty-two, tall for a girl, with soft brown hair and eyes, a lovely body. She was in St. Jean as housekeeper to her widowed father. She was also, of course, Rudi's lover . . .

Minutes later, Bruno Jacobi interrupted his dreaming: "Do you think we should call Gunther's boats down to join the party?"

Gunther commanded three E-boats based in the port where the Naval H.Q. was established, some thirty kilometres north of St. Jean. Rudi preferred his own near-independent command, out of the way of H.Q. and its Staff, but Gunther needed such close supervision. He knew the other flotilla was at sea tonight, grimaced and shook his head. "Gunther is a thickhead and charges about without thinking. He'd do more harm than good. We'll leave him up north out of the way."

Then he looked at his watch and frowned. The *Tommis* had taken enough time. Had they gone home by a different route? He doubted that. And if they had diverted by two or three miles he would still have heard those big engines. So . . . "Let's get back to business." He would run quietly back inshore and hunt for the *Tommis*, starting around the fishing-fleet.

6

"On fire!"

The man, who on his papers was described as Max Neumann, sat on the dirty wooden floor of the boxcar with his knees drawn up to his chin, his arms wrapped around them. He was fifty-three years old, unshaven and unwashed, shivering in the threadbare suit that was all he had left now.

The car was a bare box, unlit and pitch-black but for the slivers of grey that showed where there were cracks in the timber walls. Draughts sighed through the cracks but he knew the sighs would become a piercing, biting shriek when the train began to move.

The cracks had a use. By setting his eye to one of them he could see out over the dull silver gleam of the skein of steel tracks of the marshalling yard. This was a long train, he had seen that before the S.S. men kicked him aboard, and his wagon was near the end of it. There was one more boxcar waiting with its door open, empty. Then came the passenger coach in which the S.S. guards were to travel, and that was the last. He could see the guards standing outside their coach, smoking, laughing. And grumbling as they waited; he had heard them say the train's departure had been delayed by three and a half hours. When had he heard that? He only knew it was a long time ago; they had taken his watch.

The other prisoners crammed into his wagon were quiet, only whispers scurrying in the darkness and soft sobbing that tore at his heart. He was sorry for them. They did not know where they were going, but he did. Not exactly, of course; even the guards did not know exactly. Their destination might be Buchenwald, Dachau, Sachsenhausen or some other camp. It did not matter which because their fate would be the same.

As his. When he was caught at the house in Le Havre

and accused of being a Jew with false papers, he admitted it. That saved him a beating. When they demanded his real identity he gave the name of his cousin Franz. They would check their records and find that Franz had disappeared a year ago – he had taken his family and fled. They would also find that neither Max nor Franz were Jews, but as bad or worse. They were Germans and Germany was their country but Hitler was not their leader. The lies had given Max a little time. Now he wondered why he had bothered.

They would uncover "Max Neumann's" identity, no doubt of that. They would have been looking for him ever since he ran away from Heidelberg. It was not the agent who persuaded him to leave. Max knew he had no future in Heidelberg. His work was the reason they let him live like a human being and it frightened him. But he would have stayed and worked because his wife had been ill with tuberculosis and could not have survived an attempted escape. He would not have left without her. But she had died that summer, so when the agent came for him, he was ready.

There had been no sign of the agent at the house, but even if he was still free, he could not save Max now.

There were new sounds in the night outside, harsh, bawling, cursing voices and under them a softer pattering and whimpering. He squinted through the crack and saw more prisoners were coming. S.S. men herded them like sheep as they came slipping and stumbling over the steel rails, clutching pathetic bundles, and clawed their way up into the next wagon. The doors slammed shut and the men of the S.S. escort clambered aboard. The train jerked with a rattling of couplings and then began to roll forward.

This, he knew, was the beginning of the end. There would be the journey and then the identification. They might offer to let him take up his work again but he would not. It had gone much further than he had told them. He would not tell them for the sake of his immortal soul.

Ilse König and her father, the *Oberst*, talked over the dinner she cooked and served, but afterwards he apologised and grumbled, "I'm sorry, but as I've spent the day on a tour of inspection I now have to catch up on the paperwork. You must excuse me."

Ilse smiled because she knew he hated to be tied to a desk. She watched him stalk across the hall. His tall, spare body carried the uniform well. The tunic, buttoned to the neck, fitted without a wrinkle and the grey trousers were pressed to a knife-edged crease. He entered his study and closed the door.

She was used to spending her evenings alone but did not like it, only bore with it as a soldier's daughter. She read for a while, curled up in a big chair before the fire, then took the book upstairs to bed.

Her room looked out on the harbour and she stood at the window in the darkness for a minute before drawing the curtains. The house formed the bottom leg of an L, the long leg of which was the terrace of buildings – stores, chandlers, offices – stretched along the quay. That was thirty cobbled metres wide between the side of the harbour and the terrace.

The harbour was almost empty, the water still and black, the drifters of the fishing fleet at sea and the E-boats gone from their berths. There was only the old drifter, the guardship, moored to its buoys fore and aft at the harbour entrance. No one was on the quay because of the curfew, though Ilse knew there was a sentry on duty at the front door below where she stood. Three soldiers under the command of a *Gefreiter* were quartered at the back of the house and provided that sentry on the door twenty-four hours of the day.

She reached up to draw the curtains and then paused when she saw the hooded lights of a car sweep out of the main street of the new town and cross the bridge over the river to the old port. The car braked to a halt outside the last building but one at the far end of the terrace. That was the S.S. headquarters.

As they got out of the car, Schleger paused and said to Ostmann, "I have an appetite and I think a little celebratory dinner would be appropriate. I expect our new friend will be happy to wait for us." He was talking of the captured agent. Ostmann guffawed and Louis joined in dutifully.

He had never visited the headquarters before because if he had been seen entering or leaving he would have been suspected of collaborating with the S.S. That did not matter now; his work here was done. But he had often come to St. Jean, telling Albert: "I'll go crazy if I'm stuck out in the sticks all the time." That was part of the truth, but latterly he also came to see the German girl.

He looked towards the house now, where it stood at the end of the quay on the sea-wall. He could make out the sentry, pacing like a shadow before the front door. Louis had first seen the girl one evening just before curfew when she stood on the sea-wall and watched the E-boats slip out of the harbour. The wind flattened the dress against her body and he wanted it to hurt and to spoil. So he had taken to hanging about the port to watch for her and use her in the pictures in his mind. Once their glances crossed but her eyes slid quickly away.

Inside, Louis had closed both the outer and the inner doors but they all heard the second car pull up outside. Schleger pointed to the door of a side room and told Louis, "Shut yourself in my office before they fetch him in. We don't want him to see you. The less he knows, the better." Louis obeyed, and Schleger ordered Ostmann, "Tell them downstairs to bring their party out when we bring down ours."

Ostmann nodded, understanding, and strode along the hall past the stairs that led to the upper floors, then turned back to the door set under them. This stood open and the cellar steps ran down from it. Ostmann's boots clattered on the steps then his voice rumbled below.

The S.S. troopers in the second car dragged Michel out of it. His legs were cramped from his journey curled up on the floor and they folded under him. A trooper grabbed each arm and they hauled him, stumbling, up the steps and inside. They followed Schleger as he led the way, without speaking, along the hall and down the stone steps to the cellars. The rough masonry of the walls glistened with moisture and the paved floor ran with it. There were strong lights in the ceiling.

They marched Michel, shambling on drunken legs now, past the open door of a cell and halted him before another that was closed. Schleger said, "The key."

One of the troopers released Michel, kicked him and said, "Stand still, you bastard." He walked back along the passage to a small cupboard set on the wall at the foot of the steps. Another door opened at the end of the passage and two more troopers came out. They had discarded their tunics and their shirts were open at the neck, the sleeves rolled up. They carried a man between them whose legs trailed uselessly and his head lolled. As they passed Michel he saw the man's face was lumpy and discoloured, bruised and bloody, the eyes puffy and closed. Blood trickled from his gaping mouth. But Michel recognised him, and now knew who had betrayed Suzanne and himself.

He watched as Paul was thrown through the open door into the cell, then his eyes shifted to Schleger, who was smiling, thumbs hooked in his belt. The trooper unlocked the door and shoved him inside. The door slammed shut behind him and the key turned.

Michel now knew what to expect.

Schleger did not speak as Ostmann sauntered along the passage from the room where Paul had been "interrogated", but he raised his eyebrows in enquiry. His lieutenant shook his head; Paul had told nothing. Ostmann followed his chief up the stairs. But when they were in the hall again Schleger said, "Let him think about it while we eat and then sleep for an hour or two."

Ostmann nodded, seeing the wisdom of that: "And we'll take him in the dead of night. He'll be ready then."

The telephone rang and the corporal on duty in the hall snatched up the instrument from his desk, listened, then handed it to Schleger. That was the first of two calls, the second succeeding the first as soon as the receiver was replaced. When both were done he swore, pushed open the side door and saw Louis waiting.

Schleger said, "That was the *Scharführer* commanding the men hunting the girl. He says she was picked up by a British *Schnellboot*. We've lost her."

Stupid incompetence, Louis thought, but he said he was sorry.

"And the old Frenchman," Schleger went on, "was not at the café. The squad sent to fetch him found it empty. They questioned the people in the houses nearby but none of them had seen him. You're sure he went back there?"

Louis frowned, "I put him on the cart." Christ! He'll blame me for this!

"Maybe he got off again." Then Schleger shrugged, "Anyway, he's small stuff. All the men are on their way back. We'll start a search of St. Jean tomorrow." He was silent a moment, lips a thin line as he thought, then: "I think the boat came for the man we have downstairs. The girl only used it." He smiled again and Louis felt relief. Schleger said, "We have the main prize." And he added expansively, "Make yourself comfortable in there." He jerked his thumb at the corporal. "Ask the *Unterscharführer*, out here in the hall, if you want anything. We'll send in some food for you."

Louis said, "Thank you, Herr *Sturmbannführer*. I could use a drink."

Louis had already decided how to make himself comfortable. The curtained window of Schleger's office faced the harbour and a wide desk was set against the opposite wall. The floor was thickly carpeted and two leather armchairs stood before a crackling fire, a coffee table between them. As soon as Schleger and Ostmann had left for their hotel Louis stretched out in an armchair and lit a cigarette. A bottle, a meal, and tomorrow he would be paid and on his way back to Paris. He smiled contentedly.

Ilse had seen the three shadowy figures get out of the first car and guessed at the identity of two of them, saw that guess confirmed when light from the opened door flooded over the

86

group: Schleger and Ostmann. The third man came as more of a shock. She knew him, the swaggering carriage and turn of the head. She had noticed him about the town on several occasions and caught the look on his face as he watched her. He had frightened her then and now his connection with the S.S. seemed to fall into place. He was turned towards the house now, as if seeking her, and automatically she stepped back a pace from the window, though she knew he could not see her in the night.

Then the three entered the S.S. headquarters, the door closed and the light was cut off. She relaxed and realised how nervous they had made her. A second car rolled over the bridge and stopped behind the first. Two men climbed out at each side and then dragged out another. There was no light this time when the door opened but she could see that the last man was unable to walk, was pulled up the steps with his legs trailing and so into the house. The door closed again.

Ilse shuddered, remembering what Rudi Halder had told her about the S.S. and their methods. Her mind shied away from what might now be taking place behind the closed door. She pulled the curtains across to hide it but that was not enough. She left her room and crossed the upper hall to another at the back of the house. She leaned her hands on the window-sill and tried to pierce the darkness clothing the cold sea. Rudi was out there.

The cluster of lights on the sea steadily widened as Brent approached the fishing fleet. Crozier still kept station to starboard, both boats slipping along quietly at a bare six knots as their auxiliary motors eased them forward, the main engines shut down and silent. Brent lounged comfortably in the starboard corner of the bridge while Suzanne and Tallon stood unspeaking at the back. All of them watched the lights creeping nearer, and waited – until Chris Tallon said sharply, "Some of those lights have gone out."

David Brent answered quietly, "And then they come on again. It's mist, drifting in patches, that comes between us and a light, then moves on."

Jimmy Nash climbed up from the wheel-house, a rolled chart under his arm, and stood at Brent's shoulder. He asked, "Any sign of them yet?" Brent had sent Dent and Tommy Vance circling around the drifters to create a diversion on the other side.

Brent shook his head, "Give them time. We'll know when they go into their act."

"Suppose the patrol-boat is one of those – " Jimmy nodded at the lights, " – right ahead of us? At six or seven knots it'll take her ten minutes to waddle around to the other side of the fleet."

"She can take a week so long as she's out of our way. But I think she's cruising, or lying, to seaward. That way she's stopping any of them trying to slip away. She isn't carrying a light, remember, and they won't see her, just know she's out there somewhere. And her skipper will be nicely placed to run down either side of the fleet if need be, or to herd them all back to port come the morning."

Jimmy nodded agreement and stared out to sea. He jerked, startled, as the machine-guns opened fire two miles away on the other side of the spread lights. The tracers arched like tiny red shooting stars and Jimmy said, "Well, you did tell them to aim high."

"We don't want to kill any fishermen by accident," David Brent commented. But he was not watching the tracer; his eyes were searching ahead of his boat, seeing the drifter taking shape slowly beneath her masthead lamp as the gap of glinting black water between the two craft narrowed. This drifter was out on her own, no other within a quarter-mile and those others were on the far side of her. Brent's boat would be hidden from their sight by the drifter. Crozier had stopped, to wait in the outer darkness.

The drifter was close and on the port bow; Brent could see a man on her deck now, but his back was turned to the M.T.B. as he peered at the distant, winking tracer. Brent told Grundy shortly, "Alongside."

"Alongside, sir." The cox'n spun the spokes of the "coffee-grinder" and the bow swung. The boat curved into

the pool of yellow light cast by the drifter's masthead lamp.
Brent worked the telegraph and the engineer below obeyed
its order and threw out the clutch. The M.T.B. slid gently to
rest and lay beside the fisherman, rubbing against the rope
fenders hung along the drifter's side.

The man on the deck under the light gaped across at the
boat and David Brent ordered, "Hail him, please!"

Suzanne called, in clear, ringing French, "This is a British
ship. Her captain wishes to speak to yours."

The man on the drifter's deck looked to be young, though
he had a blue stubble of beard. He glanced towards the
wheel-house set aft and another man shoved out of its door
and dropped down the short wooden ladder to the deck. This
one was in his fifties, short and thick-set, heavily moustached
and with an old beret snug on his head. He glowered across
at Suzanne and charged her, "You're French."

Suzanne was not, but she was supposed to be so she
agreed, "Yes. You are the captain?"

"What are you doing aboard an English boat?"

"Fighting Germans." That short answer silenced him
for a moment and Suzanne pressed, "You are the captain?"

He nodded, then gestured at the young man. "This is my
son. My cousin is the engineer. He is below."

Suzanne took a breath and told him, "We want to take
your boat and use her against the Germans."

She waited for this to sink in. The machine-guns still
clattered in short intermittent bursts, the tracer looping.
The young man looked at his father, who asked, "Will we
get her back?"

Suzanne translated quickly for David Brent and he answered, face expressionless, "That's unlikely. I will try to
see they are compensated but I can promise nothing. This
is wartime."

The captain, nodding slowly as he listened to Suzanne's
reply, seemed to have expected nothing better. His son
asked, "Will you take us to England?"

Suzanne gave David's reply: "If I can. Or I can put you

89

ashore. If you stay on the ship it will be dangerous. I've told you I want to use her against the Germans.''

Now there was a third man on the drifter's deck, of the captain's age but smaller and thinner. He wore a boilersuit and wiped his hands on a lump of oily waste. He listened as the young man rapidly explained. Meanwhile the captain said, with a jerk of the head towards his son, "That one wants to join de Gaulle and the Free French.'' Then he was silent, looking up at David Brent on the bridge and rubbing at his stubbled jaw as he thought. Finally, he said, "Life is not too bad under the Boche. They let us live, so long as it suits them. In the town today we saw some of their S.S. catch a man they wanted. They kicked and handled him worse than any animal.''

Tallon grumbled savagely, softly, "We haven't got all bloody night!''

David Brent murmured, "Shut up!'' He listened to Suzanne's translation as the captain went on, "That could happen to any one of us, in our own town, our own country.'' He glanced at his son and his cousin. "We are all men without close family, now. My wife, the boy's mother, is dead. My cousin never married. So you can take the ship and we will stay aboard and crew her.''

Brent drew a breath of relief. He had been prepared to take the drifter by force if need be, but this was better. "Give him my thanks. Tell him he must act as this officer orders.'' He slapped Nash's shoulder. "Over you go, Jimmy. Good luck.''

The spare skipper dropped down from the bridge and climbed over the drifter's bulwark, held out a hand to be gripped by that of the captain.

Suzanne asked, "Does he speak French? Do you want me to go with him?''

David shook his head, "Jimmy has a few words and the chart. He'll manage.''

Then he straightened as the distant machine-gun bursts were overlaid by the cracking of cannon fire. The looping tracer became not just red but also laced with green. Jimmy

Nash spun to stare at it then looked over his shoulder to shout back at Brent, "The patrol-boat has found them!"

But not just the patrol-boat. Brent could see six or more curving green chains on the other side of the fishing fleet. He swore savagely under his breath then answered Jimmy, "That looks like those E-boats as well. Get under way and we'll see you later." His hands worked the telegraph and the main engines roared into life; the boat surged ahead as he shoved the throttle levers forward. He caught a glimpse of Jimmy Nash waving a hand then, unrolling his chart, spreading it out for the French captain to see. Then Brent's boat was swinging around the bow of the drifter, turning towards the distant firing. Little Dent and Tommy Vance were outnumbered. They needed him.

Crozier swung around the drifter's stern and tucked himself neatly into place off Brent's starboard quarter. David took the short route, the two boats jinking and swerving through the scatter of drifters of the fleet. Soon they were running at forty knots with bows riding high out of the sea to show a third of their hulls above the water. They all felt the exhilaration of tearing into action as if riding a runaway train.

Then they encountered mist again, a bank of fog rolling ahead, and they ran into it as if into a tunnel. It wrapped around them and made the engines bellow in their ears. They ripped out of it and a lamp loomed, the drifter beneath it leaping at them. David yelled, "*Port!*" The helm went over and they skidded past the drifter's bow, a man gaping at them from her deck only yards away. Then she was left astern, rocking wildly in their wake.

David squinted his eyes against the flying spray. For a moment saw only yellow lights ahead, swinging suspended against the sky, then he ordered, "Starboard! Steady! . . . Port! Hard over! Midships!"

On the bridge they clung to any handhold as the boat tilted madly one way, swung back the other. They flashed past the last of the yellow globes marking drifters and before them was darkness laced with the streaks of tracer. David could

91

not make out any of the boats in the night and had to work by
deduction and guess-work. He thought the patrol-boat was
ahead and to starboard, Dent and Tommy Vance ahead and
to port and the E-boats beyond them. "Starboard! Steady!"
Watching the flickering tracer. Was the nearer green lacing
coming from the patrol-boat . . . ?

She lifted out of the darkness close on the starboard bow
and they were up with her, passing her within a hundred
yards or less while the gunner in the turret aft sprayed her
deck with one long burst. Then they were past her. David
cast one quick glance astern, saw her fading black shadow
and more red tracer streaming into it at short range. That
would be from Crozier, forced to swing around the other
side of her but so able to engage her with that cross-fire.
The shadow merged into the night astern and David faced
forward again.

He stared into blackness through a silver mist of spray,
seeing the curving, shifting necklaces of red and green off
the port bow and closing rapidly. He thought, but could not
be sure, that he saw the boats of Vance and little Dent to
port showing as twin grey V's of up-thrown spray as he raced
across their bows, a quarter-mile ahead of them. Then he
saw the E-boats.

They were three or four hundred yards beyond the two
M.T.B.s, their black shapes running flatter in the sea, bows
not lifted so high out of it. There were three of them in
a narrow echelon that was almost straight ahead and they
were engaging the two M.T.B.s with cannon-fire. He would
pass across the leader's bow at less than a couple of hundred
yards' range. He just had time to draw breath then the twin
Vickers in the turret aft of the bridge opened fire. A second
later Crozier's guns joined in and both streams of tracer
converged on the leading E-boat.

It held on its course for a bare second then twisted away
from that fire, turning to port. David ordered, "Port ten!"
and he copied its turn. The other two E-boats followed
their leader, as Crozier trailed Brent, so for seconds the
two opposing forces ran parallel and less than two hundred

yards apart, exchanging fire in a spider's web of threads of tracer. Brent's boat was being hit; he could feel the tremor of those shells striking near the bridge and knew there must be others. Crozier would be suffering too. Vance and Dent had been left somewhere astern.

The leading E-boat turned away again and Brent's mouth opened to give the order to follow, then closed. For a moment, in the heat and terror of battle, he had forgotten his orders, but now he remembered: "*Bring that man back!*" He said instead, "Starboard ten!"

The boat's bow slid around as Grundy turned the wheel. She heeled under the helm then ran level as David ordered, "Midships . . . steady." The E-boats were already vague silhouettes mounted on white wakes, rapidly receding . . . gone. He shouted, "Look out for the other two!" Then glanced astern and saw Crozier was still off the starboard quarter. He saw that, but little else, his night vision destroyed by the recent action. Beyond the loom of Crozier's boat was only darkness and the lights of the fishing fleet. His eyes changed focus, registered the girl in the corner of the bridge but only feet away so he could see the pale blur of her face turned to him.

He swung away to search the sea around him with his eyes. There was the fishing fleet – on this course he would pass the drifters well to seaward of them, and of the patrol-boat if she kept on station, as she should. His own, or borrowed, drifter, would be miles away on the far side of the fleet now and heading steadily northward, following the line of the coast. His hands closed on the throttle levers, bringing down the speed of the boat but still running at better than thirty knots. If Vance and little Dent obeyed their orders, if they *could* obey them, they should –

He saw them as the hail came up from the deck below him: "Boats . . . Port!" They came surging up on the port quarter, still charging along at a full forty knots, then fractionally slowed and fell into station in the arrowhead again. Brent drew a sighing breath of relief. They might have been disabled, sunk. But they were here and keeping up, though they must have been hurt.

He thought that they had been ambushed by the E-boats – for the second time. He was certain the same three E-boats had carried out both attacks because it was highly unlikely that two such flotillas would be operating in the same waters. When Suzanne had told him of the defences of St. Jean she had said that three boats operated out of the old port. It fitted.

For the second time that night he wondered uneasily: Where are they now?

Rudi lowered his binoculars and looked round as Bruno climbed up to stand beside him on the bridge. Rudi asked, "Damage?"

"We've got some holes, but they're small ones and nothing's broken that matters. We got the jump on them again."

Rudi nodded and glanced out to starboard where the other two boats ran in echelon, apparently none the worse for the fighting. He recalled how he had seen the firing near the fishing fleet, closed it and found the two *Tommi* boats running down the side of the fleet and on a landward course. They had turned to head out to sea, going back on their tracks, when he charged out of the night with his flotilla and hit them.

They had fought back but he had them – or would have, but for the other two boats that came out of nowhere to cross his bow and pour in a terrible fire. Neither he nor the signalman on the bridge were hit, but that was a miracle because the bridge coaming was chewed to splinters. He'd swerved away, fought on but then turned away again when he could not see the first two M.T.B.s and thought they might come in on his port side and take him in a cross-fire.

Bruno said happily, "We ripped them up. Those first two, I mean. One or both of them could be stopped now, maybe sinking."

Rudi Halder agreed cautiously, "Maybe. We'll see."

The signalman handed Rudi a flimsy passed up from the wireless office below. He read: "Report of enemy agent embarked enemy S-boat . . ." That was short for *Schnellboot* – fast boat. The time and position given accorded with the distant firing that Rudi had seen first that night. So the *Tommis* had been there to pick up an agent – and would be taking him home. But why had they attacked the fishing fleet? Maybe a jittery lookout aboard an M.T.B. had sighted one of the drifters and thought it was the escort boat? Or the escort had fired on the *Tommis*?

The signal also asked for a report of his actions. He passed that on to Jacobi. "Tell them at base what we've been doing."

Another flimsy was pushed at him. This was from the escort reporting to H.Q. that three enemy S-boats had attacked the fishing fleet but had been driven off. It told him nothing. He decided his original plan was still sound. The *Tommis* would head for the other side with their agent and Rudi, with luck and foresight, would be listening and waiting for them.

He led his flotilla out to sea again. Two actions, two successes. The third to finish the job.

Brent looked over his shoulder at the lights of the fishing fleet now far astern and just pin-pricks in the night once more. He was aware again of the girl's white face, small above the voluminous oilskin. And of Tallon, shifting about the back of the bridge, peering at the luminous face of his watch and impatient or worried – or both? Tallon knew as well as Brent that whatever they attempted this night, the boats had to be on their way home before the morning light came and brought the airstrikes down on them.

The drifter should be close now, only two or three miles ahead and inshore, lying off that prominent feature, of the cape jutting out to sea, that marked the inlet. David Brent intended a landing at the inlet. He thought that his men would know, when they set out on the attempt, that the enemy could be at their backs. That was not a comfortable feeling and kept men looking over their shoulders. He had avoided action, obeying orders, but action had come to him. You could not go on being at the wrong end of the deal, always taking the blows. That was bad for morale —

Bill Emmett shouted, "Vance is signalling, sir!" And as David's head snapped around and he saw the tiny, dim blue light flickering its message, Emmett read it: "On fire!"

They saw the flames then, short streaks of yellow jetting from Tommy Vance's boat beneath the bridge, the thin tongues lying horizontal as the wind of the boat's passage laid them on their sides. Fire was the great hazard, the great fear, in a petrol-driven boat and each of these carried more than two thousand gallons of hundred-octane.

David gripped the throttle levers and hauled them back. The speed of the boat fell away and the bow slumped. As the last of the way came off her and the clutch was thrown out he saw that the other boats had followed suit. All were stopping in a loose group. He made a funnel of his hands to shout over to Vance, "Can you put it out?"

For a moment the flames had subsided to a glow, but now there came a *whump*! from inside Tommy's boat and the yellow tongue climbed higher. He bawled his answer, "Not a chance! We've been on fire since that last action and used all our extinguishers. We thought we'd beaten it once but then it flared up again in another place. And that was the forward fuel tank igniting!"

David saw the engineer and his two stokers climb out of the engine-room hatch aft of Vance's bridge and scurry forward. He called, "I'll take you off!"

He saw that Dent and Crozier had wisely drawn away to a safer distance. If the burning boat exploded then any other near it would go the same way. He worked telegraph and throttles, standing at Grundy's side, and the young coxswain took the boat in to lie alongside that of Vance, bow to bow. Tommy's crew were gathered there, waiting, and with them the eight commandos they had carried aboard. The soldiers carried rifles or sub-machine-guns and some had huge rucksacks slung on their shoulders. David called to the two seamen of his own crew who waited in the bow to help in the rescue, "Look out for those soldiers!" If they fell between the boats they would sink like stones.

But one by one they all came across as the two boats rubbed together, Vance last of all. They brought with them the blanket-wrapped body of Garbutt. David and Grundy eased the boat away from the burning M.T.B. and Tommy Vance came to the bridge. He said, "You'll sink her, sir?"

"No." The three surviving boats were lit targets in this circle of light under the spreading smoke. He did not know where the E-boats were but they knew where he was. "She'll burn and she'll sink but we've got to get out of here. I'm sorry."

Tommy rubbed glumly at his bearded chin and nodded reluctant agreement, knowing the reason for Brent's decision but not wanting to leave his boat, possibly to be boarded and captured by the enemy.

David led the other two boats away from the light and into the darkness, heading towards the distant, unseen shore. They turned when they had gone a half-mile and stopped, lay with engines silent and bows pointed out to sea and the distant glare of the fire. David told Vance, with Tallon standing by, "I want your crew and the soldiers you had aboard shared out between these three boats." There was no sense in having too many eggs in one basket, particularly a small, overcrowded basket like this M.T.B. "And quickly, please."

Vance and Tallon climbed down from the bridge and the soldier went to the sergeant and the seven men waiting aft. Tallon sorted through them rapidly: "You . . . you, and Sergeant McNab – Mr. Dent's boat . . ."

When it was done the group split up but Sergeant McNab lingered. He was tall and heavy-shouldered, hard-faced and cold-eyed, a regular soldier with ten years' service behind him, some of it as a bandboy in barracks but a large chunk of it spent on the north-west frontier of India. He asked Tallon, "Can you tell us what's going on, sir? The men are getting curious."

Tallon thought: I'll bet they are, and I don't blame them. He said, "The beach where we intended to land was occupied by the enemy, but we have an agent aboard who knows a better place. I'll brief you all as fully as I can, when I can. We may be going ashore soon. Be ready."

Up on his bridge, David Brent called over to little Dent, "What damage?"

"More holes, but nothing serious." Dent paused, then finished, "But my signalman is wounded, hit in the leg. Nothing left in there, but it's a nasty gash and he can't stand. He's below."

"Take Tommy's signalman." David asked Vance on the deck below, "Did you hear that?"

Vance answered, "I'll send him over."

David turned to Crozier, who reported, "Like Mickey, some new holes, but otherwise all right."

The three boats rubbed briefly together, manoeuvred on the auxiliary engines, as the detailed soldiers and members of Vance's crew were transferred. Then they edged apart, though with still only yards between them, and lay silent once more.

David Brent ran his fingers through his hair then pulled on his old cap. He stood in the starboard corner of the bridge with his hands dug deep in his pockets, his shoulders hunched, balancing to the slow roll of the boat as the swell rocked her. Grundy glanced at his captain's scowling face and, looking away, said to himself: We're in a right bloody temper.

Brent was again considering morale and the danger of making a landing in the presence of the enemy, an enemy who knew where Brent and his little force were, or had been until a few minutes ago. The burning boat marked the spot. To attempt a landing when they might come under attack would be taking a huge risk – and he was committed to enough risks already. If he could remove this threat, this risk . . .

He waited here for that purpose.

Grundy's head cocked on one side and he did not have to speak, the gesture was enough. David said, "Quiet!"

All movement, and the whispered exchanges, ceased. Suzanne, tucked away at the back of the bridge, heard the slap-slapping of the halyards against the stumpy mast, in time with the beating of her heart. She watched David Brent, tall and strong, as his head turned, trying to penetrate the darkness, and listening. She heard the low rumble of engines.

7

Ambush

Tension froze them all on the three boats as they listened to the engine noise approaching. The captains, each on his bridge, stood like statues with their binoculars held to their eyes. The distant rumble steadily grew in volume, until Crozier said in a conversational tone, but with his voice lifted so the words carried clearly above that rumble, "Broad on the starboard bow."

Brent answered as evenly, "Seen." There was the grey "ram's horn", like a V with its uprights turned out at the top. That was the phosphorescent bow-wave of a boat, its hull still invisible in the night, its stem cutting through the sea at the point of the V. There was another, and a third. He had last seen them nearly ten miles to the south. They were coming down from the north so must have made a wide circle out to sea.

He had to fight one decisive action to clear these waters of the enemy before he attempted a landing. Without lowering the glasses from his eyes he ordered, "Get those soldiers and any spare hands below." There was movement now, and growled commands as the decks were cleared but nobody noticed Suzanne in the dark corner of the bridge. Then the stillness held them again but she could no longer hear the halyards as they tapped against the mast, the sound drowned by the deep note of the diesels that seemed all around them now.

David Brent lowered the glasses. The E-boats ran into the spread of firelight around Vance's boat, blazing along its length now, their speed fell away and their bows dropped. They ran level and slowly as they closed on the burning boat, moving in a tight group. Brent thought: To talk to each other. Two of the boats stopped, but with their engines still idling, while the third edged in nearer Vance's boat. With, possibly, some vague idea of salvage? That hope seemed to be abandoned as the third E-boat also stopped.

The crews of the E-boats would not hear Brent's engines above the rumbling of their own. Their eyes would be fixed on the burning boat or blinded by its glare. Now was the time.

He worked the handle of the engine-room telegraph and the three big main engines crashed into life. As the boat moved ahead he shoved the throttle levers wide open and ordered, "Port!" Grundy turned the wheel, the bow swung and then Brent checked it with a shout to the coxswain: "Steady . . . steer that!" His boat was on a course to run to the left of Vance's and the group of E-boats. He glanced to starboard and saw Crozier there, and that Dent had moved over to run to starboard and astern of Crozier, the three craft in echelon. Their bows were lifted, already they were planing, had shot from rest to nearly a full forty knots in little over ten seconds. The big plumes of spray curved up on either side of each bridge.

Brent faced forward into the salt water that drove inboard, narrowed his eyes against it and blinked it away. He watched the E-boats rush towards him, their hulls standing in black outline against the orange and yellow blaze under its umbrella of dirty smoke. His own flotilla had now burst out of the darkness and was running in that shifting light. It was bright enough for him to see the droplets of spray running down Grundy's face.

The range was down below four hundred yards and now the twin Vickers machine-guns in the turret aft of the bridge opened fire. A second later Brent saw the red lines of tracer also sliding out from the other two boats – and all were hitting. The gap of black water between the two flotillas, one tearing in at forty knots and the other still at rest, narrowed swiftly. In seconds Brent was racing past the bow of the nearest E-boat and clearing it by less than fifty yards. In the wavering yellow light he saw men moving jerkily about the bridge, then the sea was churned into white foam at her stern. She was getting under way – but the men had disappeared from her bridge and it stood empty.

"Hard aport!" He bellowed the command at Grundy and the wheel went over, the bow swung. The machine-guns in their turret were briefly silent as the gunner lost his target, then he worked the control column inside the power-operated turret, it spun around and he opened fire again.

Brent glanced astern and saw Dent and Crozier follow him into the turn and the E-boats beginning to move, white water at their bows. He clung to the bridge coaming as he held the tight, skidding turn, then shouted, "Midships!" Grundy put the wheel over again, reversing the helm, met her, straightened her as Brent ordered, "Steady!"

The flotilla tore down on the E-boats again, steering to cross their bows once more, guns hammering in short bursts. One of the E-boats was out of control, her coxswain or captain, or both, dead or blinded by the glare. Brent sucked in his breath as he saw her ram into one of her consorts forward of her bridge then swing away. Both boats swerved erratically before steadying on a consistent course with the third once more. Brent swept past them as close or closer than before, saw no man on either bridge and knew they were being conned from the armoured wheel-houses below. The red tracer sprayed along them but this time there were answering muzzle-flashes aboard the E-boats.

The rounds were from 20mm. cannon. He felt the shuddering punch of them through the wooden fabric of the hull for perhaps three or four seconds then that stopped. And so did his engines. The ear-blasting roar was cut off as if a switch had been thrown. The bow sank into the sea again and the boat wallowed on the swell thrown up by the high-speed manoeuvring. Dent and Crozier charged past and the boat lay

over on her side as their wakes slammed into
her.

Brent called into the voice-pipe, "Engine-room!"

But then the engineer said from behind him, "I'm up
here, sir." And as Brent turned to question him, he added,
shouting between the bursts of the machine-guns, voice
shaky after his experience, "No good down there, sir. I
think there were half-a-dozen rounds came in. Some of them
banged about inside and made a right mess of the motors.
Some went out the other side and we've got leaks all along
below the waterline. She's filling up fast."

Brent stared past him at the E-boats. All three were on
the move now, but he thought they were only making
ten or fifteen knots. Their after-cannons winked red and
the boat shivered under him again. Something punched
a hole in the bridge coaming between him and Grundy,
splinters howled and clattered. Then Dent and Crozier
powered past, still at full speed with bows high and
spray like a diaphanous curtain hung about each bridge.
They were between him and the E-boats now and he was
no longer under fire. He saw them engaging again, the
red lines of tracer pointing the way to the E-boats that
had run out of the circle of light and were now in the
darkness.

That circle was shrinking as the flames died on Vance's
boat. The sea was extinguishing them as she slowly sank.
Vance himself showed now on the bridge behind the engineer and reported, "She's like a colander, above and below
water. You can see it reaching up inside her."

Brent nodded. He had lost another boat. There was no
point in trying to save her because she would only be a
burden in her crippled state. He had enough problems
already. "All right. Abandon ship."

Tommy Vance said, low-voiced, "And Bill Emmett; he
was just aft of the bridge. He's dead. Cannon shell."

That shocked Brent. He heard himself say, "I'm sorry.
Will you see to him, Tommy, please? And the charts and
books."

The commandos and the wireless operator came up from below, then the two stokers climbed out of the engine-room hatch, wet to the knees and swearing as only stokers can. Tommy Vance brought up the charts and confidential books. The men gathered on the deck in the waning light cast by Vance's boat.

The firing had ceased out in the darkness and they heard the growl rise into a roar as the other two boats returned. They ran into the light with bows high out of the water; then the roar was cut back to a rumble, the bows sank and they ran in slowly to stop alongside. The two bridges flanked Brent, Dent to port, Crozier to starboard.

He called across to them, "I'm abandoning ship; she's sinking fast."

Dent, diminutive beside his coxswain, answered, "They looked to be in a bad way, sir. They were still firing but not making any better than ten or twelve knots, I think; crawling along. We overtook them as if they were standing still, shot them up as we passed then turned in a big circle to come back here."

Crozier called in his deep voice, "They were heading north when we left them. I thought we'd better see how you were, rather than harry them. But one of 'em was listing and I reckon she'll sink."

Brent thought: So one possibly sinking, certainly two not fit to fight, holed when they collided. But had he gained the decisive victory he'd wanted, to leave him free to attempt the landing? He now had only two boats. As if in confirmation he felt the bridge lurch beneath his feet as this one settled lower in the water.

Chris Tallon spoke from the deck below where he was marshalling his men, "You've got them out of our way." He was talking of the E-boats, so he had appreciated the threat they might be to a landing. Brent only nodded; not agreement but an acknowledgment.

Grundy had climbed down to the deck now and was checking off his own men, making sure not one was missing.

He glanced up at Brent's set face and muttered to himself, "Well, cheer up, sir, for Gawd's sake. We gave them a belting and they had to run for it. What did you want, another bloody Trafalgar?"

They transhipped to the other two boats, Brent's crew and Vance's survivors, Suzanne, the commandos, the wounded – and the dead. At Brent's order they unlashed the dinghy from aft in the sinking boat and manhandled it across to Crozier's. Vance's craft burned down to the waterline and sank under a cloud of smoke that drifted down on the wind and set them coughing.

David Brent stood on Crozier's bridge and watched the sea now washing in over the stern of his own boat. He was conscious of the girl, standing at the back of this bridge as she had stood on his. He thought that he should have sent her away with Jimmy Nash when she had offered to go. She would have missed the dangers of the last two actions. But it was easy to be wise after the event and she was all right – so far. He shifted uneasily, then was still.

His orders were unchanged. He was to rescue the prisoner on the train. He had to put Tallon and his men ashore and without delay because time was also an enemy. This was what was known as a calculated risk, or bloody folly if it went wrong.

Tommy Vance came to stand beside him and murmured, "We only caught sight of those E-boats for a few seconds each time we met them. So I wouldn't bet money on it, but I don't think this last lot were the ones we met earlier, and they must still be out there, some-where."

The boat alongside, deck awash, now sagged and her port side went under, her bridge dipped into the sea. David Brent did not take his eyes from her but he told Vance, "Between you and me, that's right."

Vance glanced sidewise at him and asked tentatively, "Are you still going on with it, then?"

"Yes, Tommy." Because he had to. And quickly, before

this action brought down the other E-boats. And because time was running out.

The engines grumbled and the boats moved ahead. Brent gave a course to meet Jimmy Nash and the drifter off the inlet where they were to make a landing.

Rudi had waited with his boats five miles to seaward of the fishing fleet. When Bruno Jacobi saw the glow on the horizon he reported it to Rudi, then suggested, "One of the *Tommi* boats burning?"

Rudi stared at the red wash in the sky and answered, "Let it burn. They won't be sitting around watching it. We'll run due north till we're abreast of it, then wait again." They were cruising northward when they saw the firing in the distance, the looping tracer. Rudi swore and slammed his fist on the bridge coaming. "An action! I'll bet you anything you like that's Gunther, come down from his own patrol area to stick his nose in."

The firing ceased and Rudi stopped his flotilla, listened for the engine-noise of other boats headed seawards, towards him, but heard nothing. They watched the glow of the fire slowly dying in the sky and Bruno said hopefully, "Maybe Gunther has cleaned them up."

Rudi snapped bitterly, "And maybe he hasn't."

Then the wireless operator came up to the bridge and handed him a slip from a signal pad. "Just picked this up, *Herr Kapitänleutnant.*"

Rudi took the signal and read it: "From Gunther to his base. 'In action. Three enemy boats heavily damaged. My boats forced reduce speed. One sinking. Enemy broke off action headed north-west.'"

Bruno nodded. "Going home."

Rudi said again, "Maybe. What I'm sure of is that Gunther charged in, greedy for pickings, when he saw that *Tommi* boat on fire, and they were waiting for him."

He led the way below and leaned over the chart, one finger on the pencilled cross marking his present position. He thought a moment, then: "If Gunther was right and they turned for home then we're too late and we've missed them. But I think Gunther didn't know which way *he* was headed, never mind the *Tommis*."

Bruno asked, "Do you think they might be trying to be clever?"

Rudi scowled at the chart, "I don't know. It might be that this *Tommi* is another Gunther and doesn't know what he's doing. But I doubt that. It seems he laid a cute little trap for Gunther and chewed him up. The *Tommi* should be running for home." Taking back the agent he had come for. "But maybe he's in trouble. So – we'll continue north, keeping out to sea and stopping frequently to listen." He was not going to be caught like Gunther. "If we haven't sighted them by the time we're due west of this point, we'll run down to it and sweep south from there." He jabbed a finger at the chart where the prominent cape stuck out from the coastline.

When Albert had reached the inlet he had waited in the trees near the path that wound along the cliff-top. The inlet lay just north of the cape. A stream ran down to the sea through a steep, narrow ravine and where it cut through the cliffs it was crossed by a wooden footbridge that carried the path. Albert watched the path as he had often watched it from this position, just north of the footbridge.

He had confirmed there was no guard on the coast to the north of him. If this other section running south past the cape was guarded there would be a sergeant and six men. They would take it in turns to patrol through the hours of darkness. While four men and the sergeant stayed in the guard-hut, a half-kilometre south of the bridge and on the other side of the cape, two would patrol, one south of the hut, one north. That last man had a beat that brought him as far as the bridge, where he would turn and retrace his steps.

Albert knew the routine as well as did the soldiers.

He saw his first sentry after a wait of only a few minutes. The man came trudging along the path on the far side of the bridge at a policeman's slow, measured pace, his boots nearly silent on the rain-softened earth. He carried his rifle slung over one shoulder, his face under the big helmet unseen in the darkness, but Albert noted that this was a middle-sized, narrow-shouldered man. His boots clumped as he crossed the bridge, pausing in the middle to peer down into the ravine where the stream was a streak of silver at the bottom of a black pit. Once across the bridge he paused again for a minute, staring out to sea. Albert stood still, breathing shallowly through his mouth; the sentry was only a few yards from the old man's hiding place in the trees. Then the soldier hitched the rifle more comfortably on his shoulder, trudged back across the bridge and down the path on his way to the guard-hut. He would turn when he saw it, would only go to the hut when he was due to be relieved at the end of his two-hour stint.

Albert saw a red glow in the sky now, out over the sea and south of the cape. He watched it for some time, then came a far-off crackle of firing that went on for a few minutes, before dying away into silence. Albert knew what that meant and peered anxiously out to sea, but soon afterwards a sentry came again. He, too, was faceless in the gloom but a bigger man, heavier. So the sentries had changed. Albert nodded: Good.

He watched the sentry cross and re-cross the bridge, his face always turned towards the sea and that distant glow. Then he disappeared along the track towards the hut. Now Albert moved. He took his watch from his pocket and used the torch to look at its face held inside his coat, noted the time; he had twenty minutes before the sentry would return. That was more than enough. He picked up his bag of tools and spent only five of those minutes working on the bridge, wincing all the time at the renewed pain the work sent lancing up his wrist. Then he returned to stand at the edge of the trees, in their shadow but not hidden among them as before.

He worried over the firing, knowing that Suzanne could be out there, somewhere. Was she involved in the fighting? In danger? He lit a cigarette and smoked it nervously, quickly, as the glow on the horizon faded then was snuffed out. When the *caporal* burned down he lit another from its stub and flicked that away. The big sentry returned a minute later.

Albert saw him appear on the path and walk onto the bridge. The sentry saw Albert, or rather the red glow of the *caporal* in the darkness under the trees. He unslung his rifle as he started across the bridge and Albert sucked rapidly, puffing smoke, mesmerised. The big man watched that glow and not where he set his feet as he took two strides, then a third that brought him to the centre of the bridge. As his boot came down so it went through the cardboard Albert had thumb-tacked there in place of the planks he had removed. The sentry plunged forward between the supporting timbers of the bridge and down into the ravine.

Albert heard the shriek of his falling, the crunching thud of his landing, swallowed, shuddered, threw away the cigarette and walked to the bridge. Some weeks ago he had laboriously prised loose the cross-planks of the bridge at the centre for a length of nearly three metres and replaced them only lightly nailed for their quick and easy removal – when needed. He had been wary and nervous all the time he had worked that afternoon but he had seen no one. More importantly, no one had seen him. This night he had taken up the planks after the big man had gone back to the hut, then in their place he laid the cardboard, cut from old boxes and painted black. It had been hidden, ready, among the trees where the planks lay now.

He knelt on the bridge, ripped away what cardboard still hung from the supports and took it into the wood. He left it there, brought back the planks and nailed them in place on the bridge again. He wielded a hammer, careless of the noise because the men in the guard-hut would not hear him at this distance and with the wind blowing from them to him. But he grunted with pain as each blow jarred his wrist.

Finally he went to the guard-rail that he had previously loosened, prised out the single nail that held it secure at one end and pushed that end outwards. He was satisfied he had set the scene of the "accident". When the sentry was found it would be clear he had leaned on the guard-rail and it had given way under his weight.

He picked up his bag and slung it onto his back. The cliff dropped sheer some thirty feet to the beach so he walked inland along the side of the ravine to a place where it had crumbled for several yards. There he was able to climb down in a shower of sliding shale. At the bottom he walked by the side of the stream until he stood beneath the bridge. He shivered as he looked down at the body. He did not touch it, did not need to. The sentry lay face down on the rocks of the stream-bed with the water washing around and over him. He would have drowned if the fall had not killed him.

Albert edged past the body and walked on by the stream that led like a black, silver-glinting pathway to the beach. He left it there and crossed the sand and shingle until he stood near the water's edge. He still shivered so he took the bottle from his bag, drew the cork and gulped cognac, felt it burn down into his belly. That was better – a little.

He peered out to sea but saw nothing but the big rollers curling over to break on the shore and those that followed ranked back until lost in the night. He wondered if Suzanne was out there, if she would come. It was one thing to say she would get the British boat to bring her here, another to accomplish it.

She had to land within the next hour. At the end of that time the sentries would be changed and the absence of one of them investigated. But she would appreciate that and knew what he had to do, the time it would take. He did not like this business. It had been easy to promise in haste but he had not known how hard it would be to keep that promise. Contriving the "accident" to the sentry had torn at Albert's nerves and now he was alone and afraid.

He took another swallow of courage from the bottle then stowed it away in his pocket and took out the torch. He pointed it out to sea and worked the button in the signal: short – long. He almost dropped the torch as its narrow beam stretched out over the waves, catching the broken white water on their tops and turning it into silver lace.

To Albert's frightened, squinted eyes the beam seemed to extend for miles until he released the button and darkness swept in again.

He was certain anyone on the coast would have seen that ray of light. He was sweating now, head turning but blindly, his night vision destroyed by the beam of the torch. He waited, shoulders hunched, for a dragging minute but no rifle cracked nor harsh voice challenged. He remembered that the sentry to the south could not see him because of the cape lifting between them, and there were no patrols to the north; he had made sure of that before taking on his own sentry. He wiped his slippery hand on the front of his coat, took a fresh grip on the torch and flashed the signal again.

David Brent saw the first signal but did not answer. He watched the line of phosphorescence where the surf washed the shore a quarter-mile away, and waited. Suzanne stood at his shoulder on the bridge of Crozier's boat and he heard her sigh, then say flatly, "He should send the signal twice, then wait for two minutes before sending it again, but reversed: long – short. That was the arrangement we agreed on" – agreed when she and Albert had planned possible landings and the trap for the sentry.

David thought: So that might not be our man. Have the S.S. got him down there, forcing him to use that torch? Brent knew if that was the case then he and Tallon had lost their last slim chance of carrying out their orders; the casualties and the lost boats would have been for nothing.

The two M.T.B.s flanked the drifter, lying close alongside with their bows pointed out to sea. They had only been on station five minutes, after meeting Jimmy Nash in the drifter then creeping in on the muttering auxiliary engines along the side of the cape, its mass looming to starboard. They had stopped a scant quarter-mile from the shore. The darkness and the silence were their only protection.

The commandos stood on the decks of the M.T.B.s and the drifter, their webbing ammunition pouches strapped over their khaki battledress, woollen cap-comforters snugged close

111

on their heads. They cradled Thompson submachine-guns in their arms. Seven of them had big rucksacks standing beside them: the demolition team.

David could see the compact figure of Chris Tallon standing on the deck below. Both had discarded their oilskins but while Tallon was armed and dressed like his men, Brent wore a navy sweater and trousers with a pair of plimsolls borrowed from Crozier. Private "Johnson", a Sudetan German, now interpreter and commando, stood by Tallon.

David knew Chris would be recalling once again that action of a year ago and the murderous cross-fire. Suzanne claimed there were no guns sited on this section of the coast, but it would not take long to manoeuvre two or three mobile 40mm. guns into position. If the S.S. had set a trap –

"There it is!" Crozier said it, along with a dozen others.

This time the beam held for a long second, blinked out, then winked again, shortly. Suzanne said, "Albert!" It came as a gasp of relief.

Brent used his torch to send an answer, a winking, orange glow. Then he crouched inside the shelter of the bridge-screen, pulled the girl down beside him and shone the shaded beam of the torch on the face of his watch: "I make it we have just two hours and ten minutes."

Suzanne had also sloughed off the oilskins and the sleeve of her trenchcoat was damp under his hand. She extended her arm so her own watch was lit by the torch. Her wrist wavered as the boat rocked and David Brent gripped her hand, steadied it under the light. She agreed, "The train is due then."

David held her a moment longer then released her, straightened and called softly, "Boats over the side!" Their crews waited, ready, by the three dinghies and the pulling-boat carried by the drifter. Besides Brent's own party there were thirty-two commandos, with Tallon, to be put ashore.

Brent was going ashore because he was the senior officer. He knew the country; it was his plan and his responsibility. He turned to Jimmy Nash where he stood on the deck of the drifter only feet away. "I'm taking Grundy, an

112

engineer, a stoker and two seamen." He saw their heads turning.

Grundy said under his breath, "I might ha' known! Here we go!"

Brent went on, "The rest of my crew, Tommy and all of his, will go with you. Take all the spare arms." That was a miscellany of light machine-guns, carbines and pistols, salvaged from Brent's boat or gleaned from the other two. He looked from Nash to Tommy Vance. "You know what you have to do. Jimmy will command in and from the drifter."

Jimmy objected, "I'd have more mobility in one of the M.T.B.s. Tommy could – "

Brent cut him off: "The boats will stay out but the drifter has to go in. That's where you're needed: I need you."

Jimmy thought that this was not a man afraid. Whatever he had seen on Brent's face when they had been forced to abandon the original plan, it had not been fear. Recent actions had proved that. And now – Jimmy nodded acceptance of this frightening responsibility.

Brent said drily, "You might have to use a bit of initiative."

Jimmy tried to copy him: "I'd thought there might be that possibility."

David grinned at that, then told him crisply, "Get away as soon as you've recovered the boats."

"Aye, aye, sir." Jimmy Nash did not like lying this close to an enemy shore. He would be off as soon as he could.

The boats were ready. David went down into the dinghy that held his party and took the tiller. Grundy crouched in the bow with the engineer, the stoker and a seaman who would bring back the boat – if all went well. They all carried carbines. Cullen and another seaman pulled at the oars and Suzanne sat by Brent in the sternsheets.

The dinghy bucked over the rollers towards the dark shore while the drifter and the M.T.B.s receded astern, blurred black silhouettes gradually merging into the night and the shadow of the cape. Brent gripped the tiller with one hand, held in the other the Colt .45 automatic he'd strapped on.

113

The line of breaking surf was just ahead and he could see a figure standing there. He narrowed his eyes, trying to probe the darkness, searching for any other men hidden further up the beach, but he could make out nothing beyond the man at the edge of the surf. He was conscious of Suzanne at his side. He had wanted to leave her behind, but he needed her. She was the only one who knew the man who should be waiting on the beach and she had an important part to play later. Brent glanced at her quickly. She was leaning forward to peer over the lifting and dipping bow as the boat drove in. Then she nodded: "That's Albert."

A second later the dinghy took the ground. As the prow grated on shingle Grundy leapt over into the surf and dragged it higher on the beach. The others followed, Suzanne and David Brent last of all. Only the seaman who was to take back the dinghy was left aboard. Grundy and the other men fanned out, watching the beach breathlessly with carbines held ready.

Suzanne shot quick questions at Albert, then turned to Brent waiting at her side and said, "He has – dealt with – the sentry here. No one will come for an hour or more. We can go on."

All David Brent could see of Albert in the night was a bony face and the glitter of eyes above a slight, stooped figure. He wondered how this skinny little man could have "dealt with" an armed sentry, but did not ask. It was sufficient that it was done. He pulled the torch from his pocket and flashed the signal out to sea, then shoved at the bow of the dinghy. Grundy came running to add his weight and as the bow slid clear and the dinghy floated free he warned the man in the boat, "Don't get lost, Charlie."

Charlie replied as he bent to the oars, "I'll take bloody good care I don't!" The dinghy turned and headed out to sea as he pulled strongly.

Brent ordered Grundy, "All of you up to the cutting in the cliff. Get into cover and wait for the rest of us. I'll meet the boats." He watched them hurry up the beach in a loose group, Albert and Suzanne at their head, until their dark shapes blended into the blackness of the shadows at the foot of the grey cliff.

He and the girl had lain on a shore like this, not far from this place, on a hot, sun-bright day. They swam, they ate and drank a bottle of dry white wine. He had made love to her.

He turned and stared out to sea. As the other boats landed and the men scrambled onto the beach he pointed them towards the ravine. Then as the last of them trotted away he sent the boats back to join Jimmy Nash where he lay hidden in the shadow of the cape.

Now he ran across the shingle then over soft sand. At the mouth of the ravine he found the others. They crouched in what cover they could find and in the night he could only see the indistinct shapes of a few of the men. Then Chris Tallon rose from the ground almost at his feet and whispered urgently, "Let's get on with it!" Suzanne and Albert were standing now and she saw Brent's nod to her. She turned and led the way into the deeper darkness of the ravine, the old man a pace behind her, David Brent at her shoulder. Tallon and his commandos followed in single file. Chris still had some doubts, but faith in Brent now. He had saved Tallon before. Then at the briefing he had not said: "We will attempt," nor: "There is a chance." But definitely: "This is what we will do." Brent had made them a team.

They walked quick-striding by the side of the stream. As they passed under the bridge Brent heard the sudden catch of the girl's breath then he, too, saw the body of the sentry lying in the bed of the stream. But there was no break in Suzanne's stride.

David Brent thought that he had not literally burnt his boats, but they had gone. As soon as Jimmy Nash had recovered them he would be on his way. For Brent, Tallon, Suzanne, all of them, there was no turning back now. And as if in emphasis there was a sudden, long burst of firing in the darkness behind them and then the roar of engines. The column halted, heads turned, listening. Chris Tallon said softly, "Cannon fire. E-boats." Brent nodded, and there came another burst, the hammering reports echoing inside the walls of the ravine. Then the sound of the engines ceased and there was silence.

Tallon and Suzanne were looking at David Brent and the column of men waited on his decision. There had been no machine-gun fire. He thought that he could not help Jimmy Nash, whatever trouble the spare skipper was in. Brent had decided on his course of action. He was committed and would carry it through. He asked, "Where is this path?"

Suzanne answered, "A few yards ahead." She led on to it; they climbed out of the ravine and the padding file wound along the track through the night, headed inland to the river.

8

Like jumping without a parachute

When Rudi Halder had sighted the black mass of the cape lifting off the starboard bow of the E-boat he had told Bruno Jacobi, "There's our landfall. We'll run in close along this side of the cape. If the *Tommis* are hiding in there we've got them bottled up, with the shore on two sides of them."

The engines of the three E-boats were throttled back for silent running and they crept in towards the cape. Rudi glanced briefly to his left and saw the other two boats spaced out on that side and in echelon astern of him. Then he returned to staring out over the bow, as did the two-man crew of the 20mm. cannon just forward of the bridge. He could sense the tension in their bodies crouched over the breech of the gun.

But the cannon fire came out of the night to starboard in a long, hammering burst that shattered the silence, tearing tracer that blinded with its brilliance and struck home. Rudi felt the jar of impact.

He reacted after only a split second of outrage and disbelief: "*Hold your fire! Hard aport! Full ahead!*" The main engines boomed as the throttles opened and the boat surged forward but at once heeled in the turn to port. Rudi saw the other two boats following his example so the three of them ran away northwards as a second burst of cannon fire tore the night. Rudi bawled at the signalman on the bridge behind him, "Send the reply!" Then he saw the man already had the lamp lifted and was triggering off the recognition signal for that night. The signalman had also realised that they were under fire from another E-boat.

That firing came again, dazzling, shrieking overhead so all of them on the bridge instinctively crouched and Rudi blasphemed and shouted at the attacking boats astern, "Hold your fire, you stupid bastards!" He knew that was

a useless display of fear and fury – but the firing ceased.
The signalman was still triggering off the "reply" and now
there was an answering flicker of light out in the darkness.
Rudi ground out between his teeth, "So they've woken up
at last. Stop her!"

The other two boats of his flotilla saw his speed fall away
and conformed. All three E-boats slowed, slumped to rest
but with engines still rumbling, idling.

Rudi demanded, "Any casualties?" He waited, raging and
anxious, hands clamped tight on the bridge screen. He had
been on active service since the start of the war in 1939, first
in the Baltic when the *Wehrmacht* overran Poland, then in
the North Sea. He had learned his craft and some of the
lessons were hard. He knew the terrible effect of gunfire on
the human body, had suffered casualties in his crews, buried
them, mourned every one.

Now he received "negative" reports from the other two
boats, lying within easy calling distance, and from Bruno
Jacobi, climbing back onto the bridge after a lightning tour
of his own command. Rudi heard them with relief but then
Ernst Fischer, provoked, shouted across from his bridge,
"What the hell is going on?"

Rudi bellowed back at him, "*Shut up!*" And thought:
What a bloody foul-up. But he would not have a whining
session, not in his flotilla, by God! "I want a sharp look-out
all around because we may be in the presence of the enemy.
And keep silence, every one of you!"

He got it. Bruno Jacobi had opened his mouth to vent his
anger but now shut it and swallowed the words. Not a voice
was raised as two more E-boats took shape out of the night
and closed to talking distance. Rudi waited. He could make
out the bulky figure of Gunther on his bridge, could picture
the face with its heavy jaw, usually thrust out for an effect
of determination and aggression, but it would be chewing
uncertainly now.

Gunther's voice came across the narrow neck of sea
between the boats, "That's you, Rudi?"

"It is." An even, patient reply.

"I thought you were *Tommis*."

"Did you see my signal?"

"Yes. That's why I stopped firing – "

"That was the 'reply' for the night." Rudi stood with hands jammed in his pockets, his tone still patient, reasonable.

"I know – "

"There is also a 'challenge'."

"Yes, I know – "

"Then why the *hell* didn't you send it instead of shooting up my boats!"

"I've already been hit by the *Tommis* – "

Rudi mimicked, "Yes, I know."

Gunther went on, complaining, "I lost one boat. I headed for the shore to try to beach her but she sank before we reached shallow water. The other one is holed and pumping all the time, can't make better than ten knots. I was on my way back to base and when I saw these boats ahead – "

"You thought you'd sink one of mine to even things up!"

"Well, I wasn't expecting to see you here."

"I'm here because I thought the *Tommis* could be lying close under the cape." Rudi saw Gunther's head jerk around to peer at the black mass astern, and went on, "Forget it. If they'd been there they'd have grabbed the heaven-sent opportunity of shooting hell out of us while we're lying here like sitting ducks." And regretted it, if they had tried; his gunners sat with fingers on the triggers as he had ordered.

Rudi dismissed Gunther contemptuously, "The *Tommis* are miles away and on their way home. You'd better follow their example before you do any real damage."

"I'll make a full report of this conversation!" That was bluster and the silent, listening men in the boats knew it.

"I will also make a full report, Gunther, and if they ever give you another boat they'll never let you out of the bath with it!" Rudi turned away and ordered, "Half ahead." As his boat eased forward he saw the other two of his flotilla getting under way and tucking themselves into the echelon formation, swinging to port to copy his own turn as he

119

growled it down the voice-pipe at Bäcker, the coxswain, in the wheel-house below the bridge.

Gunther! That thick-headed blunderer! Rudi fought down his anger. He had to think clearly. He went over the events of the night in his mind: the *Tommis* had picked up an agent south of St. Jean and he had hit them twenty miles out as they were passing the fishing fleet. Rudi had waited in ambush again but instead of continuing on their course for home the *Tommis* had attacked the fishing fleet. After that engagement they had headed north, one of their boats had burned and the survivors had jumped Gunther when he charged in bull-headed.

Conclusion: after that first action the *Tommis* had suspected the trap he had laid for them and to avoid it had headed north before turning for home. Somehow he had missed them as he had swept northward – maybe they had changed to silent running? But no; if they were on their way back to England they would not creep along on auxiliaries.

He had told Gunther that if the *Tommis* were still around they would have jumped the E-boats while they were stopped. But would they? Suppose picking up the agent was only part of an operation to be carried out on this coast and which now demanded they avoid action? What kind of operation? He did not know, but now he thought uneasily that the *Tommis* could still be somewhere off this coast. Had they been lying quietly in the black shelter of the cape while he bawled out Gunther?

Bruno Jacobi thrust another signal at him and Rudi muttered irritably, "There's too much wireless traffic."

This one was from his senior officer sitting at his desk at base and ordered, "Pursue enemy along course . . ." Rudi scanned it quickly then slapped it into Bruno's open palm. "They want us to chase along a course to England, and try to stop the *Tommis* getting that agent back – if it takes all night. Send: 'Submit believed enemy still in my area of coast and continuing operations. Request permission to search.' And we'll do that."

The E-boats turned and started back towards the land,

but five minutes later Rudi received yet another signal from his senior officer, curt but explicit: he was to carry out his orders.

He swore and turned the boats again, on course for England.

Jimmy Nash had recovered only one of his dinghies when he heard the engine noise muttering out at sea. He stood on the deck of the drifter, head turning as he listened. Then Crozier called softly from his bridge only yards away, "You hear it, too?"

Jimmy warned, "Be ready to fight your way out, the pair of you, but fire only on my order." He heard the quiet acknowledgments from Crozier and little Dent on either side of the drifter, was aware as they were that all of them were pinned against the black loom of the cape. They waited for their boats, as he waited for that of the drifter to return from the beach.

He jerked as the cannon fire hammered and tracer slid across the sky. Then the engine noise grew from a mutter to a deep booming and he saw the grey brush-strokes in the night that were the bow-waves and wakes of E-boats running at speed. A light flickered rapidly, unceasingly, and there was another burst of cannon fire but the light winked on without pause. Jimmy called, "What was that morse flashing?" He had read it but sought confirmation.

It came from Crozier's signalman: "B.M., sir. Over 'n' over."

Little Dent called gleefully, "They're shooting at each other!"

Jimmy thought: Right. So there were two groups of enemy boats out there and Brent hadn't succeeded in removing the threat from the sea. Had he known? And landed anyway?

The firing had ceased and now the bellow of the engines receding northward dropped to a low, idling grumble. Jimmy thought: They've stopped.

But the engines were still running, would cover any noise he might make and he saw the men on the M.T.B.s alongside were hauling in their dinghies. Then the drifter's beamy boat rubbed against her side. He called to Dent and Crozier, "Follow me out. Silent running." He turned to the drifter's skipper, standing at his side, pointed to the seaward end of the cape then turned his hand at the wrist to indicate "south", and finally put his finger to his lips.

The skipper nodded his understanding, "*Oui*."

The drifter's boat was hooked onto the davits, swung up from the water and inboard. Her engine thumped softly and she moved ahead, leading Dent and Crozier. The three slowly, quietly rounded the cape, stealing like shadows over the surface of the sea, and turned southward. Now they were moving parallel to the coast but out of sight of it. Jimmy showed the chart to the skipper in the wheel-house and pointed to the cross he had pencilled. The fisherman peered at the chart in the dim light from the compass binnacle and grunted, nodded, pushed it aside. He had fished these waters all his life and had no further need of the chart.

Jimmy stepped down to the deck and found Tommy Vance waiting for him. Tommy glanced astern at the two boats, following silhouettes in the night, and at the darkness beyond. He said, recalling that Brent knew he had not driven off the original flotilla of E-boats, "We're lucky to be out of that."

"Yes." But Jimmy thought their survival might have been due to David Brent's decision to close the cape and make the landing without delaying for a preliminary reconnaissance. If he had dithered, waited out at sea, then the enemy would have found them, fallen on them while they were stopped and disembarking the soldiers. Jimmy shied away from picturing that.

But the E-boats that had hunted them through this night were still at sea, prowling, searching.

As if in confirmation they both heard the distant rumble of engines and stared out to sea. The rumble grew steadily louder – but then as steadily faded, as if the boats had turned around.

Jimmy Nash sucked in a deep breath and said thankfully, "Gone away."

Tommy asked, "What now?"

"I know what I have to do," Jimmy Nash replied. "Now I'm going to think it through, try to anticipate any pitfalls and prepare for them."

Tommy Vance mentally reviewed Brent's curt orders to him, and agreed. "Plenty of food for thought. You heard what he told me to do?"

"I was there."

Tommy muttered, "It'll be the first time I've tried to do anything like that."

"And me."

It could easily be the last.

The drifter and the two boats held to that course and creeping pace for the next hour, while Jimmy Nash paced restlessly, his handsome face sombre in thought. Tommy Vance gathered around him his little party of a dozen men: gunners, seamen, stokers, a signalman. They carried light machine-guns or carbines and wore balaclavas rolled up on their heads or pulled down so their faces only showed as ovals. Most were in thick navy sweaters but the stokers still wore boilersuits.

Tommy told them what they would have to do, and how. Then he listened to their few questions and the muttered comment, "Bloody hell!" He tried to appear confident as he peered into their faces, grey in the night, and in return found some comfort in the way they looked back at him, not avoiding his eyes.

Then the three craft stopped, the drifter's skipper definite that he was on station, the position Jimmy Nash had shown him on the chart. Jimmy took him at his word. The men aboard the drifter and the boats waited, listening to the wash of the sea and staring out into the encircling darkness. Silent. Thinking.

The track opened out in front of David Brent and the river lay before him. It ran wide between reed-fringed banks but here a timber wharf had been built and the barge lay alongside this. There were no lights showing aboard her.

She was about sixty feet long by ten in the beam and lay heavy-laden and low in the water. The hold ran from just short of the blunt bow for three-quarters of her length. Then the roof of a cabin lifted and aft of that was an engine-room hatch and the long arm of the tiller. The cargo stood out of the hold and some three feet above the deck, was covered by a tarpaulin.

Tallon gestured and the commandos spread out left and right along the bank. They crouched or knelt, some with their backs to the river so as to keep an all-round watch. Then Albert crossed the wharf, boots thumping hollowly on the timbers, and stepped aboard the barge. Suzanne and David Brent followed him while Tallon waited on the bank, head turning, watching, listening.

As Albert ducked down through the hatch leading to the cabin below, Brent beckoned Dobson, his engineer, and the stoker. He told them, "It's a petrol engine. Find it and see what you make of it. Got a torch?"

"Yessir." Dobson held it up.

"Keep it covered so it doesn't show outside. Use it as little as possible. There might be patrols around here."

Dobson lifted the engine-room hatch and he and his stoker disappeared below. David and Suzanne waited, staring out over the river, not speaking but each conscious of the other, almost touching. So for a long minute, then Albert came up from below and spoke quietly, rapidly to Suzanne. She translated for David Brent: "He's told them you want their barge. They don't mind; it belongs to the company." She unconsciously imitated their shrugs. "They have offered to come with you, if you want their help, but Albert says they are both married men with families."

Brent said, "I'll need one of them as a pilot. I don't remember that much of this river to be able to follow the deep-water channel."

The girl looked away then, knowing how he had gained what knowledge he had. But she spoke to Albert, and when he shrugged again and answered, she translated: "He says he has crewed on the barges many times, when they were short of a man and he wanted the extra money. He can pilot you to St. Jean." Brent hesitated and Albert saw it and nodded definitely.

Brent returned the nod, "All right." He glanced around and saw Dobson pulling himself up out of the engine-room hatch. David asked, "What about it?"

The engineer wiped his hands on an old rag and answered confidently, "No bother, sir. Ready to go when you give the word."

"Checked the fuel?"

"'Course, sir. Better than half a tank." Dobson's tone was injured. Did Brent think he was a bloody amateur?

"Start up." And to Tallon, "Get 'em all aboard. Coxswain! Take the helm."

Dobson dropped down through the engine-room hatch again and Chris Tallon muttered, "About time. We can't afford to stand around." He gestured to his men with arms held wide and they rose to their feet, closed in and clambered over the side of the barge. Private Johnson, the Sudetan German interpreter, went aboard at Tallon's side.

Grundy answered, "Aye, aye, sir!" He went aft to the tiller, cast off the lashing and worked it to get the feel of it in the water. He thought: Be different when she starts to move; won't handle like a torpedo boat. He looked from one side to the other at the banks of the river with the trees that lined them standing black against the night sky. He muttered aloud, "There won't be much room for manoeuvring, either. This river looks wide but it'll shallow near the sides."

"Still, you won't need no engine-room telegraph." Dobson's voice came from down by Grundy's feet, out of the open hatch just forward of the tiller.

The coxswain grinned, "That's a fact."

There was a churning below and then the engine fired, raced, was throttled back to a steady throb. The crew of the barge came up from the cabin onto the deck. Suzanne had called David Brent's decision down to them and the two men each carried a small suitcase. They stepped over to the wharf and stood there staring at Brent, Suzanne, Tallon and

125

the armed commandos. "They'll keep their mouths shut till morning?" David asked Suzanne.

"I told them. They've agreed. Albert's warned them not to go near his village, that the S.S. were there. They know a farmhouse where they can spend the night. They'll make the excuse that they had a small fire aboard so the cabin wasn't fit to sleep in."

Brent wondered whether he should trust the men – or lock them below. Then one of them lifted a hand to his cap in salute and called softly, "*Bonne chance!*" and Brent remembered he was really trusting Suzanne and Albert, as he had done all night.

He saluted, then made his way aft and ordered, "Cast off. Slow ahead." Cullen and the other seaman, stationed in bow and stern, untied the lines that secured the barge to the wharf then jumped aboard as she moved ahead. She swung out into the stream as Grundy eased over the tiller.

Suzanne had followed Brent and now she looked at her watch. David saw the gesture and glanced down at his own wrist. He nodded slowly as she said, "We've got just one hour and thirty-five minutes."

Chris Tallon checked that, recalling the briefing in the wardroom, thinking that they had just enough time. And because of that briefing and the knowledge this girl had imparted, he now knew the schedule of the train, that the prisoner was in one of the last two coaches at the end of the train, and even the strength of the escort. More, she had detailed the defences of St. Jean and effectively there was only one weak company of infantry.

This mad scheme, hastily thrown together by Brent and dependent almost totally on surprise, might just have a chance in a million of success. Tallon thought it was like jumping without a parachute. But as Brent had pointed out, there was no other way.

Ilse lay awake, propped up on pillows and reading her book, unable to sleep. She had tried and failed, was restless and uneasy. She worried about Rudi, kept remembering the man dragged into S.S. headquarters along the quay, and the Frenchman who had stared up at her window and who frightened her.

When she heard someone arrive at the door she dressed quickly, ran a comb through her hair and hurried downstairs to find out who it could be. Her father's servant, an old soldier, was hanging up a greatcoat and hooking an officer's field cap on top of it. The eagle above the peak was in silver and the cap was soft-crowned because the stiffening had been taken out – for comfort and to give it a rakish look.

The door to the *Oberst*'s study was open. She went to it as she heard him saying, "This is a quiet area – " He broke off then as he saw his daughter, and smiled at her, "Ah, my dear – " But he was again interrupted, this time by the ringing of the telephone on his desk. He lifted the instrument: "König."

He recognised the voice of the duty officer at the barracks: "*Herr Oberst*, we have had a report from the guard commander at post 12 that a sentry has been found dead."

König did not need to consult his map. Post 12 was ten kilometres north of St. Jean. He had visited it only that morning on his tour of inspection. He also thought he knew the sergeant who would be in command there this night. "You have the *Unterfeldwebel* on the line? Then put him through."

A hoarse voice this time, of a man somewhat out of breath: "*Herr Oberst!*"

König recognised the voice. His memory had not let him down. This N.C.O. was solid and stolid, maybe a little slow but reliable. "Report."

"An hour ago I heard cannon fire at sea north of the cape and it sounded close inshore. I took two men and went to investigate. Long before I had passed the cape, the firing had stopped and there was nothing to be seen. I looked for the sentry to ask him what he'd seen or heard. I found there was a broken guard-rail on the bridge over the ravine and he was down in the stream."

König asked, "Who was it?"

"Brunner, *Herr Oberst*."

König knew Brunner as he knew every man in his command: brave, a good soldier in action so long as he was told what to do, lazy and untidy in barracks.

The *Unterfeldwebel* was going on: "He must have leant on the rail and fallen when it gave way; he was a heavy man."

"An accident."

"*Ja, Herr Oberst*. There was no sign of a struggle though there is mud everywhere – the weather – but I went down with my men and pulled him out of the stream. He wasn't wounded in any way, not shot, stabbed, or clubbed. His pockets hadn't been touched, his money and papers were still there, his rifle was beside him."

"Any other incidents during your tour of duty?"

There was a breathing pause. König could picture the *Unterfeldwebel* at the field-telephone in the guard hut on the cliff, reading the notes he had scribbled down. Then: "Forty-five minutes before the firing north of the cape there was a blaze out at sea, about five kilometres south of our position and ten kilometres out, as if a boat was on fire. Then there was some gunfire, machine-guns and cannons. We could just see the tracers. I reported to the duty officer."

"Nothing else?"

"*Nein, Herr Oberst*."

Erwin König thought for a minute, oblivious to his daughter and the other officer waiting in the room, neither speaking or moving so as not to interrupt him. Then he ordered, "Search the area around the bridge, inland and on the beach. Look for signs of anyone else being there tonight, possibly gone down to the sea. Report anything you find immediately, and to me."

He put down the receiver and turned to the others, "Excuse me. My dear, this is *Major* Kurt Ritter. Kurt, my daughter, Ilse."

The *Major* wore service dress of grey trousers and grey-green tunic with the silver eagle on his right breast, a holstered pistol on his belt. He took Ilse's hand, bent his head over it. When he straightened, his blue eyes were level

128

with hers. His fair hair was trimmed neatly short but rumpled where he had run his fingers through it after taking off his cap. Ilse thought he looked fit, energetic, tough.

Erwin König explained, "Kurt served with me in the blitzkrieg advance through France in 1940."

Ritter smiled at Ilse, "I am a disciple of your father." Then his smile faded. "I think it is an appalling waste that he should be left in a backwater like this."

König shook his head. "I had my war as a young man, Kurt, and it ended in 1918. One is enough. As for this being a backwater, I'll be happy if it stays that way, but – " He paused and gave a jerk of his head towards the telephone, " – that was a report that one of my sentries has been found dead. It appears to have been an accident but I've started an investigation. There has been fighting at sea tonight, I think between some of the British *Schnellboote* and ours. Also, the S.S. reported earlier that an enemy agent was taken off the beach south of here by the British. So it may be that this area will not be so quiet in the future. We will see. However – " he gestured to the armchairs set before the fire, " – please."

Ilse asked, "Have you been posted here, *Major*, or are you just visiting?"

Ritter waited until she was seated before he took a chair and answered, "Neither. My battalion, Panzer Grenadiers, is moving north and is bivouacked near a bridge about fifteen kilometres south of here. We entrain there tomorrow. I command an assault company, one hundred and twenty men, powerfully armed, superbly trained and tested in action. They are the cream of the army." Ritter's pride was clear.

Ilse frowned and glanced at her father. "Bivouacked. That does not sound very comfortable. We could give you a room here."

Ritter grinned, "Thank you. But they sent my company ahead to be quartered in the barracks across the river for the night. I have a bed there, only five minutes away."

9

The *Schütze*

The blunt stem of the barge threw up a big bow-wave as it thrust downstream with the engine at full throttle. The river was flowing fast and deep in winter spate, adding a knot or two to the hammering top speed of the broad-beamed craft laden low in the water.

Grundy, the tiller tucked under his arm, muttered, "You can almost see her lifting." Because the barge was being lightened. Tallon's commandos had unlashed the tarpaulin over the cargo, thrown it back and were now labouring at throwing that cargo over the side. They pulled out pockets of it, sacks and crates, so that those left still held up the tarp, draped like a tent. Most of the cargo hurled overboard sank at once but some of the lighter crates floated only half-submerged and bobbed away on the wake of the barge, leaving a long trail. When each party of three or four men had clawed out enough room for themselves they crawled into the nests thus created, pulled down the tarpaulin again and lay with their Thompson guns trained outboard.

When they were all hidden and the deck clear the barge rode perceptibly higher in the water because of their efforts. Brent nodded, satisfied, and told Tallon, "All right, Chris. First party for briefing." He went down into the barge's little cabin and Suzanne went with him. Tallon moved forward along one of the narrow strips of deck running either side of the cargo. He called out names and one by one the men slid out from under the tented tarp and dropped down to the cabin.

Grundy was left at the helm with Cullen and Albert. Cullen glanced sideways at the Frenchman and asked Grundy, "D'you think the old feller knows what he's doing?"

The coxswain answered grimly, "He'd better, for our sake."

"That's a bloody fact." If the barge ran aground or was wrecked then the operation was aborted. And if it wasn't? Cullen stared out over the bow at the darkness between the black ranks of trees that flicked steadily past on either side, at the river running oily ahead and humped under the bow. He thought, What are we doing *here*, in *France*? What the hell did Grundy bring me for? I'm not one of his mates. He hauls me over the coals every chance he gets. Couldn't he have found somebody else?

He stood glumly, hands dug deep in his pockets, shoulders slouched. And Grundy growled at him, "Get your hands out of your pockets and stand up straight. You're standing a watch, not hanging about in some pub."

Cullen said to himself, "Bullshit," but complied. Then thought: Still, as we're here, anything to keep from thinking how we might finish up tonight. He asked, "Want me to take her for a bit?" While thinking: He won't let go of it, bloody old woman.

But Grundy had suggested to Brent earlier, when Cullen was working forward, "Better have two men able to take the helm, sir, just in case. And better for him to get his hand in now, while it's still quiet." Brent had agreed and now Grundy said, "All right. You've got her."

Cullen hesitated a moment, taken by surprise, then moved to the tiller and tucked it under his arm.

Albert noted the change-over without comment and kept his gaze to his front, watching the river ahead. He stood with his arms folded, hugging the old overcoat around him. That gave some comfort to the ache in his wrist and also hid the nervous twitching of his fingers. His face was set in a dour scowl of concentration but behind that stolid front, Albert was afraid. It was no instinctive, unreasoning fear. He knew what Brent intended because Suzanne had told him on the way from the beach, so Albert knew he would almost certainly die before the dawn, along with most of the others aboard the barge.

The cabin below, with its single oil lamp hanging from the deckhead, was meant to house two men, three at the most, in close comfort. Now a dozen commandos were packed in, some perched on the edges of the bunks while others stood, stooped under that low deckhead. They were the first of three parties to be briefed. Each would be given the details of its own part in the overall plan, and then told how the other two groups would fit in.

Tallon and Suzanne were there, to listen or add what they could, answer questions. But David Brent conducted the briefings. He would start by pointing at the sketch map drawn by Suzanne, where it lay on the table: "Memorise that because you won't see it again. You won't have light, or time, to map-read your way tonight. But every party will have a guide . . ."

That first time when he reached the point, "We leave the barge here," his finger tapped the map but his eyes were on Chris Tallon. At the first briefing, held in the wardroom of the boat now lying on the bottom of the sea, the soldier had objected: "We should go on foot before then."

He said so again now, stubbornly: "I still think we should leave the barge sooner. The nearer we take it to St. Jean the more likely it is to be reported, because there'll be more people to see it. Few barges travel at night – " he glanced at Suzanne and saw her nod " – and I doubt if any tear along at this speed. If we go ashore and do the last mile or so on foot we'll get closer without being spotted."

Brent shook his head, "No. The barge is quicker and it'll take us right there."

Tallon said, "Where they could be expecting us. The whole success of this scheme depends on surprise."

"Exactly. So we go right in."

"I'm thinking of casualties," Tallon snapped.

"I know about casualties!" Brent growled that and saw Tallon blink; he went on: "I'm thinking of bringing out the man we were sent for. And of time; we can't afford to waste it by moving on foot." Then he saw Tallon about to speak again and forestalled him: "We go right in." He held Tallon's cold glare for a moment and then Chris's eyes went back to the map.

132

He did not raise the objection again. When all three briefings were done David Brent climbed to the deck and stretched the cramp from his body. He saw Chris Tallon doing the same and the soldier grumbled, "Like a bloody rabbit hutch down there."

David grunted agreement, his thoughts still on the encounter at the briefing. Chris was wrong. If they tried to cover the last mile at the double they might still run into a patrol that would halt them for precious minutes. David stared at the dark banks of the river sliding past. There could be a watcher on the riverside anywhere between here and St. Jean, more and more likely the closer the barge got to the town, and the watcher might well telephone a report. It would be another matter for the enemy to stop the barge, but discovery on the river would mean the end of this attempt to rescue the prisoner from the train. And of Brent and his command.

He had laid out the plan, harsh-voiced, clearly and concisely so every man knew exactly what he had to do. But there were so many calculated risks. He worried about Jimmy Nash. Would he be able to carry out his vital part? Was he alive? Brent remembered the burst of cannon fire soon after the landing. Had the drifter, Dent and Crozier, been taken by surprise, shot up, annihilated?

He peered at his watch again, for something like the tenth time since setting out on the river, his face stooped close over the dial to make it out in the night. The rain had started again, driving in over the bow as the barge butted into it and he turned his back to it, the better to see the time. Then he looked up and saw Suzanne experiencing the same difficulty, her head bent over her lifted wrist.

"This part is new to you, of course." That was Chris Tallon, grinning wryly at David and not bearing a grudge. Brent was in command and had taken his decision, for good or ill. And he had brought them this far. Chris went on, "Coming ashore, I mean, to see how the other half earn their money."

David returned the grin, "Yes." But then it faded. This place was not new to him. His eyes were on the girl and now hers lifted to meet his stare. He knew she had heard his reply to Chris's comment, must be remembering his earlier reference to the river: "I don't recall it that well." He knew they were both a year ago from now in their thoughts.

Then, she had been pretty and chic, passionate, a hungry and eager lover . . . But once he had found her sitting at the window of the cottage in the dead of night with the tears wet on her face. She had told him she was crying because she was happy. He was sure she was lying to him, but said nothing. There was worse to come but he only found that out later. At that time he had held her in his arms through the rest of the night and did not make love to her again. In the morning the boy had ridden up to the cottage from the village on his bicycle, bringing the telegram recalling David Brent to Paris. From there he would go to join a ship. Now they stood together in the night again, only a yard apart, the rain slanting on the wind between them.

Albert spoke nasally and this time did not point to right or left as he had done so far, indicating to Cullen or Grundy at the helm the heading for the deep-water channel. Instead he made a downward, dampening motion with the flat of his hand.

Suzanne said huskily, "He says we must slow; the lock gates are just ahead."

Both she and David remembered them. He had leapt ashore to open the gates and had laughed down at her as she took the dinghy through the lock.

Brent looked at his watch. They would lose time at the lock and there was none to spare.

Otto Meissner was eighteen years old and peered nervously out at the world through round, steel-framed spectacles that gave him an owlish look. He was a *Schütze*, a private soldier, and just out of recruit training. He had hated that training and done badly, partly because his instructors terrified him, mainly because he did not want to be a soldier and knew he lacked the necessary qualities of nerve, stamina and aggression. He reasoned that by character and physique he was a clerk, so if they wanted him in uniform they should put him into a divisional office. But now he was a rifleman in an infantry battalion. That was the army for you.

He blinked through the rain that speckled the lenses of his glasses and hunched his narrow shoulders against it inside the greatcoat that was too big for him. The night was dark, cold, wet and he had to keep his eye on the *Gefreiter*, Solz, at the head of the file. Otto was at the tail of it and he watched Solz over the shoulders of the two men between. The *Gefreiter* was an old soldier, with ten years' service but still only a corporal, foul-mouthed and evil-tempered. Tonight he was drunk again, and dangerous. He had already put the butt of his rifle into one Frenchman they had met, though his papers were in order and he had a pass to be on the streets after curfew.

Now the lane opened out onto the bank of the river and Solz turned left to follow the path that ran downstream at the riverside. Then one of the others called, "There's a boat in the lock!"

Solz swung around and stared at the closed lock-gates thirty metres away. "How can you see a boat in there from here?"

"Well, I can't see the boat, but I can hear an engine. And look at the man on top with the rope."

Solz grunted, "Ah!" He, too, could hear the low throb coming from inside the lock. Now he saw the figure silhouetted against the lighter background of the night sky, with a mooring line hitched around a bollard and easing it out. So the boat inside was descending as the water level fell; he had not noticed the sluices emptying because water was only running out at the bottom and falling only inches into the river downstream of the lock. So it was almost empty. That was confirmed now as the man on top unhitched the mooring line and tossed it down to the unseen boat. Then he went quickly to the wheel that opened the lock gates and wound it furiously.

Solz said gloatingly, "We'll turn the bastards over, show them who's boss around here. And there's bound to be a bottle aboard." He moved forward towards the lock-gates

135

and the foot of the iron ladder running down from the lock above to the path on which he stood. The other two followed him, unslinging their rifles as he did, and halted by him close to the foot of the ladder.

Otto Meissner hung back at first then only trailed along at a distance, because he didn't want to "turn over" anybody but suspected that if his lack of enthusiasm showed he might be next. So he was hunched in the deeper shadows under the trees and some twenty yards from Solz and the other two, when the lock gates swung fully open and the man above came down the iron ladder as quick as any monkey.

The idling engine inside the confines of the lock now quickened. Otto caught a glimpse of a snub-nosed barge, with a tarpaulin-covered cargo, easing out from the side of the lock and towards the open gates. Then Solz was growling menacingly in bad French, "What's the hurry? Why are you running cargo at night?" He had stepped in close as the man swung around at the foot of the ladder, so he stared into the *Gefreiter*'s scowling face only feet away behind the muzzle of the rifle.

Cullen did not answer. For one thing, he did not have a word of French. For another, the only thought in his head was: "Christ! It's a Jerry!" He had never seen a German before.

The bow of the barge crept out of the lock and slipped past him. In two strides he could have stepped aboard her. He could hope for no help from the other man who had come ashore with him, to snub the after-mooring line as the water ran out of the lock and the barge sank steadily lower, because he had already climbed down the ladder inside the lock to the barge. And now Cullen saw the big German's expression change.

Solz may have become suspicious of this strange seaman wearing what looked like a *Kopfschützer*, a woollen cap, or finally noticed that he had a pistol belted around his waist. He pointed his rifle at Cullen and worked the bolt to drive a round into the breech for firing.

The three commandos, squeezed in among the sacks and

crates under the tarpaulin right forward in the barge, saw him a scant six feet away as the bow slid out of the lock. One of them opened fire and the other two a split-second later. The three Thompson guns swept the river bank like a metal flail. Solz fell forward and his rifle exploded a bullet into the mud of the path. The two men behind him were punched backwards as if by an iron fist, to lie in the mud.

Tallon snarled, "What the hell is going on?" He ran forward along the narrow strip of deck beside the covered cargo, his Thompson gun held two-handed, chest-high, ready to fire. The barge was still moving ahead so he was only half-way along the deck when he was clear of the lock and could see the bodies on the shore.

Brent, standing aft by Grundy, called down the engine-room hatch, "Stop her!" Then as the stern of the barge cleared the lock he ordered, "Lay her alongside!" He jumped ashore with the after mooring line then passed it to the seaman who followed him. Tallon was already on the bank, with two of his commandos who took up defensive positions, down on one knee and back to back at the edge of the trees, facing up and down the path. He trotted up as Brent turned on Cullen and rephrased Tallon's question: "What happened?"

Cullen rubbed a hand across his face that felt numb. "I came down the ladder, turned round and there was this big Jerry poking a rifle at me. He said something, I don't know what, then he put one up the spout – " he looked at Tallon " – and that's when your blokes fired, sir."

Tallon called to the two kneeling by the trees, "You shot them?"

"Sir!"

"How many of them were there?"

"Just the three, sir."

Tallon went quickly to the bodies, crouched over each in turn, finally rose and looked at Brent: "All dead."

"Put them out of sight and get aboard." David stepped onto the deck of the barge and stood by the engine-room hatch. Suzanne was there, her hands in the pockets of her trenchcoat, one gripping the pistol. Now she released it and brought out a handkerchief. David saw her wiping her palms. Her face was still but he heard her trembling sigh.

Tallon and his two men dragged the bodies into the trees and threw the rifles in after them. Then they returned to the barge and Chris jumped aboard beside David Brent to ask one question: "How long?"

Brent answered him flatly, "We've lost ten minutes coming through the lock."

Chris swore, then: "That firing could have been heard, reported, and another patrol on the way to investigate."

"We'll be gone when they get here." And David Brent ordered, "Full ahead!"

The *Feldwebel* in the guardpost in the village a kilometre away had brought along his portable gramophone. He and the two dozen men who had recently come in off patrol, or whose turn was not due for another four hours, were seated around the stove, bawling out the chorus of the marching song as the scratched disc revolved. No one heard the distant, short rattle of machine-gun fire.

In St. Jean, north of the river in the old port, another group of four wet and mud-spattered soldiers stood listening. The *Gefreiter* muttered, "Just that one burst."

One of the three men with him laughed, "Somebody let off a magazine. Forgot to put his safety catch on. He'll be on the carpet in the morning."

The *Gefreiter* grumbled, "I just hope he didn't shoot anybody but himself. They should put the fool inside." He started off again and the others followed him.

Otto Meissner listened to the receding drone of the barge's engine with his gloved hand stuffed in his mouth. He had gagged himself thus after the first awful shock of being hit, finding himself prone in the inches-deep sludge and leaf-mould under the trees, seeing the men leaping ashore from the barge. He bit on the glove against the pain and to stifle the shrieks that rose like bile in his throat. When one of the men came to peer at the bodies only feet away, Otto hid his eyes and face inside his sheltering arms. He did not raise his head to look around until the sound of the barge had faded into the distance.

He knew he had been hit in the legs, was afraid to move at first but then tried and pain screamed up from his feet. He made one tentative effort to stand, using his rifle for support, but abandoned the attempt. He thought he could feel broken bones grating in his ankles. He could never walk, even with the rifle as a crutch, so he tossed it aside. He thought that he had not fired a shot, had just hidden in panic and terror. Solz would have fought if given the chance. But he wasn't Solz, knew he wasn't a soldier at all. It did not occur to him that if he had tried to fight he would have died.

He had to report. He still could hardly believe what he had seen, what had happened to him, though the pain was real enough. He had to raise the alarm.

He forced himself to his hands and knees and began to crawl. He whimpered in agony at every grinding movement of each dragging boot and after a dozen yards collapsed and wept. Then he crawled on again.

The train rattled and swayed northward. Max Neumann sat with his jacket collar turned up against the wind that whistled through the cracks in the side of the wagon, his hands tucked under his arms to try to keep some warmth in them. Soon he would stand and flap his arms, stamp his feet to restore circulation to the blood that seemed to be freezing inside him. He did that every few minutes and tried to encourage the others to do the same. They would all die if they did not maintain this discipline until the train halted. They would all die anyway, but he obstinately refused to give up. He did not know why.

He shoved himself upright as the train slowed. Were they stopping? Would the torture be reduced to mere misery for a while? He set his eye to one of the cracks and saw the train was running slowly past a siding. Dozens of vehicles were scattered around; he could make out the humped shapes of the nearest and saw others vaguely in the background. There were lights in some of the vehicles, showing as thin slivers where they leaked through the carelessly closed tilts. Then the wagon trundled past a soldier, a sentry standing close by the track with rifle slung over one shoulder. Max realised this was a body of troops, possibly a battalion, in bivouac. And the train was not stopping.

It rolled on slowly and he wiped at his eye that watered from the draught coming in through the crack. He looked again and now saw the reason for the train reducing speed. They were passing over a bridge. As it slid away behind, the clacking of the wheels gradually quickened.

Max turned to face the blackness inside the wagon. He thought: What's the point? But then he started clapping his hands, running on the spot clumsily and staggering on the rocking train. He shouted breathlessly, "Come on! Keep warm! Keep *moving*!"

10

"All patrols to close on the river!"

The young *Major* Kurt Ritter was enthusing over his assault company of grenadiers: "They are all men under the age of thirty, every one of them in the peak of physical condition . . ." Ilse, watching him, thought that he made a good example, fresh-faced, seemingly packed with energy. He sat straight-backed in the chair as if copying his teacher, the *Oberst*, sitting opposite him, but looking ready to leap from it at a word of command. He addressed Erwin König but now and then would glance at Ilse, to include her in the conversation – or to assess her. Ilse recognised one more example of the stallion male but this one did not frighten her, as had the Frenchman now sitting in S.S. Headquarters. This was a man like Rudi Halder. Maybe tomorrow she would tease Rudi about the handsome and virile *Major*. She smiled to herself at that, thinking of Rudi, then remembering that he was out at sea.

The telephone rang, cutting off Ritter in mid-sentence, and König rose to answer it. He stood by the desk, lean, straight and tall, listening to the report relayed through the barracks, the hoarse voice of the *Unterfeldwebel* who commanded at post 12.

He had trudged up the path from the guard-hut to the bridge over the ravine, splashing through the puddles and slipping in the mud, his men at his heels. Before they reached the bridge they were soaked by the pouring rain, hunched and miserable, but he snapped and snarled at them like a dog herding sheep and they spread out to search.

Their torches probed into the undergrowth and under the dripping branches of the trees, the jerking beams cones of jewelled brilliance in the darkness of the ravine and reflecting from the stream. One man found the cigarette stubs, wet and shredding, where Albert had waited. Another kicked at the cardboard he had used to mask the hole in the bridge, but saw no significance in it. The cigarette stubs were reported, the man on the cliff bawling the information down to the *Unterfeldwebel* where he prowled about the beach at the mouth of the ravine. He barked an acknowledgment and went on with his own search. The sand was churned, rain-sodden, but showed signs of bootprints. He found more on his way down to the surf but no sign of a boat grounding; the tide had washed that away.

But he had seen enough, trotted, slipped and slid along the half-kilometre of greasy path back to the guard-hut and telephoned the *Herr Oberst*.

König listened to the concluding words of the *Unterfeldwebel*, who paused now and again to catch his breath: "I think someone was taken off, or landed tonight. Those prints would not last long in this weather."

König agreed, "Well done. Now get off the line." Then he spoke to the officer on duty at the barracks across the river, "There is evidence that an enemy agent may have landed in the area of post 12 tonight, and one of our sentries was killed so the landing could be made. Alert all patrols. And at first light I want a search of all houses and farms within five kilometres of that post. Start organising that now."

He replaced the receiver and scowled down at the desk. One of his men was dead and it was no accident. There might not be any mark of assault on the body but murder had been done, König was certain.

Kurt Ritter was on his feet, tugging down his jacket. "I could not help overhearing. It seems you will be out long before dawn." He did not doubt that the *Herr Oberst* would lead the morning search. "I'll leave you to take your rest."

But König waved him down. "I sleep little and certainly not this early. I have some fine cognac. You'll take a glass?"

That was only half a question and half a command. Kurt Ritter grinned and sank back into his chair. He asked, "You said an agent 'may' have landed. It is not certain?"

Erwin König stood with his back to the fire and watched his daughter busy with the bottle and glasses on the sideboard. He knew she was a beauty and had seen the glances cast at her by Ritter, but he was sure poor Kurt was too late. The girl saw a lot of Rudi Halder. König suspected the affair was more serious than it might appear, but he would not pry. His daughter, and the young *Kapitänleutnant*, had to live their own lives.

He shrugged. "Someone landed or was taken off. We're sure of that. So I'm assuming the former until I'm proved wrong. We'll see what the searches turn up tomorrow."

Ilse brought the glasses of cognac, handed them to Ritter and her father. Someone. She thought that it would be a man, of course, out there in the night, hiding and hunted. Then she saw again that other man being dragged, legs trailing, into the dark house along the quay. She shivered.

König moved aside from the fire and reached out to touch her hand. "Are you cold, my dear?"

Ilse was about to say that she was sorry for the agent, but thought that while her father might understand, the *Major* would not. Instead she said, "Only a draught of cold air, I think." What kind of man could this enemy be?

David Brent stood by Grundy, who had the helm, one arm embracing the long tiller. They both watched the river ahead, black and glittering in the night, but David could see the girl out of the corner of his eye. She and Tallon stood by the rail only a pace away. The rain had stopped and she had taken the sodden scarf from her hair which now blew out behind her.

Albert, on the far side of Grundy, shifted from one foot to the other and chewed his lip nervously. He glanced around at Brent, appealing, and David saw that look but shook his head, as he had answered Albert's spoken plea some minutes ago. Suzanne had said, "He wants you to reduce speed. He says we are getting close to the town. If we have to stop – "

"We don't stop until you show us the place. Then we'll run her into the bank if we have to." He had to make up the time lost at the lock.

Now he told the coxswain, "Steady as you go."

Grundy thought: Steady? Christ! The barge was foaming along under the twin pressures of engine and current, the trees spaced on the bank flicking past one by one. "Aye, aye, sir."

The girl watched David Brent and recalled that one day he had hired a little boat, sailed it all the way down the river to St. Jean and had complained that the rented dinghy handled like a cow. A barge leaving St. Jean in the late afternoon had towed them back against the stream. They had sat in the sternsheets of the dinghy, eaten the bread and cheese they'd bought in the town and taken it in turns to drink from the litre of red wine, rough and dry, until the bottle was empty. It had been dark when they got back to the cottage and he had carried her to bed.

That night she had wept as she always did, because she was counting the days, but he did not know about that. She had always stolen from the bed and gone to sit at the window so as not to waken him. Only that one time he had chanced to wake and gone to her at the window, taken her back to bed, and that had been the last time.

Now she realised Chris Tallon had muttered a question and was staring at her. She answered it, her voice low but clear, "We have sixteen minutes before the train is due."

The *Feldwebel* in the village stood at the telephone and listened to his orders from the officer at the barracks in St. Jean. Then he sent out almost every man to patrol, keeping only two in the guardroom to act as runners. One file of four splashed through the puddles on the track leading to the river. The rain had stopped but the sky hung low and heavy with more. They marched in silence, fed-up because they had looked forward to a few hours sleep before going out on patrol again. The weary cursing had ceased before they left the village and now there was only the rasp of their breathing and the irregular thud and slither of their boots in the mud.

Then Pohl, the senior soldier trudging in the lead, halted and the others crowded behind him. He whispered, "Listen!"

They stood, breath held, peering at the track ahead that became a tunnel of shadow under overhanging trees. Now they all heard the low moaning and the slow dragging. The hair lifted on the neck of one young soldier and he said huskily, "My God!"

Pohl, nerves on edge, snarled, "Shut up!" Then: "Stay back and cover me."

The other three spread across the track as he went forward cautiously with rifle trained ahead. They watched his hunched figure blend into the shadow beneath the trees and listened to the moaning and scraping that still came out of the darkness. Then he called urgently, "Quick! Give me a hand here!"

They ran to join him and found him stooped over the kneeling body that was still trying to crawl but edging forward only inches at a time, legs dragging through the sucking mud. Pohl ordered, "Let's get him out of here." So they lifted the man between them and he squealed with pain but they carried him into the open and laid him down again, now on his back with face turned to the sky. His eyes were closed behind the round lenses and he was silent now.

One of them said, "It's Meissner!"

Pohl, crouched over Otto Meissner, straightened. "He was with Solz."

Another knelt with his face close to that of Otto and said, "He's fainted – out cold." He looked around and up. "What d'you think happened?"

"How the hell should I know?" Pohl snapped. He thought quickly, staring down at the body, then said, "He's hurt in the legs. You two put dressings on them then take him back." He jerked a thumb at the fourth man of the patrol. "You come with me. I'm going to look for Solz."

The *Feldwebel* jerked to his feet and swore when the two kicked open the door of the guardroom and staggered in. They carried Meissner between them on a stretcher made from the greatcoat of one of them, buttoned around their two rifles as shafts. It only supported his trunk so his legs and arms dangled loosely.

"Put him on a bunk!" The *Feldwebel* shoved at the two men he had kept with him and they helped the others lay Meissner on one of the camp beds set up against the rear wall. The *Feldwebel* quickly examined Otto while the men who had brought him in told their story, then he pointed at one of his runners. "Raise the barracks on the phone. Tell 'em we've a badly wounded man here. Gun-shot wounds in both legs and he'll need blood."

He patted Meissner's white face but without result except that the head rolled on the shoulders. So he reached for a bottle on the table and dribbled a thin stream of schnapps into the open mouth. Otto coughed and gagged but did not waken. The *Feldwebel* cursed softly, crossed to the tap above the sink and began to fill a basin with cold water.

The runner turned back from the telephone and reported, "The medics are on their way." He looked at the basin and protested cautiously, "Maybe we should leave him alone till they get here."

The *Feldwebel* answered tersely, "Balls to that. I want him talking. I want to know who shot him." He turned with the basin. The runner was now talking to the barracks.

The door opened and this time Pohl, the senior soldier of the patrol, entered with the fourth man. The latter's face was yellow in the light. Pohl said, "I found Solz and his other two men at the lock. Shot dead. Shoved under the trees."

The *Feldwebel* stared at him, then down at Otto Meissner. "He's a gutsy little bugger to have crawled all that way with his legs shot to bits. But still – " He turned the basin over and the icy douche hit the unconscious man full in the face. He spluttered, coughed and his lips curled back from his teeth in pain – but his eyes opened. They squinted and would not focus, but he was aware and able to pass the message he had crawled a half-kilometre to deliver.

When Erwin König answered the telephone this time he listened to the voice of the officer at the barracks for a second or two with his usual studied calm. Then it cracked: "*What!*"

Ilse stood up quickly, startled, a hand to her throat and eyes on her father. Kurt Ritter put his glass on the mantelpiece and watched the *Oberst*.

König snapped into the telephone, "Cancel my earlier orders. Searches will not be necessary. Issue orders now for all patrols to close on the river. Inform them that an enemy force is on a barge last seen four kilometres north of the town and headed towards it. There may be a dozen men or more than fifty. Then turn out every man in the barracks and bring them down to the bridge – "

König paused as he saw Kurt Ritter lift a hand. The *Major* said, "My men, too, *Herr Oberst*."

König added, " – also the company of Panzer Grenadiers. They will join *Major* Ritter at the bridge, where I will be waiting for you. We'll patrol in strength from there on both sides of the river. Now *move!*"

The gently sloping, grassy and reed-patched banks of the river had given way to stone retaining walls. The wash from the barge rolled out from it to slap and break on the walls. There were no trees marching by the side of the river now but on the left and a hundred yards or so inland a line of telegraph poles stood like sentries. David Brent, standing by Grundy at the tiller and looking ahead over the length of the barge, saw the last lock before St. Jean. Its nearer gates were open but the further ones were closed, making a narrow footbridge over the river. The retaining walls narrowed in to the bottleneck of the lock.

Suzanne said, "The railway track runs there, by the tele-graph poles. We're just outside the old port. It lies behind the wood." Her pointing finger swept from the telegraph poles, across the river to the right bank. "You might just make that out."

David Brent thought he could see the ragged black outline of the trees against the night sky a quarter-mile away – or was he just remembering? He looked at his watch as the lock slid towards them, then nodded to its left-hand wall and told Grundy, "Lay her alongside." He called down into the tiny engine-room, "Stop her . . . slow astern . . . stop her!"

He turned to Chris Tallon as the throb of the engine died and the helm went over, "Get 'em out. Go as soon as we touch." He spoke in a conversational tone but it carried in the sudden near-silence. There was only the sigh of the wind and the wash of the river at the bow of the barge as she ran in towards the bank with the last of the way on her. So the commandos heard him, threw back the tarpaulin and crawled out of their nests in the cargo. They waited, poised along the side, their eyes on Tallon.

He asked, low-voiced, "Have we time?"

Brent saw the girl watching him, but nodded, "Just."

"But we wouldn't have done if we'd tried to cover the last mile on foot, as I wanted to." Tallon grimaced: "So I touches me cap and stands corrected."

Brent shrugged, "We might have been stopped on the river or run aground. Luck of the game. We had to gamble."

Tallon wondered, "What's so bloody important about this man we're here to get?"

David Brent could not tell, wished he knew, but as the barge closed the wall of the lock he called softly, "Good luck, Chris!"

Tallon looked over his shoulder seriously, then grinned and for a moment looked only his twenty-five years. "And you!"

The barge ground against the wall, Tallon leapt ashore and his men followed him over the side in a wave. Half of them went with him as he ran off into the darkness, headed for the railway track, but a party of nine under Sergeant McNab, one carrying a rucksack, waited on the bank and watched Suzanne. Another group, two only carrying Thompson guns but the other five laden with big rucksacks, trotted over the foot-bridge of the closed lock gates with Albert puffing stiffly at their head. On the far side they turned onto the tow-path running along the side of the river and making for the old port.

Cullen and the other seaman had secured the barge. David Brent and Suzanne stood on the bank and now the engineer and his stoker stumbled up out of the confines of the little engine-room. They came ashore with Grundy, and Brent led them all away at a fast walk through long, tufted grass that brushed wetly at their legs. Suzanne followed a pace behind him and trailing her were Grundy and the rest of Brent's crew. McNab and the commandos fanned out on either side.

In a hundred yards they came to the railway track and a crouching figure that turned and waved a signalling hand: "Down". Brent crouched beside Tallon and the others followed suit. They were only a few feet from the dull-gleaming steel lines that ran away parallel to the river to vanish into the darkness to left and right. David Brent asked softly, "Ready?"

Tallon shook his head, "I sent him off less than a minute ago." He spoke of the last demolition engineer with his rucksack. "If our information is correct and there are twenty box-cars in the train then he needs to set his charge about three hundred yards further along the line. It's still too soon." He spoke quietly, barely a whisper. He breathed quickly and that was not because of the short sprint from the barge. David Brent could sense the tension all around him. He looked for the other commandos in Tallon's group, head turning, but failed to see them.

Chris noticed that movement: "They're spread along both sides of the track, ten or fifteen yards apart, so we cover

149

about a hundred yards. Two or three of us should be opposite the last cars when they stop, if I've got my sums right."

If . . .

On the far side of the track lay more rough grassland and then a wood lifted bare branches, waving black against the sky. There was neither moon nor stars, just the low, leaden clouds and the whisper of the wind that brought a spit of rain to fall on their faces.

If the train came. If the plan worked. If any of them lived through this night . . .

Michel stood at the door of the cell and chafed his wrists that were numb and raw from the straps biting into them. When the S.S. troopers first caught him they had searched inside his mouth with thick, probing fingers for any poison capsule. Michel had never carried one. But when they threw him into the cell they left him his shoes. It had taken him some time to worry the heel from one shoe, breaking his finger-nails, but he had got the razor-blade hidden in there. Cutting through the straps with the blade gripped only between the tips of two fingers had taken him weary, frustrating, painful hours. The blade had slipped in numb fingers that could barely feel it and though he was hardly conscious of the cuts the stickiness told him he was bleeding.

There was blood on his hands now but they were free. He was not. All the while he had carved laboriously at the strap he had listened for his gaolers, and one of them had come tramping along the stone floor of the passage every ten minutes or so. He had looked in through the small grating set high in the door at the man lying on the floor under the light. Michel had lain still, watching the grating, and the trooper had gone away.

Michel heard the clack of boot-heels now, turned and lay down again, hands behind him, eyes on the door. He was not ready but there was an important decision to be made soon. If he tried to escape and failed then he would talk. He had no doubt of that. He might hold out against the pain for a day but then the body would overrule the will and he would talk. Men and women would die as horribly as he. So if he could not be absolutely certain of getting out and away he must make the razor-blade serve the purpose of the capsule he had not carried.

He had to be absolutely certain.

He stared blankly up at the face behind the grating. And prayed.

11

"That'll stir things up!"

David Brent stood close by the silver rails. His head was turned towards St. Jean, watching for the train that would come through the town but there was neither sight nor sound of it. He wondered if it had passed, or was not coming at all. How long could he and his men wait?

How could he tell them that the boats lost and the men killed had all been for nothing?

He turned from the town and saw Chris Tallon a few yards away, but the girl was nearer. The soldier was looking up the track and waiting for word that the man he had sent there was ready. Suzanne had been watching the track from St. Jean and so her eyes met those of David Brent now. Her hands were hidden in the pockets of the trenchcoat she wore and its collar was turned up to frame her face. Her blonde hair was ruffled by the wind coming in off the sea. He could have reached out and touched her.

They had stood as close that last time in Paris but he had leant from the window of the train while she had stood below with her face turned up to him. She had been pale then, her eyes wide, dark and shadowed, miserable. But she had spoken up: "It's over, David. I haven't been fair and I'm sorry, but I would do it again. Go with my love, but it's finished."

The words came without warning, shattering his plans and dreams, a blow to the heart. He could only stare dumbly as the train began to move, knowing there was no use in arguing, no going back. He could see that in her face though her mouth trembled, hear it in her voice though it caught. So he only asked the one question and she gave him no answer.

He asked it again now, as they stood in the cold night, about to put their lives at risk: "Why? You told me it was all over. Why?"

And now she answered, "Because of my husband."

"You're *married*?" He did not raise his voice but his tone laid the emphasis on the word. He had never thought of her as bound to another man. But why not? She was desirable so would have been desired by others. Yet he had never imagined her with another man. He wondered: Was that unconscious arrogance? And admitted: Maybe. But that was the fact.

She said, "You never saw my ring. I was wearing gloves when I met you and the ring came off when they did. I got you out of Paris the next day so you wouldn't meet anyone who could tell you."

Now he remembered when they had left the party at which they met, a voice had called, "Goodnight, Madame." He had thought they were speaking to someone else.

She said, "I did it because – " She broke off, then started again, "I'd been married a year. He was young, French, handsome. His family had money and he worked for the family firm. We had a whirlwind courtship. I think "swept me off my feet" is the expression." One corner of her mouth went up, self-mocking. "It sounds romantic and I believed he loved me. I think he did, in his way. But I soon realised he'd married me because that was the only way he could get me into bed."

She could see the glitter of David's eyes, the tight line of his mouth. Her fists were clenched in her pockets and she went on with it: "He travelled a lot in his work. A few weeks after the wedding he was involved in a terrible accident when driving his car. The girl with him was killed instantly. She was half-naked. Then I found out she wasn't the only one by a long way. Lyons, Bordeaux, Nice – wherever his business took him, there was a girl.

"He was very badly injured and became a permanent inmate in a hospital where most of the patients had been since the war with Germany twenty years before. They were all human wrecks. It is possible that devotion can keep such a man alive; the doctors said so and I proved it, visiting him every week, writing every day. So I would

153

not abandon him when I met you. And I had made my vows.''

The girl paused, her eyes on his, looking for some change of expression but seeing none. She said quietly, simply, "But I'm human. It had been a year. I wanted you, needed you. So I let you think I was single.''

The long, mournful whistle came faintly from beyond St. Jean and Chris Tallon spun around, "It's coming!" He saw Suzanne and said, "You should be on your way. Sergeant!"

"Sir!" McNab rose from where he crouched by the track and his little group of commandos rose with him.

The girl still looked up into David's eyes but now she said, "I'm sorry.'' She stepped past him and walked away quickly towards the lock gates and the river. McNab followed close behind her and a pace to one side so he could see ahead, while his men fanned out on either side.

David Brent watched her go: another man's wife. The whistle had trailed away into nothing but now he could hear the distant rumble of the train.

Albert had led his small party of commandos across the foot-bridge of the lock-gates and then along the path at the side of the river that curved around to the right to run into the harbour. They moved at a trot, a stiff-legged canter in the case of Albert. When they came in sight of the bridge and the harbour beyond, they halted. Albert was glad to catch his breath as they stared at the bridge, looking for sentries and patrols.

They stood on the old port side of the river. Across the bridge was the new town, an open square surrounded by buildings and the openings of streets. There was not a soul nor a crack of light to be seen, the town and port blacked-out and under curfew. On the far side of the bridge was a small hut. Albert pointed to it and wheezed, "*Soldats.*''

The corporal commanding the group nodded, "Right-oh, mate.'' He muttered to the rest, "Sentries in the post t'other side o' the bridge.'' They all glanced in that direction, the five carrying the big rucksacks and the two with their

Thompson guns at the ready; the latter were the protection party.

He said, "Looks like they're inside having a smoke. Come on." He started towards the bridge a hundred yards away, the two Thompson gunners trotting ahead. The river lay to their left and they ran in the deep shadow of a retaining wall rising on their right, until the gunners swerved in to flatten themselves tight against the wall and the others followed suit. A sentry had come out of the hut and now he walked to the parapet of the bridge. He stood there, facing upriver and towards them, one hand holding the sling of the rifle hung over his shoulder. They only saw him in dim silhouette against the night sky but they could make out the big helmet, that one jutting elbow and the barrel of the rifle poking up above his shoulder. They could picture him as if he was brightly lit; they had stood that way themselves.

They waited, tense, breathing softly as the seconds ticked away. The corporal whispered, "Bugger off, will you?" They had work to do and dared not move.

"If he doesn't go soon we'll have to do it the hard way," the corporal said softly. By shooting the sentry and trying to hold the bridge while the work was done.

Nobody fancied that.

The breathing stopped as the soldier on the bridge turned full-circle, looking over the old port, the harbour and then the square of the new town. It started again as he walked away from the parapet and disappeared inside the hut. By then they were running.

They halted again under the bridge, its web of supporting steel girders criss-crossing a yard above their heads. The two Thompson gunners of the protection party knelt on either side of the shadow of the bridge and against the wall. The corporal whispered, "Remember, he said this was vital." He referred to Brent. "If we cock this up, Jerry'll be all over us."

He shrugged off his rucksack but kept the Thompson gun still hanging on his chest. He set his back against the wall, cupped his hands and the other four commandos with packs climbed up him as if he were a ladder, one boot on his

clasped hands then another on his shoulder. The last two
to climb up waited above him, grabbed the corporal's pack
as he lifted it at arm's length, then gripped his hands to haul
him after it.

Albert was left with the two gunners – and his thoughts.
They were not pleasant. He listened to the faint slithering
sounds in the steel mesh above him as the corporal and his
men went about their business, and thought about Brent's
plan. Suzanne had explained it to him in French, twice to
be sure it was clear to him. He understood it, but did not
believe it could work. A handful of men thrown ashore in
enemy-held country? No.

He hoped Suzanne would be all right, that was all.

The corporal working above called softly to the others,
"How are you lot getting on?"

He listened to the whispered answers as he worked,
moulding the explosive, inserting the detonator, attaching
the fuse: "Four done, four to go . . . Five done . . . Three
done . . . Three done."

Then the rustling whispers again as one asked, "What do
you think of our chances?"

And another countered cynically, "What chances?"

The corporal hissed, "Shut your traps and get on with
it!" Then in the silence that followed they heard the distant
whistle of the train.

Suzanne led Sergeant McNab and his men across the foot-
bridge made by the lock-gates, and then the quarter-mile of
rough pasture beyond, soaking her legs to the knees once
more. She turned left when she reached the wood, skirted
its edge and so came to the old port. From there she led
them through the narrow, twisting streets and alleys, keeping
always a score of yards ahead. Before McNab took his men
into another street he watched for her to signal from the next
corner that the way was clear.

He watched her now and the signal did not come. The
girl stood rigid, pressed against the wall. McNab pleaded
under his breath, "Get down, lass! You're right in our field

o' fire if they come round that corner!" As if in answer to his prayer he saw her slide down the wall to lie at its foot, her face buried in her arms. He lifted a hand, pointed with two fingers and a pair of his men silently crossed the street to hide around the opposite corner. That would double their rate of fire. But they did not want a fire-fight yet.

McNab still watched the corner at the end of the street where the girl lay. The patrol appeared, four soldiers crossing the end of the street in single file, pacing slowly, not talking. The leader and one of the others glanced into the street and McNab caught his breath as their heads turned, but neither saw the slim body prostrate in the deeper darkness by the wall. When the last soldier had gone from sight and the thud of their boots had faded away, the girl rose to her feet. She looked around the corner again and this time gave the signal, a beckoning lift of her hand. McNab started along the street as she moved on and the others padded after him.

They halted at the end of one last alley, crouching in its cover and looking out onto the quayside and the harbour. To their left and a hundred yards away lay the bridge across the river to the new town. An equal distance away but slightly to their right ran a terrace of buildings facing onto the quayside and the harbour. The buildings were of a height though they all looked to have been built at different times and in various styles. Some had windows like shops or chandlers, others had the look of offices. Suzanne pointed: "The second one."

McNab nodded. So that was the butcher's house, the S.S. headquarters. All, so far, as he had been briefed. He stared along the quay at the sentry outside the house at the end that faced him. In the night the sentry might have been just another shadow, but McNab had been told where to look for him. He muttered, "See him, Jacko?"

A thickset commando answered, "Aye."

"Get that one first off when we go."

Jacko set the Thompson gun to his shoulder and took a practice sight along the quay, then waited, ready.

McNab was a professional soldier. He accepted that jobs would be thrown at him without warning, but they should be the exception to prove the rule. An operation of this kind, to have any chance of success, had to be meticulously planned to the last detail and rehearsed. This was all being played off the cuff. He thought grimly: Definitely not on, Jock. Mind, that big lad Brent seemed to know what he was doing and made sure everybody else did. And there was surprise on their side. But still . . . He turned to the men lined behind him and whispered to the only one carrying a rucksack, "Sure you've got enough, Phil?"

The rucksack swayed as Phil shrugged his shoulders inside its straps. "Enough to flatten one or two of those shops, if you like."

McNab faced out onto the quay again, measuring the distance to the butcher's house. It wouldn't be long now.

Suzanne thought that she should have told David before, told him in Paris. But she had shied away from admitting she had led him on and lied to him. He must have hated her, must hate her now and it was too late to put right. Her head lifted, listening to the rumble of the train.

Tallon licked his lips and glanced at Brent. The train was still hidden from sight around a curve but they could hear the steady beat of its engine and see the advancing plume of smoke lifting in the night sky. Tallon thought that what had started as a planned and comparatively simple operation had turned into a succession of leaps into the dark. Now they were about to take the biggest.

Grundy turned and eyed Cullen, who thought: He's not going to tell me to stand to attention or get a flamin' shave. Not now. But Grundy said, "Keep close to me and the old man, and watch out for yourself." He grinned at Cullen, winked, then moved on to give his message to Dobson and the other men from the "old man's" crew.

The old man, David Brent, saw the train sway around the curve in the line and then it was running down on him. He was conscious of Chris Tallon just a yard away, lifting his Thompson gun. He heard the commando next along the line call to Tallon, "Ready, sir!"

That was the report passed down from the demolition engineer sent further up the line. Tallon answered, "About bloody time!"

Brent heard that above the panting of the train, still muted by distance but growing with every second. So that when Tallon called some order, Brent saw his mouth open and close but the words were drowned as the train pounded towards them. He felt a rhythmic tremor in the earth beneath his feet, the locomotive lifted high above him and the roar and rumble were deafening.

Then the train was roaring by with a sliding of pistons and a hissing of steam, a smell of coal-smoke and engine-oil. David Brent glimpsed the driver standing on the footplate, and his fireman lit by the glow from the open door of the fire-box as he shovelled coal onto the flames. When the locomotive had passed the box-cars came *clack-clacking* by.

The last coach rolled past Brent and Tallon. They swore and started after it. Commandos on both sides of the track were up and running hard, cursing. Then, above the noise of the train, they heard the explosion and a long, rolling, thunderous crash and screech of metal as the train ground to a halt. The box-cars and coach jumped the line but stayed upright.

Far up the line the demolition engineer, rucksack slung from his shoulders, turned his head to watch. The locomotive lurched drunkenly and slid to a halt as it left the rails cut by the explosion then came to rest tilted almost onto its side as the box-cars behind crashed into each other and jack-knifed. The train concertina-ed and box-cars swung sideways across the line with the force of the impact. The engineer ran on back down the line.

Tallon and his commandos pounced on the last coach from both sides, men reaching up to grasp handles and tug open doors, others lobbing in grenades. The doors slammed shut again and they all crouched, waiting until the grenades burst inside, a succession of orange flashes and ear-ringing detonations. Then they yanked open the doors and went in. They found no one alive. The coach was catching fire in several places so they hurriedly dragged out the bodies and laid them clear of the track.

Max Neumann was sitting on the floor of the wagon when the train stopped dead and he was thrown flat. His shoulder was bruised and the breath knocked out of him. For a moment he was dazed and bewildered, then the screaming broke out all around him and the black box of the car became a bedlam. That was no good. He shouted, "Stop that row! Keep still and you'll be all right! Listen to me!" And because they recognised his voice now, and trusted it because they had nothing and no one else to trust, they became quiet.

He did not get time to say more. He heard the locking bar knocked off on the outside of the box-car and then the door was dragged open. He saw a man standing at the door. He wore a close-fitting woollen cap pulled down on his forehead and carried a submachine-gun. He bellowed, "Out! Out!" He gestured with the gun and Max set an example and led the way, swung his legs out of the door and dropped down to stand by the side of the car. The rest scrambled out after him, as the others were scrambling out of the next box-car, so Max became the centre of a rapidly growing crowd. And the man with the gun stared at them and said, "Jesus Christ!"

Tallon stared at them in disbelief then turned to David Brent and said, "No trouble in identifying our man." Private Johnson was leading Max Neumann out of the crowd.

David answered, "No." Max was not a tall man but his head and shoulders lifted above those around him. Then he stood before Brent and Tallon. David asked him, "You are Max Neumann?"

"*Ja.*"

"And these?" David gestured at the crowd, huddling close to each other and silent.

Johnson put the question in his native German and translated Neumann's matter-of-fact answer in his guttural English: "He says they are Jewish children being taken to a camp to die."

Tallon jerked out, "*Die?*" He looked at his watch, then at Max: "What do you mean?"

Johnson again asked, listened, answered: "They will die from cold, beating, starvation."

That was monstrous, beyond credibility, but there had been reports . . . Chris Tallon looked past Johnson at the children. He judged them to be aged between five and ten but that was only deduced from their varying heights. In the night and crowded together they were a shapeless, dark mass with a grey surface of pale faces and huge eyes. He thought that there were more than fifty of them, maybe getting on for a hundred.

The fire in the coach was gaining and now flared, shedding light that reached out to show the common expression on the faces and Tallon saw it was fear of him and his men. His eyes shifted to Max Neumann, shabby, dirty, unshaven, bruised – and meeting his gaze. Tallon said reluctantly, already seeing the awful decision to be made, "I believe him." He looked at David Brent.

Ilse asked, "What was that?" They stood in the narrow hall of the house and she looked from her father to the *Major*.

The men, in urgent conversation, paused and exchanged glances. Kurt Ritter said, "I didn't hear anything."

Ilse frowned, "It sounded a long way off, but it was a – a crash."

Erwin König shook his head, "Never mind. Whatever it was, it will be reported." He shrugged into his greatcoat as his servant held it, then told him, "Fetch the guard. On the double."

"*Ja, Herr Oberst!*"

König called after the old soldier as he hurried away towards the guardroom at the back of the house, "And bring your own rifle as well!" He buttoned the greatcoat, telling his daughter, "I'm taking every man. We don't know how many of the enemy have landed."

Ilse smiled reassurance, "I'll be all right. Don't worry."

Kurt Ritter agreed confidently, "It may become a little noisy, but we'll roll them up."

König had strapped a pistol around his waist and now

took the Luger from its holster, checked the load and then smacked the magazine back into the butt with the heel of his hand. He looked from the pistol to Ilse, then said quietly, "There is another gun in the drawer of my desk. I wouldn't leave you if I thought you would need it, but you know it's there and how to use it."

Ilse said again, "Don't worry. *You* take care."

The *Gefreiter* came running, the other two soldiers of the guard behind him, all with rifles held across their chests. They halted and the servant joined them, rifle slung over one shoulder while he pulled on his cap. He was old in soldiering with twenty years of service behind him, but still only forty and younger than his commander. Ilse looked at them and was glad her father was taking them all. They were a tiny force, hardly a bodyguard for him, but he would join the company from the barracks and Ritter's assault troops at the end of the quay by the bridge.

She went with them to the door and there her father bent his head to kiss her. He told her, "Lock it when we've gone." She obeyed, hearing him call to the sentry outside, "You, too. Come on!"

Schleger and Ostmann had eaten leisurely and well in the restaurant of their hotel in the new town. They were relaxed and at ease. The manager was not; he and his staff stayed up to serve the two officers of the S.S. because they had to.

Early in the meal Schleger ordered food to be taken to his headquarters for Louis. Ostmann waited until there was no waiter in the room, then said of Louis, "Our French friend is very co-operative. And a little bit smug tonight, though he tries to hide it."

Schleger smiled, "He has to be co-operative but shouldn't be smug. He thinks he is going back to Paris, but he isn't. He stays here until I have no more use for him."

Ostmann twisted a mouthful of bread from a long stick with his thick fingers. "Think he might sulk?"

"You mean drag his heels, not try as hard as he should?" Schleger's smile widened. "He'll work as if his life depended

162

on it. He's wanted by the French *gendarmerie*. That's why he needs the papers and the protection we give him."

"What do they want him for? He didn't kill that *Wehrmacht* soldier, did he?"

Schleger shook his head, swallowed, drank wine and dabbed at his lips with a napkin. "He started working for us in the autumn of 1940. He found a family hiding a British officer and turned them in. As part of the deal with him we – that is our section in Paris – fitted him up with some false papers in the name of Labrosse. He was using them when he committed the offence the *gendarmerie* want him for. I believe that was not the first time and the other victims kept quiet for one reason or another, embarrassment, not wanting to talk about it."

Schleger smirked, then went on, "Anyway, if somebody down here checked on him in Paris then all they would find under his real name would be the charge of murder of a German soldier that we trumped up against him. But if he steps out of line then we tell the *gendarmerie* where they can find Labrosse."

Ostmann asked, "So what was the offence?"

Schleger's smirk was still there. "Rape."

After the coffee and armagnac the two officers kicked off their boots and stretched out on couches by the fire, leaving instructions that they were to be called in two hours. At that time they rose, drank more coffee and washed, then set out to take up their duties once more.

The streets of the new town were dark and silent, the men's boot-heels clicking loudly on the paving as they walked slow striding and in step. Their thoughts also marched in time. These hours in the dead of night were best for the work they were to do now, when a man in a cell was at his coldest, loneliest, weakest. They talked quietly, thoughtfully, of technique and approach. The walk gave them time to plan both. They were experienced, optimistic and confident.

They came to the bridge and were too absorbed in their conversation to notice that the sentries appeared quickly from the hut in which they had been sheltering from the night's cold. Then there was a flash in the dark sky to the north and beyond the old port, and a distant *thump* like a gentle blow on a big drum. It was followed by a long drawn-out grinding and crashing that died out, then a staccato popping sound. Finally there was only the moaning of the wind from the sea funnelling under the bridge.

The sentries' heads jerked around and Schleger said, "That was an explosion."

Ostmann suggested, "A bomb?"

Schleger shook his head, "No aircraft, no raid. It sounded faint – a long way off." He ordered the sentries, "You'd better phone in a report."

"*Ja, Herr Sturmbannführer.*" One sentry ducked into the hut to the telephone there, thinking: That last lot sounded to me like grenades.

Schleger told Ostmann, "That's the army's business; we have our own." As they strolled on across the bridge the engines of trucks muttered far behind them, but they took no notice. They could see their headquarters now and quickened their pace with a growing sense of anticipation. Schleger said with certainty, "They sent a boat from England to take him back." He was talking of the man in the cell. "That's why he was at that rendezvous tonight. He's a king-pin, I know it. He'll talk before morning and we'll rake in the rest of his gang."

Ostmann said, "Pity we didn't get the girl, though." They were his last words. The bridge exploded under their feet.

Albert lay close against the wall a hundred yards away with the corporal and the other commandos. He shuddered as debris rattled and rained down all around them.

The corporal thought: That'll stir things up. Then he was dragging Albert to his feet and all of them were running.

12

Assault!

Chris Tallon's head turned as the blast-wave shook the ground, then the flare and bellow of the explosion cracked the silence of the night. The children cowered as if under a lash. They stood, body pressed to body, surrounded by the armed men and they stared fearfully at the two officers. They were familiar with the authority that held the power of life and death.

David Brent said, "We'll take them." The bridge had been blown and the old port severed from the new town and the troops in barracks. That had been vital and Brent had stressed it: "If the bridge doesn't go those troops will pour over us and bury us!" Now they all had a chance.

Chris reasoned, "We only have to take one man, but at all costs. Those were our orders." His eyes flicked to Max Neumann then back to Brent. "We can't risk him for anything – anybody else."

David answered reason with a statement of responsibility, simply: "We have to take them all, haven't we?"

Or leave them here, to be sent on another train. Tallon looked at them, lit by the yellow light from the burning coach, then at the faces of his own men. They showed nothing, but he knew the thoughts behind those masks. The awful decision had been made.

Brent was gambling on Jimmy Nash taking them all off in the drifter.

Chris Tallon said, "Right."

Brent led them all away, the children in a scurrying huddle inside the flanking guards of soldiers. They hurried down to the river then across by the foot-bridge on the lock-gates, treading in single file. Tallon's demolition sapper jumped aboard the barge and disappeared below to emerge a minute later. As he stepped ashore Grundy and Cullen cast the barge loose. The sapper set a charge on the winding mechanism of the gate then the three of them crossed by the foot-bridge. Cullen wound on the wheel on that side, which also opened the gates, so the river raced through and the barge drifted downstream. The sapper set another charge on the wheel.

The corporal had come running up the path from the bridge he had blown, Albert half-loping, half-carried between two of the commandos. Tallon told them, "Well done." He ordered the corporal and his men out as a screen on either side of the children, sent Albert to walk with Max Neumann, then stationed himself in the lead with a vanguard of his men. But Brent went ahead as they moved off again.

They hastened over the rough, wet grassland towards the wood that hid the old port. Almost immediately they heard the scuttling charge detonate aboard the barge lower down the river. The sound was muffled and distant but Tallon's sapper muttered with satisfaction, "That's the bottom blown out of her. Jerry won't get her afloat again in a hurry." Then behind them first one charge on the lock-gates, then the other, exploded with echoing *cracks*!

The men with the Thompson guns were widely spread, wary, eyes searching. The children scurrying at the heels of Max Neumann in a long, narrow crowd inside the screen, were too frightened to weep or make a sound. They were as fearful of these escorts as of those that herded them onto the train. At the rear were Grundy and Cullen, and Brent led them all. Cullen thought: Like the bloody Pied Piper. I hope to God he knows what he's up to.

David Brent wondered and worried about Jimmy Nash. They had got the man they had come for but still had a long way to go. And in the end all would depend on Jimmy, whether he was able to carry out Brent's orders. If he lay dead ten miles north where they had come ashore . . .

Suzanne had heard the crash of the train and then the flat *popping* like the bursting of balloons. She had glanced at

McNab and the nine commandos with him, lined along the wall of the alley, its doors closed, windows shuttered. She saw their heads turned, listening, the sideways slide of McNab's eyes in his stone face. He said softly, "Grenades."

They waited, Suzanne and the sergeant with watches held up before their eyes, seeing the long second hands ticking steadily around the dials.

Jacko whispered, "Somebody coming out – five or six o' them."

The eyes shifted, refocused on the house facing them at the end of the quay. The door had opened and then closed – Suzanne thought she had glimpsed a woman inside the house – but there was a group outside now. They started along the quay, t ie sentry coming with them.

The cobbles of the alley shivered under Suzanne's feet and then there came the second-long flash and booming roar of the explosion as the bridge blew up. For a second they hesitated, blinded, and Jacko swore because he could not see the group on the quay. McNab had not anticipated that but now he bawled, "*Move!*" He led the way, running hard and bent over in a crouch, across the hundred yards of the open quay.

Suzanne tried to keep close behind him but some of the soldiers overtook her. She trailed McNab by a few strides when he took the steps in one leap and kicked open the door of the butcher's house. He shoved through the black-out door inside and light wavered over the steps as the door swung. Two more commandos followed him, then Suzanne. The rest were panting at her back, Jacko and those at the rear pausing to set the Thompsons to their shoulders and send sweeping bursts along the quay.

König and Ritter had gone only twenty yards from the house when the explosion blinded them. They halted, and König said, "The bridge!" Then the Thompsons rattled and flamed, and bullets whined around them.

Ritter shouted, "Cover!" He broke left, ran bent almost double to the nearest building and into the low shelter of the

167

steps leading up to its door. König and the soldiers crowded after him, down on one knee and close against the wall. The *Oberst* peered over Ritter's shoulder, their heads lifted above the steps. There was light from an open door at the far end of the quay.

König said, "The *Tommis* have blown up the bridge and they are in the S.S. headquarters." He could see the broken silhouette of the bridge and the trucks stopped on the other side. They were his reinforcements from the barracks and Ritter's crack troops. He was cut off from them, could not even communicate. He knew that if he ran back to his house he would find the telephone dead because the lines were carried over the river on the bridge. He remembered his daughter, alone in the house, doubtless frightened and bewildered by the explosion and the firing. But he could not go to her. His duty lay here.

When the railway line was cut the sound of the crashing train was not heard inside S.S. headquarters because the corporal seated in the hall had the telephone clapped to his ear and was laughing. He asked, "Know any more?" His opposite number on duty twenty kilometres away always had a new repertoire of lewd stories. The corporal listened on, whiling away the boredom of the night shift, until he had heard them all.

He finally put down the telephone reluctantly and took a dog-eared book from a drawer in the desk. Reading bored him, but he had nothing to do but man this desk and run after that French pimp sitting in Schleger's office as if he owned the place. But he had to be more than just an informer. He had come in with Ostmann and the chief as if the three of them were old pals.

The telephone rang and he recognised the voice of the operator at the barracks: "I've been trying to get through to you for the last ten minutes."

"I was answering another call."

"Give me the *Sturmbannführer*."

The corporal said, "He's at the hotel; him and Ostmann."

"Well, listen: There's been a report that a party of *Tommis* has landed. The *Herr Oberst* has ordered out the troops from here and he's meeting them at the bridge. You'd better alert your detachment because he might call on them. Got that?"

But the line went dead before the corporal could answer. The explosion as the bridge blew up rattled the front door in its frame and shook the floor. The lights went out and windows shattered in a crash of falling glass. The corporal jumped up from his chair and groped for the switch on the wall behind him, threw it and the emergency lighting came on. It had been installed the previous winter on the order of Schleger, infuriated by a succession of power cuts. It was weak and yellow but it served. Now the Frenchman shouted from the room behind, "What the hell's going on?"

The corporal went into the office. Louis was down on one knee picking up the tray and the empty plate that had fallen from the coffee table. In this kneeling position Louis could see his bottle and glass that had rolled under the armchair. He had dined well.

The corporal glanced at the window where the drawn curtains swayed on the breeze, the glass blasted from the frame lying in fragments on the floor. He snapped, "Some *Tommis* have landed. That's all I know. Now shut up and don't bother me!" Then he heard the front door burst open and he swung back into the hall, pulling at the pistol in its holster on his belt. The inner door was kicked wide against the wall and a tall man in khaki glared at him.

McNab did not hesitate. His finger was ready on the trigger and the burst from the Thompson threw the corporal back into the office. Louis grovelled behind the armchair, saw the soldiers in their khaki filling the hall – and Suzanne among them.

McNab jumped into the office and landed crouching with the Thompson gun sweeping in a swift arc. He saw Louis behind the chair and the gun twitched onto him. Louis screamed, "*Français*!"

Suzanne shouted, "No! He's one of us!"

Louis, staring into the muzzle of the gun, saw it swing away. McNab ran back into the hall. Commandos were racing up the stairs, another through to the rear of the house. One lay bellied down at the front door looking out towards the bridge while Phil, with his rucksack, knelt by the desk. Two more stood at the head of the stairs leading to the cellar; they ran down beneath the flight lifting to the upper floors. McNab joined those two and nodded at the one holding a grenade. The clip sprang free as the pin was pulled and the grenade was lobbed down the stairs.

Other grenades burst first on the upper floors and firing racketted from there. Suzanne recognised the rattle of Thompsons now, like a stick drawn across railings. She went to Louis as the grenade boomed hollowly in the cellar below. He was curled up in a foetal position, knees drawn up to his chin. His face was contorted with fear – he had seen his death in the muzzle of the gun – but she took it to be pain. Her mind was asking questions already, but Louis was thinking with the speed of terror. His hands clutched his private parts and he moaned, "He kneed me. He said I was going to talk, shoved his gun in my face, then kneed me."

Suzanne said, "I thought you were dead."

"Back by the wood, when they jumped us?" Louis nodded, "I went down when the shooting started. I'd never been in anything like that before. No warning, no time to – to get ready. When I was down I just couldn't move. I thought I'd wait and see if I got the chance of a shot, but it was too late and I – I couldn't move." He averted his eyes from Suzanne's. "I'm sorry. I was supposed to be the escort and I was useless. I wanted to be some help but I just didn't realise what I was getting into. I saw them take the other man away. Then they came for me." He said again, "I'm sorry."

Suzanne could not feel sympathy for him; she simply did not like him. But he had volunteered for a task he was unable to handle, though in fairness, no one in Louis' position could have fought his way out of that ambush. She said, "It wasn't your fault. They were waiting for us. Someone sold us out."

Louis stared up at her. "Who?"

Suzanne shook her head. "I don't know. Come on, get up." She helped him, groaning, to his feet and he staggered to the door with her, though he was still bent over and holding himself.

McNab appeared in the hall and said tersely, "Two dead down there. Must have been the warders on duty. Grenade got them."

Jacko called from the head of the stairs, "Bloody mess up here, but it's clear."

McNab asked, "How many?"

"I counted fourteen. We're covering front and rear from up here now."

Phil still waited, down on one knee by the desk in the hall. McNab jerked a thumb at him. "Up you go." Phil rose and took the stairs at a run despite the weight of the rucksack on his back. McNab glanced back towards the cellar steps. "We found these two."

Suzanne saw Michel, and behind him two commandos carrying the limp body of a man between them, his arms around their shoulders, his legs trailing. Suzanne stooped to peer into his face, for a moment did not recognise him, then whispered, "Paul!"

Michel said, "He knew we were meeting?" He spoke in French.

Suzanne replied in that tongue, "Yes."

"He held out a long time." He gestured at the battered body, "You can see that."

Suzanne said, "You remember Louis?"

Michel did not. This hunched figure with the pain-wracked face was a stranger to him. Then Suzanne prompted, "Our escort." Now he recalled the tall, cock-sure young man

171

with a swagger, standing at the edge of the wood with his face half-hidden in shadow. Suzanne repeated Louis' story and finished, "They'd just started on him when we got here."

McNab had listened impatiently, not understanding a word. Now firing broke out overhead and he shouted above its hammering, "Get down behind the desk!" He flicked at switches and the lights on the ground floor went out. The rest of the house was already in darkness. McNab pounded up the stairs while Michel and the others crawled into the meagre cover between desk and wall. There was some faint, diffused light from a single bulb that had somehow survived in the cellars. Suzanne sat with Paul's head in her lap.

Louis had his back to the wall, knees drawn up as if still in pain but his hand was close to the pistol in his pocket. He did not want to use it, saw no way out of this place. These were the network of British agents Schleger had talked of, all of them here except Albert. Where was the old man? Louis could not ask, had earlier told Suzanne he had sent Albert back to his café.

Louis thought that his story had been accepted – or was that only because they believed the wireless operator had betrayed them under torture? He had seen suspicion on Suzanne's face when she first saw him in Schleger's office. That suspicion had been allayed, but did it still linger? He would have to be on his guard.

Michel sat opposite Louis, watched his face and said, "I didn't hear you brought up from the cells."

Louis stared at him blankly. "I don't know anything about cells. They put me in that room, gave me a drink and a cigarette, even a meal. The one guarding me, he told me not to worry, that they knew I was nobody important. He said he thought they would ask a few questions and then let me off with a warning. After a bit I think I believed him. I started to relax, you know? And then – " He looked at Paul and then turned away quickly, shuddered. "I was next."

172

Michel nodded. That was one method of breaking down a suspect: get him to relax, to hope, to trust. Then shock him by a sudden attack. Another was to let him see the results of "interrogation" then leave him to think about it, look forward. As they had let Michel see Paul when they took him down to the cells earlier in the night. He said, "So was I."

Out on the quay the four soldiers of König's guard stood or knelt close against the wall, firing steadily at the windows of the S.S. headquarters. The windows offered only a narrow target from this angle but by the same token König and his men were not under fire. The commandos inside would have had to lean out to see them.

Ritter glanced sideways at the building by which they sheltered. It looked to be an office of some sort. He said, "I'll reconnoitre the rear of this place, sir." He jumped up onto the steps and kicked at the front door until it swung open. There was a passage inside and he blundered along that in the darkness, cursed when he stumbled and fell down a step he had not seen, finally came to another door. His groping hands found the key still in the lock, turned it and he emerged into a yard. He started down the yard, walking quickly, but then came the *bang*! of a bullet passing close overhead and the *crack*! of the report. He threw himself down and squirmed on elbows and knees into the shelter of a wall. He was able to stand up then, panting obscenities. He had been fired on from the rear of S.S. headquarters, so the *Tommis* were up there and keeping their eyes open, had spotted him as soon as he was clear of the house and in their field of view. They were still firing – and now he could hear other voices cursing, in German.

There was a gate in the wall at the end of the yard and he was able to reach it without edging into that field of fire. He shouted, "Who is it out there?"

A moment of silence, then a voice answered from the alley beyond, "Patrol."

"I am *Major* Ritter, Panzer Grenadiers. Hold your fire."

He opened the gate, eased through and saw the four men kneeling against the wall of the alley for cover. In the darkness they were no more than silhouettes of big helmets and rifle barrels. Ritter asked, "Any more of you?"

The nearest soldier answered, "No. We're the only patrol in the old port. The others are all across the river."

Ritter swore again, but under his breath. Aloud, he ordered, "Some *Tommis* have landed and they've occupied the second house from the end." On the other side of the alley was a stack of logs cut to size to feed a stove and looking as if a cart had been unloaded there. They made a wall that was waist-high and four to five metres long. It ran along the opposite wall of the alley but an arm's length from it. Ritter pointed, "Take cover behind that lot and keep the *Tommis* under fire. I'll be back."

König worked the button of the torch, its beam pointed at the trucks on the other side of the bridge, sending the morse slowly because he was out of practice. He ended: " – König." He waited, wondered if anyone over there had noticed the flickering light through the smoke and among the muzzle-flashes. And if they had, would they recognise it as a signal? He was about to repeat the message when another light stuttered from the far end of the bridge: an acknowledgment.

A sharp signals *Gefreiter* had picked out the hesitant dots and dashes, read their message and reported it to the commander of the force from the barracks: " – ends 'König', *Herr Hauptmann*."

"Acknowledge!" He snapped that, though he was glad to know the old man was all right. But he had already anticipated König's order and tried to bring a boat round from the harbour to ferry his men across the river. The first men to make the attempt had been raked by fire from the S.S. headquarters when they began rowing the boat. Now he had swimmers in the water, shoving the boat around and sheltering in its cover. When it was clear of the harbour and hidden by the bridge he would ferry some men across.

He had also sent Kurt Ritter's young *Leutnant* running up the side of the river with a dozen of his assault troops. He had no way of knowing how they had fared. The *Hauptmann* glowered at the wreck of the bridge and wondered how many *Tommis* had landed, were waiting for him on the other side of the river.

The *Leutnant* had panted up to the lock with his men hard on his heels. In the light from the burning coach he saw the train some two hundred metres away, saw that there was something wrong in the irregular outline of the boxcars; but the train was not his business while the lock was.

The gates stood open and when he attempted to close them he found the mechanism mangled and jammed. He blasphemed then ordered, "We'll swim it!"

Ritter came out of the front door of the house, jumped down from the steps to stand by König and told him, "I found a patrol of four men in the alley at the back. They're keeping the *Tommis'* heads down."

Erwin König smiled wrily, "That's about the best we can do for now. I think there are more of them in there than of us out here. So we bottle them up until we get more men – and grenades. That shouldn't be too long." He still held the torch and now trained it towards the guardship by the harbour mouth. "But we can bring a little more pressure to bear." He started sending again in his slow, careful morse.

McNab moved crouching into the upstairs room at the front of the house. It was pitch-black, the darkness of the night thickened by dust hanging on the air and drifting smoke from the Thompson guns. They were firing from the window, a dark grey rectangle, and McNab picked his way carefully towards it; there were dead men littering the floor, some of the fourteen S.S. troopers who had been quartered in the house.

In a break in the firing, he said, "We've got company at the back."

Jacko's head turned, "Many?"

"I reckon three or four. What about here?"

"They tried to row a boat a few minutes back but we stopped that. I think they've got one, though. Can't see much out there but I thought there was a shadow that could be a boat went round towards the bridge; somebody swimming and pushing or pulling it, maybe."

"So we'll have a lot of them on our necks soon." McNab winced as a dull explosion overhead brought more dust and plaster raining down from the ceiling. There was a clatter of falling rubble.

Phil's voice called faintly from somewhere above, "Right!"

McNab muttered, "Thank Christ for that." He hurried, stooping, back to the door and bawled down the stairs, "Everybody up to the top floor!"

The commandos came scurrying from front and rear of the house. Michel and Louis lifted Paul between them and Suzanne followed them up the stairs.

The captain of the guardship was on his bridge, that was no more than a big wheel-house set right aft in the drifter. He stooped over the mouth of the engine-room voice-pipe and shouted into it, "How long before we have steam?" He had called for it an hour before when his wireless operator picked up a signal from the boat policing the fishing fleet: one drifter was missing after the fighting round the fleet and might have run for home. But if she didn't turn up then the guardship might be ordered to sea to search.

Now he listened to the metallic voice coming up the pipe and bellowed, "Ten minutes! It had better be no more than that. We're sitting ducks, tied up here!"

He straightened and looked out from the open wheel-house, its glass windows lowered to save them from blast, and narrowed his eyes as a light winked from the quay. The signalman behind him on the bridge started, "Somebody's sending – "

The captain cut him off, snarling, "I can see that, you fool!" He read the slow, hesitant signal himself, word by word, and swore at the end, "Damned soldier!" Then he bawled at the crew of the 40mm. gun mounted in the bow of the guardship, "The *Tommis* are in the second house from the end!" He thrust out a pointing finger, "Fire!"

The slender barrel of the gun was trained out to sea but now it swung around, rose and fell as the crew found their point of aim, steadied, and then fired. The captain saw the shells bursting low on the house with vivid orange flashes, spurting smoke, clouds of dust and shards of stone. Then he felt a tugging at his arm, turned and saw the signalman shouting at him, mouth opening and closing but the words blotted out by the hammering of the gun. He stared past the signalman and out to sea in disbelief.

13

"I – am – sinking!"

Jimmy Nash, on the drifter lying out in the cold, rainswept darkness, knew the timetable of David Brent's plan. When he looked at his watch for the fifth or sixth time he calculated, believed – no, hoped, that the barge was hurrying on its way downriver to St. Jean. He finally decided: Don't want to be early but, by God! better that than too late. He nodded to the French skipper of the drifter and got a lift of the hand in reply. Moments later the engine of the drifter churned, coughed, then settled into grumbling life. She moved ahead and Jimmy looked astern and saw Crozier's and little Dent's boats under way, using their auxiliaries so he could not hear them. They kept station on either quarter of the drifter, like ghost ships with only grey ripples at bow and stern as they slid through the sea.

The rain had stopped save for occasional showers of drizzle drifting on the wind. Tommy Vance had the men of his party striding about the deck again as he had done every ten minutes or so all through the long hours of waiting. They carried their carbines slung over their shoulders and moved easily because of the constant exercise. They had to be ready. Tommy walked with them because he could not stand still.

The three craft crept along parallel to the shore but out of sight of it, for a half-hour. Then the French skipper called a halt and the drifter's engine puttered into silence. He beckoned and Jimmy Nash joined him in the wheel-house, and peered at the chart where the skipper pointed with a pencil. Jimmy nodded and stepped down to the deck again. He found Tommy Vance waiting there for him.

Tommy asked, "How far?"

"We're about a mile out." Jimmy wasn't sure but he

thought he could make out a deeper shadow in the night ahead that could be the loom of the land.

"How long will it take us to cover that?"

"Should be ten or twelve minutes from the time we go. This old girl makes a comfortable six knots and we can't seem in too much of a hurry."

Tommy said, "I'm not." He was thinking of the task ahead of him, afraid for himself, his men, Brent and the others ashore.

Nash grinned at him. "Want my job instead?"

"No." Tommy had enough responsibility on his shoulders already and shied away from the thought of commanding all this little force at sea. He only wished he had Jimmy's cool bravery and confidence.

Jimmy Nash was wishing for those qualities now as he acted his part to encourage the others. So much hung on the success of the drifter, slow, unarmoured and unarmed except for the weapons in the hands of the men aboard her. And Brent had singled him out to command on the drifter: "That's where you're needed, I need you." Jimmy voiced his thoughts to steel himself, "We can't let the old man down, can we?"

David Brent. "No," said Tommy, "we can't." And that was all there was to it.

They both saw the flickering light on the inshore horizon even as a dozen voices called softly from around the deck, "See that, sir?"

"I saw it!" Jimmy Nash snapped that without taking his eyes off the distant shore. The flash, tiny and thin, had come and gone in the blink of an eye.

They waited again, as they had waited before on this night. Jimmy was aware, without looking round, that the two boats lay close alongside. He could hear the small sounds of movements that were not aboard the drifter. He lifted his watch so its face was before his eyes and he could read the time without losing sight of the shadow of the shore. That flash had been the first, surely. Just about when it was due. But the second . . . That should have come by –

179

This time the glare on the horizon was bigger and spread wide, seemed to stand for seconds in the sky. Then it died and the rumble of the explosion came rolling out over the sea.

Jimmy whispered, incredulous, "They've done it!" He shivered with apprehension, then shouted at the skipper, "Now!" Seconds later the engine fired and Jimmy turned forward, ordered, "Hoist those lights!" He watched as the two big lamps swayed up to the masthead and bathed the deck in a yellow glow. "Take cover! Safety catches on!" Tommy Vance's men, expecting the order, checked their carbines and lay down behind the starboard gunwale.

The drifter was picking up speed now, stubby, high bow nodding as she rode the seas. Jimmy, apprehension now overlaid by excitement, gave Tommy Vance the raffish grin that had turned many a girl's head: "Do you ever wonder why you joined?"

The guardship's skipper glared at the drifter with its two big lamps at the mast-head, closing the harbour mouth. He recalled the message that one drifter might be on her way home, but he swore, "Bloody stupid Frenchman! Wanting to come in *now*!"

His signalman ventured, "Maybe he's got engine trouble – or something."

"I don't care what he's got! There's chaos already in here without him adding to it! Tell him to haul off!" The signalman worked his lamp, the order blinking out. The 40mm. gun still banged away at the house on the quay while the rattle of small-arms fire rose and fell like the waves breaking on a beach. Smoke billowed from the guardship's funnel as it had since the captain demanded steam and now it rolled down over the sea as the wind took it. For a few seconds the drifter was hidden, then the smoke lifted and the captain saw her, the deck under the lamps empty of life but still coming on.

He thumped the side of the wheel-house with his fist and shoved the signalman towards the ladder, "Tell them to put a shot across her bow. The fool will understand that!"

The signalman ran forward and the gun fired a final round then the barrel swung away from the quay and through a half-circle until it pointed at the harbour mouth. It fired two rapid rounds over the drifter, but she still came on. The captain blinked as the gun-smoke wisped over the wheel-house. It was not surprising that there was no one on the drifter's deck now she was fired over, but odd that there hadn't been a single man to be seen before. There was always a hand or two on deck as a boat entered harbour –

He suddenly had an awful suspicion and shouted down to the gun crew staring up at him, "Shoot into her! *Fire!*" The barrel of the gun dropped and then it opened rapid fire. The drifter was barely a hundred yards away now but the gunlayer had over-corrected and the first rounds kicked up the sea under her bow. He raised his sights but she was still closing the range so the next rounds screamed high over her deck, harmlessly except that one carried away a lamp from the masthead. The layer desperately lowered the barrel again and this time the shells slammed into the drifter's hull on or below the waterline. Then a man rose from hiding below the gunwale.

Tommy Vance had flattened himself on the deck as the drifter ran in, jerked as the shells burst on her hull and he felt the vibration through the timbers. He was prey to fear and uncertainty. He had not trained or prepared for this. Not only did he have to do it himself, he had to inspire his men. But David Brent had thought he could, had given his orders without a trace of doubt, wholly confident that Vance would carry them out. And knowing that if he failed then all of them were lost and the operation as well.

He found himself on his feet, standing straight. He had no need to shout his commands. His men lay with their eyes fixed on him. He lifted one open hand with the palm uppermost and they rose from the deck to line the gunwale. The carbines twitched in their hands as they fired and worked the bolts.

The guardship's captain saw the crew of the gun fall away from it and the signalman scramble for cover at the back

181

of the wheel-house. The sea behind the drifter was churned into foam as her screw raced briefly astern, taking the way off her. Then she scraped against the guardship's side and men from the drifter jumped across while others held the two together.

The voice-pipe squawked and the captain stooped to it, listened, then answered, "It's too late now. Come up, all of you." He had a wife and four children of school age in Hamburg. He lifted his hands high and so Tommy Vance found him.

Jimmy Nash spared a second or two for a swift, sweeping glance around the harbour. He saw the spurts of flame from rifles and machine-guns, on the quay and from a house near the far end. He knew that one was the "butcher's house". The firing was heaviest from across the harbour, on the other side of a bridge that no longer spanned the river but ended only half-way over. There was a square littered with trucks stopped in untidy confusion and the prickling flames stabbed from the darkness all around them. His head swung back. The house at the seaward end of the quay was dark.

He turned as Tommy Vance shouted, "She's ours." They grinned at each other, both breathless, relieved, elated that they had pulled it off. Then the French skipper stood before Jimmy, face dark, trying to tell him something, using gestures when he could not find the words. The miming finally became clear and the message got through.

Jimmy Nash said softly, "Oh, hell!"

Brent's orders to Jimmy and Tommy Vance had been to capture or silence the guardship then lay the drifter alongside the sea-wall. There she would take off the landing party of Brent and the others, and the two rescued men, Max Neumann from the train and Michel from the cells. Now Crozier and Dent would have to carry out that part. Jimmy thought: And it's too bad about you, Nash, Tommy and the rest of us here.

The drifter was sinking.

McNab was again in the top-floor front-room and down on his belly by the window. The commandos kneeling either side of it glanced at him. They were all coated in the dust that fell steadily from the ceiling now. Bullets smacked into the wall outside and others *cracked*! in at the window to punch into the ceiling or ricochet howling off the walls.

One of the commandos said, "That gun on the guardship gave us a pasting before it stopped, but now there's a lot more stuff coming up from this side of the river. There are blokes in the streets and houses only fifty yards away. We're keeping 'em busy but that's getting harder. We have to nip up, squirt a few off and duck down again."

"And they'll soon be knocking on the front door." McNab's eyes lifted to the torn ceiling and he muttered, "Come on, laddie, we're running out o' time."

Suzanne stooped under the angled roof of the house and wondered which one of the buildings it was. The third – or fourth? Paul lay at her feet, Michel and Louis kneeling beside him. There was room to stand upright in the centre of this attic but they were tucked in a corner under the roof-beams, away from the shattered dormer window that was a square of grey light. That was because a stray shot sometimes came close to, or in at, the window. They were also well clear of the hole, roughly circular and a yard in diameter, blasted in the wall leading to the next house.

A commando crouched to one side of the window and now another, Phil, crawled back through the hole into the attic and to one side of it. He set down his rucksack and squatted by the wall.

Suzanne asked him, "Have you seen any people in these houses?" Because Phil was always first through a newly-blasted passage into the next attic. She glanced at the small, empty bed standing opposite the window, a crucifix at its head, the sheets thrown back.

Phil shook his head. "Not a soul. Lucky for them."

Suzanne thought that was as they had expected: anyone sleeping up here had gone down to the cellars when the bridge was blown and the shooting started.

183

Phil put his hands over his ears and Suzanne covered her own. She felt the kick of the explosion through her shoes then the dust boiled out of the hole in the wall in a huge cloud. When it cleared Phil lifted his rucksack and crawled through the gap again but reappeared only seconds later to call to the man by the window, "Tell McNab to get up here!" He beckoned to Suzanne, Michel and Louis lifted Paul between them and all four worked their way through the hole in the wall into the attic of the next building in the row.

David Brent had Albert with him now as the ragged column emerged from the wood, crossed a stretch of wasteland and came to the old port. There were gardens at the backs of houses but the old Frenchman led the way to an alley between them that opened on to a narrow street. The column snaked to the right then, heading towards the sea and passing through a shadowed canyon, its walls the fronts of houses. Their windows were shuttered and not a light showed. The people behind them were waiting for the firing to stop and the light of morning before they came out.

The escorts around the column were tense, fingers on triggers and eyes hunting in the darkness, probing each side street as they hurried across its mouth. The firing was very close now, seeming to come from just the other side of these houses that sheltered them. The children straggled down the axis of the column following Max Neumann. If they wept or cried out, they were not heard.

Grundy and Cullen were still at the tail, heads continually turning to sweep arcs from front to rear. The snake ahead bent again, but left this time, and the two at the tail followed it round. Now on their right there was a chest-high wall a yard thick and beyond it lay the sea. A hundred yards ahead of them the column had halted, the children showing in the night as a low, packed crowd between the stone wall and another, on the left and higher, that seemed to bound the yard of the last house in a row. Grundy and Cullen could see the backs of the houses

184

running away to their left. Beyond the huddled children lifted the rear of another house but this one looked out on the sea. And sliding in towards the harbour mouth, just seen over the stone wall, was the mast-head of a ship with two big yellow lamps hung glowing at the yard-arms. Grundy and Cullen exchanged glances: nearly there.

They were closing on the rest of the halted column and passing the mouth of one last alley when Grundy yelled, "*Left!*" He fired and Cullen was blinded by the flash. He could not see the shadows moving among the others in the alley but he raised his carbine and squeezed the trigger. Grundy shoved him, stumbling and falling, into the cover of the wall beyond the alley's mouth, then shouted, "Rapid! Keep 'em down!"

Cullen squirmed around, poked his head and the carbine around the corner and fired into the darkness. Flashes sparked back at him and he knew he was being fired at, was deafened by Grundy's carbine slamming quickly above his head.

Brent and Tallon stood at the back door of the house. They, too, had seen the mast-head and the lights. They spun around now as the firing broke out but saw the corporal who had blown the bridge running back with two of his men to where Grundy and Cullen held the alley. Then a gun barked rapidly somewhere in the harbour, stopped, fired again, stopped, then let off one last burst that ended with a fusillade of rifle and machine-gun fire.

Tallon, ears ringing, mouthed: Jimmy Nash. Brent nodded, praying that Jimmy was all right.

The door did not budge when they tried it; it rested thick and solid in its frame, a storm door meant to keep out the sea when the big rollers broke over the wall. The windows on either side of the door were shuttered but Brent yanked at one of them and the catch inside tore loose. The shutters opened. Tallon smashed the glass of the window with the stock of his Thompson, reached in a hand, unhooked the latch and slid up the window.

For a second they listened but could hear nothing in the house because of the cracking of carbines and the rattle of Thompson guns only a score of yards away where commandos had joined Grundy and Cullen in firing into the alley. Brent pushed aside the curtains drawn across the window and swung his legs over the sill to stand in the room beyond. Tallon followed. They saw at once that the room was not completely dark. In the gloom they made out four chairs around a table, two camp beds along one wall and above them four packs hung from hooks. Tallon thought: Guardroom. So where was the guard? And where was the light coming from?

He was only a yard behind Brent as he crossed to the door. It was open and there was a passage outside, lit by a shifting radiance. The room behind them was filling with commandos, Johnson, the German speaker, first of all. Brent moved into the passage and looked into the room opposite: a huge kitchen. He could see it in detail by the red gleam that seeped out around the door of the big, old stove. But the wavering light in the passage came from another source.

They sought it, following the passage that gave onto a hall. A staircase climbed up from it but their eyes were on the room to the left. They saw armchairs around a fire in a grate, the flames casting shadows on the walls, and there were glasses standing on the mantelpiece above. The room was empty.

Ilse, at the head of the cellar stairs, saw them pass stealthily along the passage. When the explosion had rocked the house and the firing started she had run up to her own room because she would have a better view of the quay from the upper floor. She had to know what was happening outside, to her father. She peered fearfully around the curtains and saw the muzzle flashes all around the harbour and close by on the quay. There were soldiers taking cover behind the steps of one of the buildings and a lean figure crouching among them that she recognised as that of Erwin König.

Sometimes a bullet from the S.S. headquarters cracked against the wall of her house so she retreated to the hall below. The lights had gone out with the explosion. She hoped, though doubted, that the cause might only be blown fuses so she went to the door of the cellar under the main staircase. She pulled it open, found the torch hanging on the wall inside and descended the steps by its light. The cellar held some stocks of vegetables, racks of wine and the furniture moved out of the guardroom to make space for the guard's table and beds. There was a couch and two armchairs, all covered with dust sheets and they stood in a far corner almost hidden by the wine racks.

Ilse did not like the cold cellar, its dust and shadows. She went quickly to the box on the wall. She knew a little about fuses; one had blown a month or so ago and the old French electrician sent to her aid had shown her how he changed it. She inspected the fuses now and accepted what she had suspected, that this was a total failure of power.

She climbed back to the door but stopped there as she heard another stray bullet ricochet around the front room where she had sat with Ritter and Erwin König. She decided she was safer where she was and sat on the top stair, hands to her mouth, her fear still for her father, until she heard, faintly, the tinkling of breaking glass from the back of the house. That brought her to her feet. She heard movement in the guardroom a few yards down the passage, switched off the torch and pulled the cellar door to, leaving only a crack. She peered through it, heart thumping.

The two men prowled like hunting animals into the light of the passage. One carried a pistol in his hand, the other a submachine-gun. They darted glances about them, eyes glittering, but did not see her where she stood with the stillness of terror behind the almost closed door. They were the enemy. In her house. She was alone and the pistol her father had left her was still in the desk.

187

They passed from her sight. Ilse closed the door softly and tip-toed down the steps. She halted at the foot of them because here the darkness was total and she could not see a hand before her face. Dare she use the torch? That was decided when she heard a skittering in the cellar and she kept the beam pointed down, sweeping the floor as she crossed to the far corner. She pulled the dust-sheet from the couch, shone the torch underneath it and then sat down. She could barely hear the firing now; it was very quiet in the cellar and there was no more skittering. She thought she might have imagined it. Or it was just a draught fluttering the dust sheets. The enemy would not come down here. They would not think of a cellar. She gradually became calmer, her trembling stopped, and she worried again for her father. She buried her face in her hands.

Commandos following Brent and Tallon worked their way, light-footed and cautious, through the house until Tallon, dogged by Johnson, joined Brent where he stood at a side window on the ground floor and reported, "It's clear. I'll lay a pound to a penny that's the *Oberst* and his guard out on the quay. We're holding the front." That meant his men were stationed at all the windows facing along the quay.

Brent said, "You've told them to hold their fire."

"They know, and why." Because it was vital their presence in the house was not suspected for as long as possible. Chris peered over David's shoulder. From here they looked out over the harbour mouth to the guardship and the drifter alongside her. Smoke hung in a pall over them, so while Tallon thought he could see the scurrying, stooping figures of men on their decks he could not be sure.

David had drawn the curtain aside and now he stepped back a pace from the window so the beam would be seen only from the two vessels and not from inside the harbour. He worked the switch on the torch, then waited.

A commando trotted up behind them and told Tallon, "All in the two back rooms." He was talking of the children – and the little man Tallon and Brent had come for – now crowded into the house. "Covering party is up in the attic."

Tallon nodded. "The others are due any minute. See how those at the back are getting on." As the man hurried away Chris wondered how many would be with McNab and the girl.

But now he held his breath as an answering light flickered aboard the drifter and Brent read: "Guardship taken." Tallon let out the breath in a sigh of relief, but Brent was going on: "I – am – sinking."

Tallon swallowed, then said thickly, "The drifter was supposed to take us off. The two M.T.B.s can't take all of us, not that crowd in the back room." He remembered their faces. Leave them now?

David Brent could see those faces but did not answer. He stared out at the drifter, taking in the signal and its significance, then thinking, remembering what Suzanne had told him of the guardship. He lifted the torch and worked its button again.

The house quivered to a muffled explosion above them and Tallon said, "That sounds like McNab." He hurried away with Johnson following him.

Jimmy Nash peered across the mouth of the harbour at the house on the end of the quay and the tiny spot of light that winked at him. It ceased and he spun on his heel, shouted up to Tommy Vance on the deck of the guardship, "You've got your engineer aboard there?" Then as Tommy acknowledged with a lift of his hand, "Fetch him!"

"Sarge! Come on up!" The call came from the attic.

McNab, standing on the landing below, heard the message he had been waiting for and bellowed, "Everybody upstairs!" He counted them as they came back from the front and rear windows, and passed him to climb the steep stairs to the attic above. He followed the last man, crossing the floor of the attic, ducking to work his way through the hole in the wall into the next building in the row, then the next, until he came to the room where all his men were stooped under the angled roof beams, along with Suzanne and the rescued prisoners.

Phil stood a few paces from the rift in the wall and McNab glowered at him. "You took your time."

Phil only grinned, teeth white in a face coated with a paste of dust and sweat. He lifted his hands to cover his ears and the others copied him. The floor shook and dust squirted from the hole like steam under pressure. As it drifted aside and settled Phil ducked through the rift and crossed the attic beyond. There was a new, raw fissure a yard wide and nearly the height of a man cut in the wall ahead of him. A voice challenged hoarsely from the darkness on the other side, "Who's there?"

"Phil, with McNab and the rest."

"Come on in."

But Phil stood aside as Louis and Michel eased Paul's loose body through the gap and Suzanne followed. They were in the house of the military commander of St. Jean and Suzanne thought that David Brent should be here. Had to be.

McNab counted his men again as they filed after the girl, their faces expressionless and eyes staring. He thought that they were showing the strain now. Then he turned on Phil, down on his knees on the floor and delving deep into the rucksack. "How long are you going to be?"

"Couple of minutes. I want to make a proper job of this one."

McNab said, "I'll keep an eye open in case we get company." He went back to the hole through which he had come and knelt there with his Thompson.

The *Gefreiter* pinned down in the alley with his three men turned his head as a burst of rifle-fire came from behind him, but it was directed at the S.S. headquarters. He called, "Somebody's got around behind them!" It was Kurt Ritter's young *Leutnant* and his assault troops, shaking from exertion and the freezing wet clothes dragged onto their bodies after swimming the river.

The firing from in front of the *Gefreiter*, at the end of the alley by the sea-wall, intensified now in response to that of the *Leutnant*'s party. The *Gefreiter* hugged the ground behind the stack of logs that was the only cover he and his men had. He shouted, "One of us has to tell that *Major* on the quay about these *Tommis* back here!" He had said that twice already, given a direct order, but no one had moved. He had screwed up his courage to try to cross the alley himself, but his legs would not obey him.

Erwin König, at the front of the house, stared along the quay and said abruptly, "Their fire's slackening." And now no muzzle flashes showed at the windows of the S.S. headquarters.

A man broke from cover at the far end of the quay and ran, crouching and weaving, across the open ground. Another followed him and they flattened themselves against the wall on either side of the front door of the headquarters. Kurt Ritter recognised that weaving run, was certain they were his assault troops. He saw their hands go back and the grenades lobbed in at the door. Seconds later there was a stab of flame and a double explosion. The two men by the door plunged inside and more came running across to it.

Ritter said grimly, "Now we go." And to the soldiers kneeling around him: "On your feet."

But Erwin König frowned, "Strange. No tiles fell that time." Ritter paused and König's gaze ran along the row of buildings. Tiles had fallen at intervals all through the action, from the roofs of the buildings in front of him, alongside – they crunched under his boots – and finally behind him. He had assumed they fell because of grenades but they had cascaded down in succession. *In that order*. His head went back as he shouted, "They've broken through the attics of the houses! Bombed their way!"

Ritter leapt up the steps of the building and disappeared inside. König started to run back to his house, throwing over his shoulder at the men of his guard, "Follow me!" The scything fire from his own windows kicked sparks from the quay and ricochetted around him. Instinctively he swerved aside, fell and rolled into the cover of another flight of steps.

Kurt Ritter, pounding up the stairs, reached their head but then the blast hurled him back, bouncing and rolling to lie winded and dazed as the dust boiled about him.

Erwin König lay with his arms over his head as the rubble crashed onto the quay. Only when the last brick had fallen did he wipe dirt from his eyes and squint blearily up at the building at the end of the row and next to his house. The upper floor had gone and now there was a ragged gap silhouetted against the night sky. His house now stood alone. The enemy held it – and his daughter.

14

The cellar

Tallon was making his rounds of the house, starting with the defenders at the rear who held the end of the alley. Cover was more precious than ever to them now because the last building in the row had caught fire following the explosion that ripped away its upper floor. The flames lit Grundy, Cullen and the commandos who had to show themselves around a corner or above a heap of rubble to shoot into the alley. They breathed through open mouths and the firelight cast shadows in their hollow cheeks. They were holding against more than a dozen men now the young *Leutnant*'s party had worked up towards them, and they were paying the price.

Chris Tallon said, "Won't be long now."

The corporal warned, "Ammunition's low."

"I know." Tallon returned to the house. He crawled through the rooms at the front because they were under heavy fire now, talked to the men kneeling by the windows and had the same warning from them, gave the same encouragement. And hoped it was true. He moved on.

One of those in the upstairs rooms was Phil, who had blasted a way through the houses for Suzanne, McNab and the others. Tallon said, "You made a mess of that place next door."

Phil nodded, "Mr. Brent's orders, sir."

Tallon remembered when the original plan for the raid had to be abandoned and he had described the demolition engineers with their rucksacks packed with explosives as being: "All dressed up and nowhere to go." And David Brent's reply: "We'll need them all." They had.

He found McNab, who reported sombrely, "I brought back two wounded and lost three." He had been forced to leave their bodies in the S.S. headquarters at the far end of the quay. Tallon's weary brain did the sum, adding McNab's casualties to the others: five dead and four wounded. The wounded were in the two rooms on the ground floor at the rear of the house.

Suzanne sat on the floor in the former guardroom with her back against the wall and Paul's head in her lap. Michel sat on one side of her, Louis on the other. Albert stood close by, bewildered now and needing the reassurance of the girl's presence. Suzanne knew that, and said in French, "I want to lay him down. Can you see something we can use as a pillow? And is there a light we can use as we move him? I can't reach my torch." It was deep in the pocket of her trenchcoat.

Michel edged through the children who crowded the room and returned with a small pillow from one of the camp beds. Albert pulled his torch from his pocket, held it out and Louis took it. He switched it on for Michel to see to lift Paul's head gently so that Suzanne could slide her legs from underneath and insert the pillow instead. She said softly, "I think he has some colour now. And he seems to be breathing more easily."

Chris Tallon came to their side and said, "Don't use that torch too long. It'll spoil your vision when you go outside."

Suzanne told Louis, "All right, put it out now." She rose to her feet and moved towards Albert.

Louis obeyed, stepped back to give her room – and slipped the torch into his pocket.

Suzanne asked Tallon, "We're going outside now?"

He hesitated before saying, "Not yet."

She noted that hesitation. "What's wrong?"

Tallon admitted, "The drifter's sinking. Brent is still signalling to it. I don't know what he has in mind. But it won't be long." Casualties, a shrinking supply of ammunition, more and more of the enemy pouring across by boat from the new town. Not long. "I'm going to look at the wounded." He did not want to answer any more questions.

As he left, Suzanne translated for Albert and he shrugged, "If the drifter is sinking, then we are finished."

She shook her head, "I don't believe that. There are the other boats."

Albert waved a hand at the children. "The little boats can't take us all."

Suzanne put her arm around him, "Don't worry." She trusted David Brent but was afraid.

Louis, standing unobtrusively in the background, had listened to Suzanne's explanation. He gathered there was a plan for the raiding force and the others to escape by sea. He dared not go to England. His story had been swallowed, but for how long? Suppose the battered wireless operator survived and said he had not told Schleger about Suzanne's rendezvous with the important agent? Then Louis would fall under suspicion again. The operator might admit he *had* talked – but that was a gamble Louis would not take. The unconscious man might die, and Louis was prepared to see that he did, but there was no chance now. And later? That, too, was an unacceptable risk.

He had to get out. But only to run the gauntlet of the cross-fire? *Did* he have to get out of the house? If he could stay in St. Jean then he was safe, Schleger and Ostmann would see to that. Ostmann . . . Louis remembered and now knew how he could stay.

Brent stood at the side window and watched the guardship getting under way. Her screw churned at her stern and men forward and aft cast off her moorings. She moved forward slowly towards the mouth of the harbour. He had asked Jimmy Nash if the guardship had steam up, and she had. Suzanne had said the guardship sometimes went to sea, so there was a chance she would have steam.

Suzanne. Now he knew why she had sent him away so long ago. But he had still lost her. Another man's wife. What had been a mystery was now a sentence. He swore under his breath, strode back through the house and came on Tallon in the hall. Chris crawled out of one of the front rooms as it was raked by automatic fire and plaster fell from the ceiling, was kicked from the wall opposite the window. He shoved up to his feet and Brent told him, "I want all the seamen at the back of the house. Get ready to go. We're leaving aboard the guardship."

"The guard – " Tallon broke off, stared at Brent open-mouthed, then finished, "You're a bloody marvel!"

David Brent said grimly, "We haven't done it yet."

Chris nodded sober acceptance of that, answered in a voice hoarse with dust and shouting, "We'll be ready when you give the word. Now, if you like."

"Minutes, that's all. And two good men to take Neumann first of all."

"I hope he's worth it." Chris was remembering his dead and wounded.

Brent left him, went to the back room and edged through the crowd to where Suzanne stood over Paul and Michel. He told her, "We're leaving, starting in a minute or two." He paused, staring down at Paul's face, as the girl translated for Albert. Brent said, "His eyes are open." He could see the whites of them in the gloom.

Michel said, "He's waking!"

Louis stood close by the door and now he eased around the frame, out into the passage. He was only two paces from the open back door, the racket and whine of the firing, but he turned away from it and strode quickly into the deeper darkness under the stairs. Ostmann had said, when they sat in the car after the ambush, "All those houses on the quay have cellars." And Ostmann had then added, "I hear the *Herr Oberst* keeps a good one."

Louis found the door, opened it and stepped through, closed it behind him. He felt for a bolt or a key on the inside, but there was neither. No matter. They would all be gone in a few minutes and he would go up and show a white flag, make sure the German swine didn't shoot him. Till then he would keep well out of the way. He could use Albert's torch to find his way down –

But now he realised that there was light below in the cellar. He turned, breath held, transferring the torch to his left hand, with his right bringing the Luger pistol from his pocket. The source of the light was far back in the cellar and out of his sight, the edge of its radiance barely touching the bottom of the steps. Was one of the soldiers down here? No, that didn't make sense; they could not defend the house from the cellar. A light left on by accident? No again, because the power had failed – Schleger's office had been plunged into darkness until the yellow emergency lighting cut in. He started down the steps, carefully, quietly.

Ilse had not heard the door open and close. She did not hear Louis walk soft-footed across the floor of the cellar. The noise of the battle above her was muted but the distant crackling was still enough to cover his approach. She sensed his presence and jerked upright; her hands fell from her face and she stared into his.

Louis reached out a hand, seized her under the jaw and began to force her back on the couch. She tried to struggle but now he showed her the Luger pistol and she was still. He said, "If they find you, they'll kill you. Make a sound and I'll turn you over to them. Only I'll say you tried to grab the gun." His face was close to hers, his grip on her throat thrusting her head back. He lowered the gun and laid it on the floor under the couch, where he could reach it and she could not.

Suzanne and Michel knelt by Paul, David Brent stooping over them. The girl said, "This is Suzanne. Can you hear me? See me? We got you out."

Paul squinted up at her out of swollen eyes and his voice came thickly, "I can see you. Out? Where are we?"

"A house on the quay. There's a boat. The Navy is going to take us back."

Paul did not seem to hear that. He said, "I didn't tell them anything. Just my cover story. Nothing else."

Suzanne and Michel looked at each other over his body, then stood. Michel whispered, "Can we believe him? He might have given something away when he was only half-conscious, and doesn't remember that now."

"I believe him." She said that with certainty, suspicion surfacing again.

"Then if he didn't give us up – " Michel glanced down at Paul, then up at the girl. "Who else knew?"

"You. Me. Albert – Louis."

They turned as one and saw Albert watching them. Suzanne asked, "Where's Louis?"

The old man looked around him, and shrugged, "I don't know. He was here a minute ago."

David Brent asked, "What's going on?"

Suzanne told herself coldly that suspicion was not enough and other possibilities had to be examined. Albert could have betrayed them – but would he then have met her at the landing and acted as a guide for Brent?

Albert had told Suzanne of his accident and Louis' care for him. But Albert and herself had plotted an "accident" to a German sentry, so . . . Louis had had ample time to pass a message to Schleger. He had not been shot. He claimed to have been kneed – but there was only the one corporal in the room with him. Not two troopers in a cell, not Schleger nor Ostmann. Just one corporal. And an empty desk in the hall.

Suzanne threw at Michel, "You and Albert look after Paul." Then she pushed past Brent to the door and as he followed she explained rapidly, "We brought three men away from the S.S., those two in there and another, Louis. We've just found out he was the one who gave us up. He was in that room. A big thug."

They were at the open back door and Grundy appeared, Cullen at his shoulder. Suzanne demanded, "Did you see a big Frenchman come out of here?"

Grundy shook his head, "No, miss. But we've just come back. And out here we're all watching for fellers coming from the other direction." He turned to Brent. "Mr. Tallon said you wanted us, sir. The rest of the men are over by the wall. There's a drifter closing."

Brent saw them crouching in the shelter of the sea-wall. He ordered, "Take her lines. That's Mr. Nash. I'll be with you." Then he told Suzanne, "This Louis, he's gone, and we've no time to search for him. Wait here." She would be first out of this hell and aboard the guardship, along with

Max Neumann, he was determined on that. He ran to join Grundy and his men lining the sea-wall.

Suzanne listened to the unending din of the firing and saw the flicker of muzzle flames only a score of yards away at the mouth of the alley. She said to herself: "Louis wouldn't risk his skin. He's found a hole and when this is over he'll crawl out of it." To betray and inform again. She turned back into the house, ruled out the rooms at the front of it and started towards the stairs, then hesitated. Tallon's men were in every room in the house so there was no hiding place in any of them. She thought that if Louis got away then it would be her fault. She should not have believed his explanation when she found him in an office in the butcher's house while Michel and Paul were both in the cellars –

The word triggered the thought. She went back along the passage and found the door under the stairs. She paused then: Louis had been armed with a Luger. She stood to one side of the door and turned the handle with her left hand, her right holding the Mauser pistol, then threw the door wide. No shot was fired. She edged forward until she could see the steps leading down and the faint glow of light at the bottom of them. She descended the steps steadily, watchful. The cellar was a place of shadows, the only light coming from behind racks of wine-bottles at the far end. Her eyes probed the shadows but saw no one and now she was crossing the cellar floor, closing on the light. She checked a moment when she first heard the panting breathing, the sobbing, then moved on more quickly until she could see beyond the racks.

Louis held the girl by her throat with one hand, the other was thrust under her rucked-up skirt. She was trying to fight him. Suzanne saw the girl's face, eyes closed tight and tears on her cheeks. Suzanne jabbed the muzzle of the Mauser into the back of Louis' neck and ordered, "Stand up!" It did not sound like her voice.

For an instant Louis was frozen with shock then the pistol jabbed again and he knew what it was. He let go of the girl lying under him and pushed himself up on the couch, head

199

turning as the pressure of the pistol barrel was removed. He saw Suzanne, standing two strides away now and holding the pistol with both hands but pointed at the ceiling. She knew, he was certain. The one they called Paul had talked and she knew Louis had betrayed her. It might have been a lot worse if he had been found by Michel or that hard-faced commando who had nearly killed Louis in Schleger's office – but it was only Suzanne.

He was thinking quickly again, pretended to slip and fall as he tried to stand. His hand sought and found the Luger under the couch, swept it up. Suzanne still had her pistol pointed at the ceiling, was retreating, side-stepping away, but she was a fool if she thought that would save her at this range.

David Brent stood on the yard-wide sea-wall, lit by the red glare from the burning house, as the guardship slid in with Tommy Vance at the helm. Her lines were caught by Brent's men lining the wall and made fast. He shouted down to Jimmy Nash, ten feet below him on the deck of the guardship, "Did you bring that sail from the drifter?" And when he saw Jimmy lift his hand: "We've a bigger party than we planned." He told a staring Jimmy about the children, then gave his orders and asked, "Understood?"

"Aye, aye, sir!"

Brent jumped down from the wall and called to Grundy, nearby and listening, "Get them moving! Get them aboard!" He glanced towards the house, saw the girl had gone and strode towards the door.

Jimmy Nash said disbelievingly, "A boatload of kids!" Then he turned to the signalman waiting at his side, "Got that lamp?"

"Sir!"

"Send now."

The signalman directed the lamp out to sea and began to work the trigger.

Crozier's boat lay within feet of Dent's, the bows of both turned towards the shore a mile away. The sound of the

firing came out to them over the sea as an irregular crackling.
A house was burning and in its light they could see the mouth
of the harbour, saw the guardship turn out of it and edge in
to the sea-wall near the fire. A minute later they read the
signal flickering out from under the sea-wall and Crozier
told his signalman, "Acknowledge."

As the light flashed from his bridge he called across to
Dent, "See that? We cruise offshore and give covering fire."
That was the import of the two-letter signal flashed to them.
Brent had also told them of another two-letter combination
that would be used if Jimmy Nash failed, that would have
called on Dent and Crozier to close the sea-wall and take
off as many as they could. Crozier said "So it seems to be
working, so far."

Little Dent replied, "Bloody marvellous! I can't believe
it."

Crozier thought: Neither can I.

The engines of the boats rumbled and they ran in towards
the fire, the flames reaching higher as they closed and now
the crackling was louder and they could see the pin-prick
flashes in the night.

Brent shoved his way into the passage, going against the tide:
the commandos were bringing out Max Neumann, Michel,
Albert, Paul and a shuffling, whimpering trail of children.
He worked clear of them when he passed the doors of the
kitchen and guardroom on either side. That was when he
heard the shots. There was firing from the front and rear of
the house but these reports came from below. There were
four of them and they echoed up the steps from the open
door to the cellar.

He went down them at a run, grabbing the Colt .45 from
its holster and cocking it. He saw light at the far end of the
cellar, drifting wisps of smoke and ran towards it. He found
Suzanne standing still with her hand holding the Mauser
pistol hanging loosely at her side. A man lay on his back
with his arms flung wide. There was a couch, a girl curled
up small at one end of it, as far from the body as she could

go. Her brown hair hung tangled about her face and her eyes were big with fright.

He knew who the man had to be: "Louis?"

Suzanne nodded, "He had a gun. I believe he thought I wouldn't shoot. I nearly didn't. I had to move to one side because he was right in front of her and I didn't want to hit her. And then I knew he was going to kill me."

She was shaking and David Brent put his arm around her and said softly, "All right. Put the safety catch on that thing." And when she lifted the Mauser and obeyed, he asked, "Who is she?"

"The daughter of the *Oberst*. She lives here. Louis must have found her down here by accident. He was trying to – " Suzanne broke off there, then finished, "I'm very sorry for her."

Brent understood and stared down at Louis. "Her father would have had him shot."

"No." Suzanne knew Louis now. "She wouldn't have been able to tell her father anything when he found her. You and your men would have been blamed."

David Brent asked, "Do you speak German?" And when Suzanne shook her head he muttered, "Where the hell is Johnson when we need him?" But he knew the answer to that: the German-speaker would be with Tallon.

Suzanne said, "She understands French. I know the woman who comes in here to clean for them."

"Well for God's sake say something to take that look off her face. Tell her we're taking her out of this bloody place and she won't be hurt."

Suzanne did that and they each took one of the girl's hands. They led her up the steps and into the now-empty kitchen. It was lit by the glow from the stove but Brent pressed the torch he had brought up from the cellar into Ilse's hand. "Tell her to sit on the floor in the corner away from the windows. When we've gone she must shine the torch on herself and keep singing in German, anything, as long as it's loud." So her father's men would not indiscriminately shoot their way in. He waited until Suzanne had got that message across. There was intelligence in the German girl's eyes now and she did as Suzanne said. Brent glanced over his shoulder as he left the room and saw her face turned towards him from her place in the far corner, watching.

He found Tallon behind the house, counting his men as they fell back from their defensive positions. Johnson was with him and Brent wondered what would happen to the interpreter if he was captured. He had a good idea how the Germans would treat one of their own caught in an enemy uniform. Johnson had taken that risk from the start of this operation, but he could serve no purpose here now. Brent told Tallon with a jerk of the head towards Johnson, "We'll get him aboard."

Johnson went with him as David hurried Suzanne to the sea-wall, a hand gripping her arm. The sail had been secured as a makeshift chute from the wall to the deck of the guardship. The last of the children were sliding down it, lifted onto it by Grundy and Cullen. Some of them shrieked but most were too terrified by the clamour of the fighting, the glare from the burning house and the sight of the glittering black sea around the guardship below. When they bumped onto the deck they were grabbed by the waiting seamen and manhandled below, with rough gentleness but rapidly, steadily, like so much cargo.

Brent shoved Johnson after them, picked up Suzanne and swung her over the wall, let her go. He lifted his head and saw the two boats, or rather the soaring arcs of red tracer that marked where they cruised back and forth a quarter-mile out in the darkness. Dent and Crozier had their gunners sweeping the old port and the houses behind. They were under fire themselves from the gun on the headland; Brent could see the distant winking of flame at its muzzle and the silver-grey waterspouts lifting where the shells fell alongside or astern of the boats.

"Last of them coming now!" Chris Tallon shouted that, standing at Brent's side but facing back towards the houses, his Thompson at his shoulder. Men came running from the end of the alley and out of the back door of the house, the tall figure of McNab trotting behind them.

Brent called to Grundy and Cullen, "Cast off and get aboard!"

Grundy shouted, "Watch them other fellers forrard! Make sure they get away!" Cullen obeyed, saw the men flip the forward line loose and go down to the ship. Then he felt Grundy's hand on his back, heard the cox'n's voice in his ear, "Your turn now, chum!" Cullen swung over the wall and Grundy followed him.

Brent stood with Chris Tallon through those last seconds as the lines securing the guardship fell away and the men rolled over the wall. He emptied his pistol at the end of the alley as Chris fired short bursts from the Thompson, then, last of all, they dropped down to the deck of the guardship as she swung away from the wall and her bow pointed seawards.

Erwin König was first into the house after the firing stopped. His troops waited in the alley and on the quay as he had ordered: "Tell them to stay back and hold their fire. Ilse is in there and nobody else." Ritter was not prepared to gamble on König's certainty and would not let him go in alone. He walked at the shoulder of the *Herr Oberst* and carried a machine-pistol, cocked and ready but trained on the floor.

They paced through the house, littered with rubble and broken glass, stinking of burnt cordite and smoke. They heard the singing before they came to the kitchen, a hoarse, high, quavering voice, and they found Ilse curled in a corner, torchlight on her face. Erwin König lifted her and she clung to him.

Kurt Ritter went out of the back of the house to the sea-wall. No tracer looped in from out of the darkness. The gun on the headland had ceased firing, no longer having the tracer for an aiming point. The guardship and the other boats had gone. The sea was empty.

Blowing the bridge and isolating the old port had been

a master-stroke. Ritter felt doubt for the first time. His battalion was on its way to Russia where the *Wehrmacht* stood at the gates of Moscow and victory seemed inevitable. But now he wondered.

He returned to the house and found the *Oberst* stripping off his greatcoat to wrap it around his daughter. König glanced at Ritter, "Get hold of a runner and send a signal back to the barracks for general transmission: Enemy evacuated – no, better say 'driven out of' – St. Jean – put in the time – taking guardship and believed with two *Schnellboote*."

They exchanged cynical grins over the amendment, knowing an ill-chosen phrase could cost an officer his command, but Ritter printed the signal neatly in his notebook, ripped out the page and looked for a man to carry it. He would have to be ferried across the river and then get a truck to lift him to the barracks and the wireless there. Ritter thought bitterly: Slamming the stable door.

Rudi Halder had searched along the *Tommis*' probable course until his three boats were nearer to England than to France, then swept back and forth across that course, waiting and listening. He had not found them. He had never believed he would. The bright boys back at base had cocked it up. Logic told him that by now the motor torpedo boats would be out of his reach; whatever operation they had carried out on the coast they had completed and gone home by a different route. He had lost them and he would have to be content with that one confirmed sinking, the boat that had burned.

That was logic. But stubbornness, or instinct, told him otherwise. There was something wrong, in his reasoning or the pattern of the night's events. He shifted uneasily and Bruno Jacobi, standing at his shoulder, said, "Coffee?"

Rudi snapped at him, "No! And be quiet! There's too much talking going on!"

There was no talking, only an occasional murmur from one of the gunners forward or aft. They had been stopped and listening like that for the past fifteen minutes, the three boats lying in a spread line, one either side of Rudi and just visible. But Bruno knew his captain and did not argue; he eased quietly back on the bridge to leave Rudi alone. The old man had got his back up because they had missed the *Tommis*. So keep out of his way.

Rudi scowled out over the screen at the heaving sea. Something wrong . . . Again he recalled the sequence of events: the pick-up of the agent by the M.T.B.s, his own first ambush, the action with the fishing fleet, the burning boat and the ambush the *Tommis* laid for Gunther – He stopped there, and asked himself: Why Gunther? They didn't know about him, only of Rudi's boats. So the trap had been laid for himself?

Of course. But why was it set up at all? Why hadn't the boats gone home with the agent they had come for? What operation could they –

Why *boats*? When one would have sufficed to recover one agent? Or put another ashore. With four boats they could have lifted off a score or more but there wouldn't be a score so –

Lift off – or *land*?

He swore and demanded, "Signal pad!" And when Bruno hurriedly passed it to him he printed rapidly: BELIEVE ENEMY FORCE ESTIMATED 30 MEN LANDED NORTH OF ST. JEAN. He turned to shove the pad at Bruno, "Send that." Instead he found the signalman facing him, holding out a flimsy like the one he had just filled in. He snatched it and read: ST. JEAN UNDER ATTACK . . . He skimmed through the rest of it then ground the signal he had written into a ball inside his clenched fist and hurled it over the side. "Start up!"

It would take him more than an hour at full speed to get back to his home port.

15

In the sunlight

David Brent wondered if they would get away with it.

The guardship was an hour out of St. Jean and plugging along at a thumping eight knots as the engineers below demanded all the old engines could give. Brent, in the wheel-house, could feel the vibration through the gratings under his feet. Grundy was at the wheel, Cullen standing at the back of the bridge. The French skipper of the drifter was down on the deck with his two-man crew. It was one thing to let him steer his own boat, knowing how she would respond, but this ship was not his and Brent did not want the problems of translation while conning her. They were not yet home and dry.

The deck was littered with the bodies of seamen and commandos, sheltering behind the cover of the bulwarks. Some were stretched out and sleeping, others seated with heads hanging, nodding then jerking awake, but all held their weapons. Chris Tallon moved among them, exchanging a word here and there, but Private Johnson stood in the wheel-house. Brent had given his orders as soon as they were clear of St. Jean, and one had been that Johnson should be at his side.

Crozier and little Dent cruised astern but at some distance and unseen in the night. One deadlight had been left open a crack in the guardship's after cabin, letting out a sliver of light for the M.T.B.s to keep station. Jimmy Nash, Tommy Vance and two gunners worked around the 40mm. gun on the foredeck, practising a drill for loading and firing.

There were no prisoners. Jimmy Nash had put the guardship's crew aboard the sinking drifter in the harbour of St. Jean and left them her boat to ferry themselves to the quay. The drifter had been settling surely but only slowly and they would have reached the shore dry-shod.

Jimmy strode aft from the gun now and said, "They're getting into the swing of it."

Chris Tallon came to stand beside him below the wheel-house and reported, "They're ready." He glanced around at the supine figures then his teeth showed in a tired grin. "You wouldn't think so, but they'll stand to if we give the word." He felt numb, as if he watched himself doing what had to be done, driven on by this man above him in the doorway of the wheel-house.

Brent looked down at them. The darkness hid their faces but the loose slouch of their shoulders told the tale of their weariness. He could hear it in their voices, husky, thick.

They were ready. Brent thought that the E-boats had not been seen since the landing. They had not returned to St. Jean so they were still at sea. Somewhere out there . . . He pulled off his cap, rubbed at the tousled, sweat-flattened black hair and jammed the cap on again. "Keep shaking them up." So Tallon and Jimmy Nash turned stiffly and went back to the men and the gun.

Tommy Vance and his men had got the hang of it, the laying, training and firing. He wondered if the gun would be needed, hoped it would not. But just before the landing party went ashore by the cape he had voiced his doubts to Brent, that the E-boats they had first encountered were still prowling in the night. Brent had acknowledged that but gone on with the landing. Tommy had done as he was told and held his tongue. But Brent had remembered; his orders once they were away from St. Jean had shown that.

Brent asked Cullen, "Have you got that light handy?" His own voice sounded hoarse, slurred. He saw the glance he got from Grundy, eyes flicking quickly from compass to Brent's face then back again.

And he heard the odd note in Cullen's reply, "Aye, aye, sir."

Brent knew that he was as tired as any of them. He had asked Cullen about the signal lamp before. Twice. He remembered now and rubbed at his face, feeling the rasp of the stubble.

Suzanne said, "I came up for some air. It's crowded down there."

He saw her standing on the deck by the wheel-house; he had not seen her come up from below. She would need the air; the accommodation below deck was filled with children, crammed in cabins, curled up in passages, even packed into the tiny galley. He asked, "Is Neumann all right?" Because he was the reason for it all.

"He's asleep. I got him into a bunk with a blanket."

Brent was still thinking about E-boats with a part of his mind but he climbed down to stand beside her, said what was now foremost in his thoughts: "I used to think about you. All the time." And he had pictured her clearly in his mind.

Suzanne looked out over the sea creaming along the guardship's rusty side. "Angry? Bitter?"

"Both. But not now that I know." Just – alone. She had made her vows – and broken them once, that was true – but it would not happen again, Brent was certain.

She confirmed that: "I'm sorry, but I couldn't tell you that day you went away." Her head turned to look up at him, "There's a nasty word for what I'd done. I'd been unfaithful but I didn't want to dirty the time we'd had. I didn't want to remember it that way. I wasn't ashamed. I'd married him for better or worse, but if he had not suffered the accident I would have left him. I wasn't forgiving. *I* was bitter."

She stopped and used the back of her hand to rub salt spray from her face, then blinked and went on, "As it was – well, he needed me. I was told in so many words that I was his only hold on life. He lived from one of my visits to the next. He died the day the Germans marched into Paris but he knew nothing of that. I arranged the funeral then came down to Normandy."

It was some seconds before he took in what she was saying, then he reached out to hold her by the arms, turning her to face him . . .

"Light! Starboard bow!" That was Jimmy Nash standing just forward of the bridge. Brent saw it, a flicker of morse, and he called up to Cullen, "Give him BM!" Remembering the challenge or reply Jimmy Nash had told him he'd seen when the E-boats fired on each other after Brent had landed north of St. Jean. He thrust the girl away, "Get into cover!" As he swung up into the wheel-house Cullen was working the signal lamp, the reply stuttering out in longs and shorts. Brent prayed it was the right reply and saw the gun forward swinging on its mounting as Tommy Vance trained it out to starboard.

Brent stared out into the darkness, holding his breath, but no burst of fire ripped across the black sea. It seemed the reply had been correct and Jimmy's voice came up from below the wheel-house: "Looks like it worked." Then Jimmy moved aft to stand right in the stern. That had been in Brent's orders.

The E-boats came into sight and thundered in out of the night. One moment they were just vague silhouettes picked out by the grey "ram's horns" under their bows, then the next the silhouettes hardened and the grey turned into the silver of bow-wave and wake.

There were three of them, running in a flat echelon. They swept past by a cable's length, two hundred yards, but slowing, turning to swing around the guardship's stern. Brent called, "Port side, Tommy!" But Vance was already traversing the gun around to cover the E-boats. Brent reached past Grundy to grab the German skipper's cap from where it hung on a hook near the wheel. He shoved it at Private Johnson and told him, "Put that on. And use this."

Johnson set the cap on his head and took the tin megaphone. Cullen wondered: What the hell does he want that for? The leading E-boat had closed to within twenty yards of the guardship's port side and had throttled back so the thunder of its engines was muted to a deep rumble. She ran well within easy hailing distance without using a megaphone.

Brent saw that the other two boats were keeping station on their leader but still that cable's length beyond her and abreast of the guardship. They would not see the light in her stern now. He said, "All right, Jimmy." And Nash stamped three times on the deck.

David Brent was thinking that the E-boat's captain, if his flotilla was that out of St. Jean, would know the guardship – and her skipper. That was confirmed by the first question shouted across the narrow neck of white water: "Why are you at sea?" Johnson rapidly translated as David watched his enemy, the E-boat's captain, standing tall and straight on his bridge but featureless in the night.

Johnson passed David's muttered reply: "St. Jean has been raided. The *Tommis* landed a force of commandos and there was fighting in the port. It was reported they were taken off by drifter. We were ordered out to search for them."

This only confirmed what Rudi already knew, except the evacuation by drifter. And now the earlier action near the fishing fleet fell into place in the pattern: the *Tommis* had been capturing a drifter to use in their operation. He thought absently that Ulrich's voice sounded different, but it was coming out of that distorting megaphone. Rudi called, "You're showing a light!"

"A light? Where?"

"At your stern. A scuttle hasn't been properly secured."

"Thanks. I'll see to it." The megaphone was lowered but Rudi still heard clearly the bark of the guardship's skipper, "Fasten that damned scuttle aft!"

When Jimmy Nash had stamped on the deck the man stationed right under him in the after cabin had heard that signal above his head and started sending his own, closing and opening the deadlight so the crack of light showed short-long-short-long.

Rudi could not see that as he stared across at the old armed drifter. The gun mounted forward in her bow was manned and trained out in his direction. There was nothing odd in that; he would similarly cover a strange vessel he closed in the night and his own guns were trained on the drifter now. But Ulrich's voice –

He called softly to the crew of the 20mm. just below him in

211

the bow, "Stand by!" He saw them glance up at him, startled by the harsh urgency in his tone, then tense over their gun. He raised his voice to hail the guardship's skipper, "Werner! Was your wife hurt in the fighting?"

There was only one right answer to that question and Ulrich should ask, "Who is Werner?" Rudi saw the megaphone lifted –

Brent had his own suspicions when the question came, saw that it could be a trap. He decided he had to take it at face value and play the game out to the end – which might come at any moment. "Tell him she's all right."

But now Rudi turned as a voice called behind him, "*Herr Kaleu!*" The shortened, slang version of *Kapitänleutnant*.

He saw his wireless operator thrusting a signal flimsy at him. As he took it he heard the sudden harsh rattle of machine-gun fire above the rumble of his engines and spun around, shouting instantly, instinctively, "Full ahead!" He saw the chains of tracer, level and not looping because they were fired at close range and the targets were his own two boats cruising two hundred metres away on his port side. He saw the boats that were firing the tracer, beyond his two and moving at high speed, racing past them. He felt the surge of power under his feet, saw his guns forward and aft training around to port to face this new attack. He roared, "*No! Starboard!*" And flung out a pointing arm towards the guardship, knowing he was too late.

Brent also saw the tracer and the boats out in the darkness and realised Crozier and Dent had seen the signal flashed from the deadlight in the after cabin. The engine note of the big diesels in the E-boat alongside quickened and her stern dug in as she moved ahead. He shouted, "*Fire!*" but Vance hadn't waited for that order. When the tracer opened up he depressed the barrel of the 40mm. gun until it was trained on the E-boat, and fired.

Rudi was deafened, stunned, shocked as the gun hurled shells into the bow of his boat at point-blank range. The 20mm. cannon just forward of his bridge was mangled. As his boat moved ahead the shells marched back along its length, ripping through the wheel-house below his feet. The bulwarks of the drifter were suddenly lined with rifles and submachine-guns and their fire swept the deck of his boat clear.

Then the 40mm. shells plunged through the engine-room. His boat was so close to the gun that its barrel was pointed down and the shells smashed through the deck then into the diesels or out through the side – but below the waterline. Rudi's boat slowed as the engines stopped. The guardship quickly drew ahead and the terrible gun aboard her shifted its fire to the other E-boats; but that relief came too late for Rudi. He knew with an awful certainty that his boat was not only stopped but sinking. He looked along her length from bow to stern and could not see another living soul.

Brent had seen the appalling destruction wrought by that close range fire and he had shouted to Tommy Vance, "Shift target!" That went unheard in the din but Jimmy Nash ran forward and grabbed Tommy's arm, bawled the order at him, pointed to the other E-boats. Brent cast one glance astern as the guardship drew away and saw the E-boat's commander still standing on his bridge, the only figure to be seen on her deck. It was incredible that he had survived the fire storm that had scoured the vessel beneath him.

David faced forward. The other two E-boats had turned away from Dent and Crozier, to join their leader or to escape the Vickers machine-guns. That turn set them on a course to cross the bow of the guardship. Tommy Vance opened up with the 40mm. but these were not targets close alongside and keeping pace. They were moving at speed and from left to right; they were some two hundred yards away and he had lost his night vision. He could not see the boats themselves and laid the gun by sight of the bow-wave of the leader and the flashes of her guns as they fired at Dent and Crozier. Because he was not used to the gun he led his target by far too much so the opening rounds passed fifty yards ahead of the leading boat. But by the time he realised this the boat had run into the line of the shells. Jimmy Nash bellowed at him, "Hold it on! Hold it on!" Tommy did his best.

213

David Brent saw the green fireflies of tracer sliding into the leading E-boat. Her forward gun ceased firing. The other one mounted aft was in action for only a few seconds longer then the flicker of that muzzle flash died. The boat's speed was falling away, the bow-wave diminishing then vanishing. Jimmy Nash turned to peer back at Brent, who gestured, pointing to the last boat still under way and Jimmy raised a hand in acknowledgment.

He passed on the order again and Tommy Vance trained the gun around, seeking that last boat. Brent had barely made it out from his position aft, but Tommy had been squinting past the long, pulsing flame licking from the barrel of the 40mm. only feet from his eyes. For some seconds he could not locate the grey moustache that was the phosphorescence thrown up by her bow, and for that time her guns were not firing to give her away. Then she fired and he had a target.

The last boat had to swerve to avoid the first that had led her by a hundred yards or so, cutting inside her and so coming between her and the guardship. Her guns had ceased firing because they were being trained around. They had been trying to fight off the M.T.B.s but now they turned on the old drifter. The first shells slammed into the guardship high on the port bow and side but then the gunners raised their sights.

They fired only a short burst before their boat swerved again and they lost their target. David Brent saw the tracer sliding in and heard the shrieking of the shells, the smash of their impact. Grundy was hurled across the wheel-house like a bundle of old clothes and collapsed at the back of it. Cullen moved towards him but then remembered as Brent shouted at him, "Take the wheel!" He grabbed the spinning spokes and stooped over the compass, spun the wheel then steadied it as the needle came on. Out of the corner of his eye he saw two of the other hands come running to lift Grundy and carry him away below.

"Course nor-b'west, sir." Cullen wondered how the hell he had remembered that.

"Very good," Brent acknowledged. Both of them were bawling at the tops of their voices to be heard above the gunfire. Tommy Vance had the 40mm. in action again and the last surviving E-boat was concentrating all her fire on the guardship in an attempt to silence his gun. They failed, narrowly, and the shells that missed him savaged the wheel-house.

Brent winced and ducked so only his eyes showed above the screen, while Cullen bent his knees and peered at the compass over the spokes of the wheel. They were instinctively seeking cover but that of the screen was an illusion. The splinter mattresses around it would keep out small-arms fire but the cannon shells ripped through it.

The E-boat was passing across the bow of the guardship and Brent ordered, "Hard astarboard!", so her bow would come around to follow the E-boat.

"Hard astarboard, sir." Cullen spun the spokes.

Brent watched the bow swing and straightened cautiously as he realised he was no longer under fire. The 40mm. in the bow faltered and then was silent. Dent and Crozier were still in action; he could see their red tracer and by following the line of it he picked out the E-boat. She was going away, just a blur of white water that was her wake growing smaller and fainter with every second. Her guns were either out of action or her commander had ordered them to cease firing so as not to give away his position to the gun on the guardship.

Brent shouted, "Can you see her, Tommy?" His voice sounded thin and distant in the silence.

"Not a thing."

"Nor me." That was Jimmy Nash.

Brent glanced down and saw him still standing by the gun. David looked up again to seek the grey blur of the wake but could not find it. The tracer was no longer pointing a red finger but there was something . . .

Jimmy Nash called, "Looks like Crozier coming back."

It was. The two boats raced in out of the night and turned to run alongside the guardship. At Brent's order they dropped astern to take up their former positions and he told Jimmy Nash, "See that light is shown from the after cabin again."

There was one badly mauled E-boat limping away and two more possibly sinking, but he would be ready to fight another action if he had to.

He looked astern but he could no longer see Crozier or Dent, let alone the two E-boats left lifeless on the sea.

Rudi Halder did not stand idle. He made his way aft, dropped down into the engine-room and sent the staff on deck, the living taking the dead men along with them. While he was below he confirmed what he already knew in his heart, that his boat was sinking. Back on deck, he helped the survivors from below to search through the bodies strewn around the guns and about the bridge. They looked for more survivors but found none. He lit the boat's navigation lights and it was by their glow that Petersen found him.

Hans Petersen's boat came alongside and stopped with her diesel engines throbbing. Rudi called across, "Where is Ernst?" He had seen Fischer's boat under fire.

"I found him," Petersen answered. "I took his people off. I've got six of them below."

Rudi asked, but guessing the answer, "What about Ernst?"

"He's aft with the others."

Rudi knew what that meant, could see the bundles ranked on the deck of Petersen's boat aft of the bridge. He whispered, "Dear God!"

Petersen said, "I had to leave his boat; she wouldn't tow."

"Neither will this one."

So Rudi stood on Petersen's bridge as the boat eased away from his own that was listing and awash at the stern. Petersen complained bitterly, "A pity we didn't get that signal a few minutes earlier."

Signal? Then Rudi remembered his wireless operator coming onto the bridge just before – He dug into his pockets, found the ball of crumpled paper, smoothed it out and read it: Enemy driven out of St. Jean . . . taking guardship . . . two *Schnellboote* . . . Rudi rolled it into a ball again and flipped it over the side. "Yes." Pity. Pity. The row of bundles aft of Petersen's bridge was longer now, and one of them was Bruno Jacobi, Rudi's friend.

They came to St. Jean in the last of the night, passing the fishing fleet a mile or two out as the drifters returned to port. When the E-boat entered the harbour Hans Petersen had to manoeuvre around the wreck of a drifter, only its mast showing above the surface. He turned slowly then to run in to the quay and Rudi saw the old port was swarming with troops. They still moved cautiously, nervously. A span of the bridge had been blown out and army engineers were working on it, striving to erect a temporary crossing. The S.S. headquarters had shattered windows and its walls were pitted. The house at the end of the row, next to that of the *Oberst*, had lost its upper storey so the gap showed like a missing tooth. A fire still smouldered in the ruins and its smoke hung over the quay.

The quay. They were alongside and soldiers caught and made fast the lines thrown to them. Rudi was first ashore and he walked to where Ilse waited for him, huddled in her father's greatcoat that hung to her ankles. There was dust in her hair, dirt on her face and tears had cut runnels through it, but her mouth went up at the corners when Rudi came to her.

He put his arms around her and held her close, said gently, "It's good to know you're safe." That was the only good thing to come out of this night. "I was afraid you might have been caught in the fighting. Did you see the *Tommis*?"

"Yes." She shuddered, remembering the cellar, the tall young man and the girl who had saved her.

Rudi felt that shudder and tilted up her chin to look into her eyes, "Are you sure you're all right?"

Ilse nodded, "I'm fine now." She would tell him about it, but later.

Rudi saw from the corner of his eye that Petersen's men were bringing the bodies ashore. He had to see to that himself and he let the girl go, but before he turned away he said, "I think this will be a long, hard war. Maybe it will be too long, too hard."

David Brent saw the lift of the land in the first grey light. So did Cullen, standing beside him at the wheel and stealing a glance up from the compass. "Nearly home, sir." Brent grunted and Cullen thought: Well, he was never one of your talkers. He asked, "How's Grundy, sir?"

"Not too bad, I'm glad to say." David said that with relief, had feared the worst when Grundy was carried below unconscious with his face bloodied. "Mister Nash has seen him and he's got a nasty lump on his head, probable concussion, and a few cuts and bruises. Nothing that a few days' rest won't cure."

"Good cox'n, sir." And that reminded Cullen . . . He ticked off in his mind the names of the other seamen aboard the guardship, recalling their records. He was the senior man. He asked, "Permission to leave the wheel, sir? Legget here can stand a trick." Legget was one of Vance's men, standing at the back of the bridge now as a messenger.

"Yes, carry on."

Cullen jerked his head at Legget, and as he came forward muttered, "Take the wheel, but before you do, put your cap on straight."

Legget protested, "It's not a proper cap, just a rolled-up balaclava – "

Cullen hissed, "I don't care if it's a bloody topper! You're supposed to be under it, not alongside!"

Legget yanked the woollen hat square across his brow and Cullen nodded satisfaction, handed over the wheel. He heard Legget repeat the course correctly and then left the bridge. He looked down his nose at the men sprawled on the deck and sleeping the sleep of exhaustion despite the dawn cold. He reached out to the nearest and shook him awake: "Heave ho, lash up and stow! On your feet and smarten up." He moved to the next, "C'mon, get yourselves up and tidy. Where the hell d'ye think you are? This is the Navy, not a bumboat." He saw McNab waking the soldiers. They still cuddled the Thompsons but they had less than a dozen rounds of ammunition left among them.

One by one the men struggled to their feet, tidied their clothes and straightened caps, Cullen and McNab badgering them. So as the guardship entered harbour every man on her upper deck lined her sides, rigidly at attention. Cullen was satisfied; that was how Grundy liked it done for the skipper. Now he had to wangle it to send a man away early to light a fire in the men's quarters . . .

David Brent saw them and was proud, glad that he had brought these men home. The officers, Chris Tallon among them, stood in a little group looking up at Brent in the wheel-house.

He thought over the night's actions, slowly because weariness made his mind fumble and seize up for seconds at a time while it held on to the last thought. He had been ordered to bring out Max Neumann and the operation had gone wrong but then he had seen a way it might be done. He had been told the rescue must be made "at any cost", so that way had to be tried. It had been possible, barely, because of his knowledge of St. Jean and the country north of it – and because of Suzanne.

His mind froze for a time, then lurched on again. His original plan, set out at the briefing in the wardroom long hours ago, had been for the drifter to take off the entire force from the sea wall. But first Jimmy Nash had to capture the guardship because Suzanne had said it sometimes went to sea, so it might have been able to leave the harbour, engage the drifter and fight off the two M.T.B.s. If the drifter was sunk or too badly damaged to go to sea then all the landing force would cram aboard the two boats.

Now he wondered how he would have managed with all those kids. But he'd have taken them somehow . . .

And he'd always thought he might use the guardship *if* Jimmy Nash took her intact and *if* she had steam up – and that had seemed likely. The landing, the barge, the train, all fell or were forced into place in his plan. He had taken some calculated risks but you always had to do that. The gambles had come off and he'd prepared for eventualities that seemed to him fairly obvious. He had not so much set a trap for the E-boats at the end as been prepared to meet them if he had to.

Nothing very clever. No cause for Tallon and Jimmy Nash to look at him like that. He had lost two boats – and the men, he could not think about the men now, but later . . . He had brought out the children and Max Neumann. The children filled the deck below him, staring at the land. The shabby little man stood just forward of the wheel-house now, grey stubble on his chin, hollow-eyed, stooping and blank-faced with tiredness. The man who was so important. David Brent wondered why.

The admiral and the general of the United States Army stood on the quayside and anxiously watched them enter harbour, the guardship leading the two motor torpedo boats in line ahead. A winter's sun was up now in a clean-washed sky, giving no heat but glinting off the sea. The general muttered, "Only two boats. It doesn't look good, huh? Think they got him? And what the hell are all those kids . . . ?"

The admiral shook his head, baffled, eyes searching the men on the two boats then the drifter.

But then, as the guardship came alongside, the general identified Max Neumann, despite the stubble. He had studied the photograph a hundred times. "There he is! They've got him!"

The admiral asked, "Little chap just below the wheel-house?"

"That's the guy." The American stood straighter and took a breath. "Am I glad to see him! He may not look much right now, but I can tell you – well, it's vital he works for us and not for the Nazis. Sorry I can't say more, but you know how it is."

The admiral nodded courteously. "Of course. I have to keep my mouth shut about certain topics. Though as a matter of fact I talked to a chap I know at Oxford – the university. He knew your man and spoke very highly of him. He's in the same line of business, as it happens: splitting atoms."

Brent saw them on the quay but only gave them a cursory glance; the admiral had got what he wanted. David watched the girl standing in the bow. The stained and bedraggled trenchcoat was wrapped tightly around her slim waist, her hair was loose and lifted as the wind took it. As if she sensed his eyes on her, she turned to him and smiled in the sunlight.